Also by Judith O'Brien

Rhapsody in Time
Ashton's Bride
Once Upon a Rose
Maiden Voyage
One Perfect Knight
To Marry a British Lord
The Forever Bride
Gift of Love

Available from Pocket Books

JUDITH O'BRIEN

ENTER the HERO

POCKET BOOKS

New York   London   Toronto   Sydney   Singapore

This book is a work of fiction. Names, characters, places and incidents are products of the author's imagination or are used fictitiously. Any resemblance to actual events or locales or persons, living or dead, is entirely coincidental.

An *Original* Publication of POCKET BOOKS

 POCKET BOOKS, a division of Simon & Schuster, Inc. 1230 Avenue of the Americas, New York, NY 10020

ISBN: 0-7434-2798-X

First Pocket Books printing December 2003

10   9   8   7   6   5   4   3   2   1

POCKET and colophon are registered trademarks of Simon & Schuster, Inc.

Manufactured in the United States of America

For information regarding special discounts for bulk purchases, please contact Simon & Schuster Special Sales at 1-800-456-6798 or business@simonandschuster.com

ENTER the
HERO

Prologue

Fairfax Castle
County Mayo, Ireland
Spring 1814

Emily Fairfax dipped her quill into the crystal bottle, ignoring the small droplets of blue ink that splattered on the paper. A stray yellow tendril escaped a silken knot at the nape of her slender neck, and she brushed it aside, adding a smear of ink to her unlined forehead. Outside the constant rush of water tumbed from the marble fountain just below her window, and the swell of birdsong carried in the breeze.

But Emily Fairfax had all of her senses focused on a duel to the death.

She paused for a moment to consult the *Assembly Gazette* for yet another bit of information on Mr. L.A., her favorite character in life as well as in her own creations. He was at every duel, it seemed, a popular second if not actual combatant in battles over honor and manhood.

There were occasional, if maddeningly brief, references to his appearance. He was above average height, of course, and handsome of face, naturally. He seemed to be the most eligible bachelor in all of London, which, of course, meant he was the most eligible bachelor in the entire world.

Had Mr. L.A. not actually existed, Emily had often thought, she would have been forced to invent him. But fortunately for everyone, he did exist. It was Emily who took it upon herself to fill in any missing information with her own imagination.

> *It is reported that the ubiquitous Mr. L.A. of* _____ _____-*shire has again participated in a duel as a loyal second. The field of honor was mildly stained with the blood of Sir* _____ _____, *whose wounds consisted of a burn to the side of his nose (said to have occurred when he peered down the barrel of his pistol to see if it had indeed fired. It had.), and a slash to his thumb, incurred when he grasped the blade of his own sword to aid Mr. L.A. in his efforts to bandage the afflicted nose. All parties later retired to a nearby inn, where Sir* _____ _____ *paid the ultimate price—the tavern bill. No person seemed to recall the cause of the argument that had prompted the duel.*

"That will never do," Emily muttered. "My duel must be far more dangerous. There must be an actual threat of death." Her eyes opened wide, and she stared out the window for a long time. Suddenly, with her bright, slightly uneven grin, she began writing again.

Enter the hero, stage left . . .

Before she could continue, there was a creak on the floorboards outside of her room. She refused to have the loose boards mended, for the warning creaks were a most convenient and reliable alarm system. With the aid of the helpful floor, she was given a good two seconds notice before the impending knock on her door.

Swiftly she covered her last page with blotting paper, pulling out the letter she had prepared for such a purpose.

My dearest sister Caroline,
  I do hope this missive finds you in the best of health, and that my nephews are not being too hard upon their little sister, nor upon my own little sister, who happens to be their mother.

"Come in," Emily called, taking a deep breath.

It was her youngest sister, Letty.

"Good heavens, Letty, why didn't you say it was you? I smudged my new page," she sighed.

Letty closed the door with great ceremony, and walked toward her older sister, holding her index finger over her mouth.

"I have mail," she whispered.

"How extraordinary," Emily whispered in reply.

"I have mail," Letty repeated. Before Emily could speak, Letty raised her eyebrows. "For a Mr. Edgar St. John."

The calm expression left Emily's face. "What does it say? Surely it is too early for another payment from Mr. Giles. The new play is not yet in production."

"Well, I didn't read the letter, if that's what you mean."

"Please, Letty. No cat-and-mouse today. You read all of the mail. Here, let me see it."

"Emily." Letty seemed reluctant to hand the thick envelope to her sister. "You have been called out."

"What?"

Letty clasped her hands, crushing the letter. "You have been called out. Can I be your second? Please? I'm the only one here who knows you write plays under the name of Edgar St. John. You must let me come, absolutely must."

"I've been called out?" Emily repeated in disbelief. "May I please see the letter? How on earth—"

"Mr. Giles sent the letter along. But he's not the one who wishes to call you out. Mr. Giles simply redirected the other letter."

Emily continued to stare in amazement. Letty stepped forward, dangling the letter just within her sister's reach, then whisked it back when Emily held out a beckoning hand. "You know, Edward Giles—the man in London who produces your plays."

"I know who Mr. Giles is, dearest," she said with annoyance. "Who has called me out? Or rather, who has called out Edgar St. John?"

"This is the best part!" Letty bounced up and down, unable to contain herself. Unruly strawberry blond hair fell into her eyes, and with impatience she pushed it back, her blue eyes sparkling. "Oh, Emily! This is the most wondrous part of all!"

"Who? Just tell me, Letty."

"His name is Lord Ogilvie."

Emily blinked. "Who in heaven's name is Lord Ogilvie?"

Letty finally handed the letter to her sister.

"Lord Ogilvie?" Emily repeated, reading the words that had been slashed in bold, harsh strokes, some with such ferocity that the paper had been sliced clear through, allowing sunlight to shimmer around the words.

"And his second is to be none other than the celebrated Mr. Lucius Ashford."

"Lucius Ashford. Mr. L.A.?" Emily breathed. "*My* Mr. L.A. from dash-dash-shire? Are you sure?"

"Not *your* Mr. L.A.," Letty corrected with authority. "Edgar St. John's Mr. L.A. Or Lord Ogilvie's Mr. L.A. You really have very little to do with this, other than the fact he is a second and is quite willing to stand by and enjoy the sight of your body being riddled with gunshot."

"Has anyone ever told you what a vile child you have become?" Emily mumbled distractedly, reading the missive from Lord Ogilvie. The gist was simple. He believed the playwright Edgar St. John had besmirched his noble name with the character of Lord Oswald in the most recent play, *He Begs to*

Differ. In truth, Emily had never heard of a Lord Ogilvie, much less ever dreamed of besmirching his name. Her entirely fictional Lord Oswald was a debauched, foppish creature, and Emily could only assume her creation had hit an unintentional mark.

As for Mr. L.A., well. He was but the second, but she had followed his colorful career with delight. Now she had a chance to meet the man himself.

She put the letter down. "I know not how to respond."

"Why, you must agree to the duel, of course!" Letty exclaimed. "How can you not?"

"Impossible." And it was.

"Oh, Emily." Letty's shoulder's slumped.

"It is impossible, dear. To agree to the duel would be to reveal that the dashing Edgar St. John is nothing but a provincial Irish spinster." Even admitting those bare facts out loud was painful.

"But you *are* Edgar St. John."

"No. I pretend to be Edgar St. John. There is a big difference."

They were both silent, and then a slight smile played on Emily's lips. "Unless . . ."

"Unless?" Letty whispered with undisguised hope.

"Unless we reply to this letter as Edgar St. John, agree to the duel, and then arrive as his emissaries. We will not allow the duel to take place, of course, but just think of the story possibilities that can come from this small adventure!

Why, it can be research for the next play. We will be the emissaries," Emily continued, thinking of the plotline. "Perhaps the unfortunate Mr. St. John has suffered a sudden illness of a most serious nature."

"Or maybe he's dead!" Letty shouted with glee. "Maybe he has the pox, or the plague. Or some vile, fearsome disorder from America that causes his nose to fall off."

"Well, he certainly cannot be dead, my dear, for he must recover enough to write another play. And he will need his nose, for nothing would be more conspicuous than a playwright without a nose. We can invent a suitable illness later. The main point is to make him unavailable for the duel. And then we can actually see Mr. L.A. in the flesh."

"So you will agree to it? To meet Mr. L.A.?"

"How could I not?" Emily said simply, ignoring Letty's whoop of joy. "This is really most inconvenient. We were to go to Dublin in the next few weeks for new muslin—that lovely red dot pattern is in—but I suppose the duel will keep us here. Of course I will insist they travel here to Ireland for the assignation. I certainly cannot be bothered with a trip to England at the moment."

"Not to mention Father. You would have to come up with a jolly good excuse for Father," Letty sighed, suddenly pensive and oblivious to the glare of mild pique from her older sister. "My goodness, Emily. What does one wear to a duel?"

Emily paused, then shook her head. "I haven't

the faintest notion. We will not actually duel, of course, but one must be prepared. Perhaps a suit of armor. We could always borrow the pair in the hallway downstairs. This is a great deal of trouble, is it not?" Then, arching her eyebrows, she added, "It is also a great deal of fun. I will try my best not to kill him."

"Then I can be your second?"

"Of course, dearest. Just mind that you get to sleep early the night before. Every duel I have read about occurs at a painfully early hour. Oh, and I expect I shall have to learn to shoot. But I shall attend to that tomorrow. Now begone with you. I have a manly reply to compose."

"May I write the letter?"

"Good grief, Letty. Let me at least respond in the character I created." Taking a new slip of paper from her desk, she tapped the quill a few times. "I am Edgar St. John, gentleman playwright, and my honor has just been called into question. My goodness, this is a bit like having one's own imagination get out of hand, is it not? I can't think with you gaping at me like a gasping fish, Letty. And if you don't run along, you cannot be my second."

With that, twelve-year-old Letty skipped from the room without even glancing back.

Emily smiled at the closed door before again straightening her shoulders, the retreating creak of the floorboards confirming that her sister had left.

"Lord Ogilvie," she began in the deepest voice

she could manage. "I do believe honor dictates satisfaction on both our sides. I must warn you, sir, that I have triumphed over many an opponent, and many is the villain I have rendered one-eyed or hideously disfigured." She scribbled as she spoke, then halted to ponder her words.

"That *does* seem a bit much," she admitted to herself, crumpling the thick paper into a ball and tossing it at her feet. She began again. "Lord Ogilvie. Or shall I say Mr. Lucius Ashford?"

Looking down at his name, she imagined what his features must be, how strong and bold her hero would seem when she at last saw his face. "Mr. L.A., at last we are to meet," her voice softened. Then she balled up that paper, pulling out a fresh sheet.

It was most difficult to respond to the note without being perfectly aware that he was hers, the flesh-and-blood man she had imagined for so long. Although she wouldn't recognize the actual man if he walked into her bedroom and tapped her on the shoulder, in her mind's eye she would know him at once, his spirit, his soul.

And now she was writing actual words on paper that would find their way into his hands, to be read by his eyes and deliberated by his mind.

"Lord Ogilvie," she wrote with great authority, thinking of Mr. L.A. *"I do, sir, agree to meet you on a field of honor ..."*

Perhaps it was not the most flowery of communications, yet Emily could not help but imagine where this note would lead her, and how very pleased she was to at last have something occur in reality that approximated the excitement she created in her plays.

Finally, she was making something happen in her own life.

Chapter One

❧

Lucius Ashford bitterly regretted the last couple of brandies he had imbibed the night before.

At the time it had seemed such a good idea, to celebrate in advance, basking in the friendly lantern light of a local tavern. Now, however, with the sun rising with inconsiderate strength and blinding brightness, he wasn't so sure.

Even though he had been abused by the choppy journey across the sea from England to Ireland, then further assaulted by brandy of dubious origin and suspicious quality, he was still breathtakingly handsome. It was not so much his features, which were strong and even—with hair that was very nearly black and eyes that were very nearly the color of dark chestnut—or his physique, which was splendid, much to the vexation of the bucks who spent brutal hours with fencing masters in order to avoid the indignities of wearing a corset. Instead, there was an elusive quality to his character that both intrigued and disturbed all those who claimed acquaintance with the man. In truth, no one seemed to know him completely, even his present companion, Lord

William Ogilvie, who was counted as his closest and oldest friend.

For all of Ashford's apparent openness, there was something yet hidden, perhaps even from himself. He was of a good family, that was certain from his manners and bearing. But unlike other men of excellent lineage, Ashford was fascinating and unpredictable. One never knew exactly what to expect from the man, from a witty, if scorching comment to an almost antique defense of chivalry. And that single perplexing attribute of the unexpected, combined with an easy charm and an expertly cut and maintained wardrobe, allowed him access to the best parlors and assemblies.

Furthermore, he was the most popular second in the land. Many a hotheaded argument was lessened or even forgotten by virtue of his skillful reasoning. For Ashford was as known for his abhorrence of dueling as he was for his striking appearance and his smooth manners.

"I thought it was supposed to be cloudy in Ireland," Ashford observed, squinting at the intrusive light. His cravat was tied more loosely than usual, his dark green double-breasted superfine morning coat was not as well brushed as was the owner's custom, and the cream-colored waistcoat was misbuttoned. He had removed his hat a few moments earlier, hoping the fresh air would ease his headache.

"Cloudy in Ireland? Ah, that is a commonly held fallacy," replied Lord Ogilvie from beneath his top hat, which was covering his face and muffling his voice. He, too, had partaken of the extra brandy, and was slumped against the trunk of a large tree, his legs splayed out before him. Although Ogilvie was of an age with Ashford, a certain deliberation in his manner made him seem older. Every movement seemed to have been pondered and calculated, every gesture precise, every word carefully selected for its meaning.

"So you've been here, Ogilvie? You've never mentioned Ireland before."

Ogilvie snorted. "Of course I've never been here. I've never been in ancient Greece either, but I do have a fair idea of how they lived and thought. All those hours with books have been most helpful. I happen to possess a vast store of knowledge of the most eclectic sort."

"In that case, sir, I bow to your superior intellect. And with all of your vast, eclectic knowledge, do you know where on earth Edgar St. John is this morning?"

"If he is a man of any wisdom, he is still abed," Ogilvie mumbled, keeping his motions to a bare minimum.

Ashford, by contrast, was all movement and impetuosity, which was why in the twenty-odd years of their acquaintance, Ashford had stood as Ogilvie's second for nearly half that same number of times. Indeed, Ogilvie had been called out with as much frequency as he had been called a charming partner for the less lively country dances.

"Ogilvie, I do wish you would at least stand in an

upright position. St. John is liable to believe you are an easy mark if you are incapable of rising to your feet."

"I will stand when it is necessary, sir," was the reply. "At the present time, I believe it would be folly. Why are we here, by the way?"

"We are here because Edgar St. John requested it, because we are gentlemen, and because we both thought Ireland would present a pleasant change."

"Do we know anything of this St. John fellow?"

"Nothing. Do you recall the conversation last night?"

"I will thank you not to mention the events of last night."

"It was with the tavern maid in that village over the hill. What was its name again? Balleen-something."

"I have not the faintest clue."

"In any case, no one has ever heard of their most illustrious citizen, Edgar St. John. I find that most curious. After all, he's quite the man-about-town in London. Seen everywhere. But I have yet to make his acquaintance, nor do I know anyone else who has. Most curious indeed."

"I do not feel well, Ashford."

Ashford sighed and shook his head, realizing that any additional conversation was pointless. It mattered little what sort of man Edgar St. John was. In his mind he had already dismissed St. John as a social fop, a middle-aged country squire with a talent for composing clever, inflammatory plays. Since

Ogilvie had made his anger at St. John known, more than one gentleman had confided a desire to meet the playwright on just such a field. His only surprise thus far had been St. John's willingness to be met, although as the minutes ticked by, Ashford wondered if the man himself would actually have the nerve to appear.

Perhaps, for once, Ashford would not be required to halt yet another foolish duel. That would present a pleasant change indeed.

"If he fails to show, I shall consider it a severe breech of etiquette," Ogilvie stated flatly. "This has been a most inconvenient journey, and the least St. John can do is have the decency to show. The threat of death is no reason to display poor manners."

"Thank you, Mr. Brummell," smiled Ashford. "But I believe I see a pair of mounted figures in the distance. Do you suppose you could find it in yourself to rise to your feet? Barring any unusual bloodshed, this whole affair should be over rather swiftly."

Ogilvie grunted once and, with a wince and a groan, hoisted himself into a sitting position.

"Where? I see no one, Ashford. Oh. Yes. Here come the vile demons of death."

Ashford held his hand over his eyes to get a better view. "They may be vile demons of death, but their mounts are magnificent. Look at that chestnut on the right."

"How splendid. The horses no doubt have more breeding than their country-cousin riders."

The rumble of hooves was now discernible as Ashford straightened his cravat and swallowed. This was always the most difficult moment in a duel, the long seconds before the actual face-to-face meeting, before the measured steps to decide each other's fate. Usually he had been offered the chance to stare into the opponent's eyes before this point, to divine any hints there. Excessive redness usually meant either illness, eyestrain or debauchery—all good bets for Ashford's side. Clear and unblinking indicated a cool calculation or religious fervor, both of which were to be avoided at all costs. St. John was a complete unknown, making Ashford more than uneasy. A man as clever with words as St. John could indeed be a dangerous combatant. Ashford himself had taken this whole affair with Ogilvie too lightly, and they were both likely to pay for his foolishness. Perhaps pay very dearly indeed.

And then he smiled at his own poetic fear. He had always managed to stop a duel, or at least lessen the severity of the outcome.

"Really, Ashford. Must you grin so? It's damned irritating, especially given that we are both under the weather and there is a slight chance that I shall soon be under the ground." Ogilvie rose unsteadily to his feet, then stopped. "Good God."

"What is it?"

"Look. Squint if you must, but take a good look at the men approaching. They appear to be riding sidesaddle."

"Good God." Ashford stared in disbelief. "Those

men are women." He quickly rebuttoned his waist-coat.

"No, I'm afraid you're wrong there. Those are girls. Straight from the schoolroom, if I'm not mistaken."

Emily Fairfax and her sister approached slowly, eyeing the two men with wary hesitation. They returned the gaze with perplexed interest, Ogilvie stroking his chin and shifting uncomfortably in his boots. Ashford remained motionless, although the tension in his body seemed almost palpable.

Emily glanced from one man to the other. Suddenly this was no longer such a lark, she realized with a sickening flip to her stomach. These were actual men, and one of them was particularly large and fit.

This was real, not a scene in one of her plays that she could crumple up and toss aside should the outcome displease her.

In fact, this was all *too* real. She was alone, with her twelve-year-old sister, in the middle of nowhere, having told absolutely no one of their whereabouts, and facing two armed men. One was well-formed, the other rather pudgy, like a wad of kneaded dough. This was not simple folly, but actual danger, and she had placed Letty squarely in the center.

How very different this was from writing a daring scene, or even a duel to the death. Instead she was living it, and had absolutely no power over the outcome.

Even in the midst of panic, Emily hoped the tall one was Ashford. Not only because that would make him the mere second, but because she so very much liked his looks.

When they were within earshot, she squared her shoulders and willed her voice steady. "Lord William Ogilvie," she called. "Which one of you is Lord Ogilvie?"

Neither man responded, although the tall one crossed his arms, and she could not help but notice how very large and muscular those arms were.

Ashford stared at the girl who had spoken, realizing that she was older than he had at first assumed, perhaps five and twenty. She did not wear a riding habit, but instead seemed dressed for a country fair, all muslin and freshness and springtime. She most certainly did not seem dressed for a duel.

From beneath her chip bonnet were blond curls, and her face, even in the concealing shade of the bonnet, was strikingly beautiful.

"I am Ashford, Lord Ogilvie's second," he said at last, after concluding that her figure, buttoned into a light blue spencer, was indeed as lovely as her face.

And then she shifted in her saddle, a gesture at once elegant and childlike, and Ashford felt an odd jolt to his midsection.

"Actually, I am Ashford," blurted Ogilvie, wishing to avoid any blame for the situation, and hoping the comely older sister would look at him with the clear admiration she bestowed on Ashford. "And I wish to apologize for my brutish friend here. Ogilvie, how could you possibly call out a young lady? Despicable. Utterly ungallant. I am most dreadfully appalled at your behavior."

Emily glanced between the two men before Letty spoke.

"I think you should let me pick, Emily. I'm your second, so it is us up to me to do these things."

Ashford placed an arm on his hip. "What sort of jest of this? St. John must be a coward of the worst degree to send two . . ."—he looked first at Emily, then at Letty—"ladies ahead of him. What delays him? This is most awkward."

Letty preened at being included as a lady.

"So you are annoyed that certain death is to be delayed?" Emily blurted. Even as she spoke she recognized the line from one of her earlier plays. Oh Lord, she thought. What have I done now?

"Are we to expect an ambush then, madame?" growled the tall one. His hands had clenched into fists, although there were no other outward signs of his anger. "Where is St. John? I demand to know."

"Well, sir," she began. "You see, I fear . . ." her voice wavered slightly. With added confidence, a great deal more than she felt, she repeated, "Well, sir . . ."

"Miss," he spoke with dangerous softness, grabbing the reins of her horse. "I repeat, where is St. John? We have not journeyed from England for the sport of two schoolgirls."

Letty's face fell before Ashford continued.

"If you do not reveal the whereabouts of St. John, I will be forced to return to London with the news that St. John is an utter and complete coward. To send a woman in his place is the most despicable act I have yet to—"

"His nose fell off!" Letty exclaimed.

Ashford turned to her. "Pardon me?"

Letty grinned. "It is most dreadful, sir. Truly. Poor Mr. Edgar St. John was most brutally, gruesomely and revoltingly taken with a rare illness from America which caused his nose to fall off." She straightened with pride. "Right in the middle of tea."

The stunned silence was broken only by the cackle of a bird overhead.

Letty's smile faltered. "Well, it dangled for a moment before it fell."

Ashford was the first to recover. "Where, miss, did he acquire this illness?"

"Why, in America, of course. They have hideous, untamed things there." Letty twisted the reins. "Where else would one acquire an American disease of such a morbid variety?"

"So Mr. St. John has been in America of late? And ill? Then how did he respond so robustly, and in such a timely manner, to this issue?"

"Please, Letty." Emily began to dismount, and with only a slight hesitation Ashford stepped forward to assist. Her hands rested on his shoulders for a moment before he set her down. She curtseyed and extended her right hand for his clasp.

With a deep intake of breath he shook her hand. "So please tell me more of Mr. St. John's unfortunate nose condition." He peered into her face. Up close her features were even more extraordinary than from a distance, finely cut without being sharp.

"Thank you. Oh, and please allow me to introduce my youngest sister, Miss Letty Fairfax."

Letty, who had jumped to the ground with Ogilvie's belated assistance, bobbed her best curtsey, then beamed. "Pleased to meet you. Shall I fetch the pistols, Emily?"

"Not now, dearest. You gentlemen seem a bit perplexed. I am Emily Fairfax, and have been sent here by Edgar St. John."

Ashford was beginning to recover. "Why did he send a woman?" He bowed to Letty. "Forvive me, women."

Letty flushed with delight.

"Because he doesn't know."

"He doesn't know?" Ogilvie bit out. "God's blood, is the man blind?"

"No, I mean he has become so ill that he does not quite realize this was to be the date of the duel. You see, we conduct all of our business matters through the post. So he is unaware at present of this meeting, although he would most certainly approve. You, sir, I assume, are Lord Ogilvie?"

"Forgive my manners." Ashford stepped aside. "Lord William Ogilvie, this is Miss Fairfax, also known as the emissary of Edgar St. John, and her sister, Miss Letty Fairfax."

They smiled and nodded at each other, as if meeting over a punch bowl.

"So just what matters, Miss Fairfax, do you handle for Mr. St. John?"

"Excuse me, sir?"

"Precisely what matters do you handle for Mr. St. John?"

"Well, all kinds of matters, sir. Many kinds of matters."

"Indeed?"

The tone of his voice made her uncomfortable. "Well, you see, he is a single gentleman," she began, untying the blue silk ribbons of her bonnet. There was a knot she had difficulty untangling, and Ashford stepped forward and with a flick of his hand the ribbons came loose.

"Thank you, sir." Emily averted her eyes as she pulled off her hat. "As a single gentleman, he often needs assistance in social matters."

"So you are his social secretary?"

"No, well, what I mean is, I assist in household matters as well."

"You are his housekeeper?"

"Of course not!"

"How long is this charade to continue?" Ashford asked ominously.

"Whatever do you mean?"

"Damn it, you know very well what I mean."

"Profanity is not necessary, sir," Emily replied at once, her back straightening. "If you are reluctant to discuss the duel with me because I am a woman, let me assure you that I have Mr. St. John's complete confidence on all matters."

"This is ridiculous."

"Sir, I must say that—"

"Ogilvie, let us quit this place at once," Ashford snapped.

"Now, let us not be hasty," Ogilvie smiled at Emily. "Maybe we should allow Miss Fairfax an opportunity to practice settling duels on me. After all, they were forced to rise at an uncommonly early hour."

Ashford glared in stunned disbelief at his friend.

"What I mean is that we should not abandon these ladies in such a wild place, Lucius."

"The only thing remotely wild are the ladies themselves."

Letty, who had been busy with her saddlebag, emerged from behind her horse with two pearl-handled pistols. "Emily, I can't seem to find—"

The crack of gunshot jolted them all. Birds scattered; horses reared. Ogilvie, in an instinctive gesture, fell to the ground.

Letty's eyes filled with tears. "I'm so very sorry," she said earnestly. Then her lower lip began to quiver. "It was so loud," she said to nobody in particular. "I didn't think it would be so loud. I had no idea it would make such a noise."

Ashford grabbed both weapons from her weak grasp.

"Is anyone hurt?" he asked, removing the ball from the unfired pistol.

"Letty," Emily ran to her sister and folded her in comfort. "Are you harmed?"

"No," the girl stammered. "I'm so sorry," she said first to Emily, then to the two men. "Can I still be her second?"

Ogilvie rose to his feet, sheepishly brushing the grass and dirt from his clothing, as Ashford, after tossing the empty pistols to the ground, stilled the horses.

Emily glanced at Ashford, wondering at how very furious he must be. But to her surprise, even shock, there was a small smile on his lips.

"Miss Letty," he said, rubbing the muzzle of Emily's horse. "I believe we had best put off the notion of discussing a duel."

"No, please," the girl pleaded, tears forgotten. "Emily and I have been so looking forward to it. We sneaked out of the house like robbers in reverse. This is most unfair."

"Perhaps," Ashford said calmly. "But you see, the gunshot seems to have rattled my duelist, which puts him at a distinct disadvantage. Isn't that so, Ogilvie?"

"Indeed," Oglivie murmured, gingerly pressing a hand to his temple. "This has not done much for my head, Ashford. Not in the least."

"Well," Emily ventured. "What time is it, sir?"

Ashford consulted his watch. "It is just gone half six." He clicked the case closed and returned it to his trouser pocket.

"Have you gentlemen had breakfast yet?" Emily inquired.

"No. No we have not," admitted Ashford.

"Breakfast was the last thing on my mind," confessed Ogilvie, still tenderly exploring his forehead. "Although a jot or two of something may be of great help by now."

"Well, gentlemen, we are just two miles across the field from my home. Would we be breaking any code of conduct if we discussed this business over breakfast instead of pistols?"

"That, Miss Fairfax, is the best idea I have heard in quite some time," Ashford said. "Do you have some sort of lodgings, or live with relatives?" His question made sense. Where else would a spinster and her twelve-year-old sister be expected to reside?

"No, sir," Emily smiled. "We live with our father, who is a great believer in hearty breakfasts."

The sisters guided the way, leaving the two men to follow behind holding the horses' reins.

Cheered by the prospect of food, Ogilvie offered brightly, "A bit of rusticating may be just the thing before we set off for home, eh, Ashford?"

"Rusticating, Ogilvie, has never been a particular pastime of mine. I, for one, cannot wait to return to town. I've already been stalled for too long from urgent business."

"How delightfully vague you can be," Ogilvie smiled. "Just enjoy the fresh air while we are out in the open. No doubt the sisters dwell in some sort of picturesque rural squalor."

Ashford was silent, watching Emily Fairfax's slender form as she conversed with her younger sister, bonnet swinging at her side. And to himself he offered wordless thanks for yet another duel averted.

Chapter Two

The party of four, the men leading the horses, stood at the top of the vivid green rise. A scent of fresh grass and lush, thick leaves tingled their senses. The sun had almost fully risen and the air was crisp and clean. In the distance was one of the most happily settled estates either of the men had ever beheld, a sprawling structure of gray stone surrounded by hedges and large stretches of garden just now beginning to bloom. It was a handsome home, solid and elegant of line, and even from their vantage it was possible to see the remains of an ancient keep nestled within the large center courtyard.

"How pleasant," commented Lord Ogilvie.

Letty had skipped ahead, attempting to scoop up butterflies in her bonnet. Ashford smiled at the girl, his features relaxed in an unguarded moment, and Emily scrutinized him.

He was astonishingly handsome.

"Do you live nearby?" Ogilvie asked.

Emily pointed to Fairfax Castle.

"Good God," Ogilvie sputtered. "Do you mean to tell us this estate is yours?"

"No, of course not. It belongs to my father."

"He's my father, too," chirped Letty, examining her bonnet.

Ashford admired the beautiful grounds of velvet green, interrupted with rows of brilliantly colored flowers. There were swirling, well-defined footpaths winding throughout the gardens, dotted with graceful stone benches.

The closer they got to the home itself, the more apparent it was that the Fairfax home was very well cared for indeed. Windows glistened in the sunlight; the gray stone seemed to sparkle. Everything about the estate had a crisp, polished appearance, as if it had all been painted with a sharp brush.

Stable boys swiftly and wordlessly took the horses' reins as they approached the castle entrance. Ashford's boots clicked lightly upon the small steps leading to the door, and Lord Ogilvie made several peculiar snorting sounds which Ashford took as approval.

"I confess I am astonished at the elegance." Ogilvie stared up at the marble columns bracing the entrance. "So understated. And to think we're in Ireland. I was anticipating harps and shamrocks and little green fairies and whatnot. Why, one could easily be in Kent." His voice trailed off when a liveried servant bowed and held the doors open. He was formally attired in the custom of the last century, with satin knee britches and hose and a wig that was ever so slightly askew. Buckles twinkled on his boots—none of the new-fangled laces were in sight.

"Good morning, Williams," Miss Fairfax greeted the servant.

"Miss Fairfax. We had no idea you and Miss Letty had risen. Breakfast is within."

"It was ever so much fun, Williams! Was it not, Emily? We were up at dawn, and we almost fought a duel to the death!"

The servant did not blink, and Ashford had a strong suspicion the dignified man was accustomed to more unusual goings-on than a schoolgirl engaging in a duel.

"Very well, Miss Letty. Breakfast is within."

"Thank you, Williams," Letty tossed her bonnet in the direction of an elaborately carved banister, releasing a trio of butterflies into the hallway. Williams plucked the bonnet from midair, then returned to courteous attention, bonnet in hand.

"Well done!" Emily Fairfax smiled her crooked smile at the man, and he blushed briefly with pleasure. Letty clapped her hands in delight as the butterflies flew to the vaulted ceiling.

"Oh, Williams," Emily continued as she handed him her own hat. "These gentlemen will be breakfasting with us."

"Very well, Miss Fairfax."

"Is Edward at the table?" Letty asked.

"I believe so, Miss Letty. As is Daisy." Williams winked almost imperceptibly.

Ashford and Ogilvie exchanged glances. Edward must be their brother, perhaps Daisy a servant or companion.

But inside the room, filled with twinkling silver and mahogany furniture polished to a high gloss, was a gentleman in his late middle years reading a newspaper at the head of the table. Gold spectacles perched at the end of his nose.

He did not glance up.

"Good morning, Father," Emily greeted. She walked briskly to his side and kissed the top of his head. "This is Mr. Ashford and his friend Lord Ogilvie. This is my father, Mr. Jeremy Fairfax."

Ashford extended his hand, and Mr. Fairfax—still intent on his paper—took it without standing up, and without even glancing at his guests. Ogilvie, seeing the man's hand groping in the air, also shook it, and then Mr. Fairfax continued perusing his paper.

"Welcome, welcome," he said distractedly. "I was not aware that we had guests. But you are most welcome indeed."

"Thank you, sir," Ashford answered. Ogilvie shrugged and sniffed the air in anticipation of a luscious meal. A fire crackled invitingly in the fireplace, easing the chill of the morning.

"They're not staying with us, Papa." Letty helped herself to a plate and a roll. The sideboard was laden with enough food to sustain a good-sized militia, all hot and enticingly displayed, some dishes covered with domed silver, others were artfully arranged with sprigs of herbs. Letty continued with excitement. "They were here to kill us in an early morning duel. So we decided upon breakfast instead."

"Fine, my dear," Mr. Fairfax replied, turning the page of his paper and smoothing out a crease with great deliberation. His slate-gray wig was elaborately dressed and curled tightly above his ears, although it seemed in danger of losing its grip on the owner's head.

"How is Edward?" Letty asked.

"Very fine indeed," their father replied. "Quite nice."

Emily shook her head in resignation. "Please forgive my father, sirs. He is most interested in his recent batch of gazettes from London. He favors books and words to people and conversation."

"An interest he shares with his daughter?" Ashford suggested, and Emily smiled uncertainly.

How had he been able to guess?

"Please do help yourselves, sirs. Letty," she scolded mildly, still flustered by Ashford's attention. "You should have waited for our guests."

"Sorry. But *they* should have treated us more as gentlemen," Letty said without remorse, spreading a huge mound of fluffy butter on her roll. "Duels make me ever so hungry."

Emily again motioned for them to help themselves, and a maid entered with a silver tray of hot chocolate, tea and coffee.

Ashford, comfortable in any social situation, made himself at ease in the breakfast room, helping himself to the delicacies on the sideboard, pausing over a plate of blood pudding.

"So Miss Fairfax, is this the house where you conduct all of Mr. St. John's business?"

"Please, sir," she said softly. "No one knows but my sister. Eggs?"

"Yes, thank you. Not even . . ." He cocked his head toward her father, who was chuckling over something in the paper.

"Especially not," she cocked her head in the precise fashion Ashford had just done. "Ham?"

"Please."

Suddenly Mr. Fairfax looked up at the two men in the room. He squinted once, and then removed the glasses. "Good morning."

"Good morning, sir," Ogilvie began. "May I just say how very—"

"Oh, no." Mr. Fairfax's soft blue eyes took in the sight of Lord Ogilvie. "Emily, he will never do. Never do indeed."

"No, Father. You are mistaken. He is not a suitor."

"Indeed? I am vastly relieved."

"I say, there is no call for—" Ogilvie began.

Then Mr. Fairfax glanced over at Lucius Ashford. "Now you are a good deal more of what I had in mind for my Emily. She needs a man with strong shoulders. Those are yours, I presume, and not the work of an excellent tailor."

"No, Papa," Letty said after biting into a roll. "Mr. Ashford came here to help Lord Ogilvie shoot Emily, not to court her."

"To shoot her?" Mr. Fairfax stiffened. "Sir, perhaps I am old-fashioned in my ways, but it seems to me that there is no need whatsoever to shoot my daughter."

The servants continued to clear the used plates, pouring tea and coffee as if nothing could be more logical than the present conversation.

"It was all a misunderstanding, sir. I assure you," Ashford said, settling a warm roll onto his plate. "My friend here thought she was a man and called her out."

"Indeed?" Mr. Jeremy Fairfax thought for a moment, then glanced at his eldest daughter. "You are right, Emily. You do have need of some new gowns. Without her mother I am at a loss concerning the current fashions, although how you can mistake her for a man I cannot fathom. As you see, I prefer good old-fashioned breeches to pantaloons or gowns or whatever the young bucks are wearing in London. Now, if you will forgive me, I am going upstairs to finish my paper in peace. Good morning."

With elegance he rose and bowed, then left the breakfast room.

Much of Lord Ogilvie's color began to return as he ate. "Excellent ham! Delightful eggs! My word, Ashford, I daresay I have not had such succulent kidneys in years."

Ashford held Emily's chair as she glided into place, then sat down himself. "I take it, Miss Fairfax, that you have had many suitors of late?"

Before Emily could answer, Letty spoke. "She

always has suitors, Mr. Ashford. Emily has quite a dowry."

"Letty, please."

"It's true. Whoever gets her will also get fifty thousand pounds. Same for me," Letty took a dainty bite from her roll.

Lord Ogilvie choked, but Ashford managed to maintain a polite expression.

"And why have you not married, Miss Fairfax? You are more handsome than any lady I can imagine."

Letty answered with delight. "Why, I thank you! But as I am only twelve years of age, I suspect I should wait at least a year before embarking on marriage." She suddenly crinkled her nose, then rubbed the tip violently to prevent a sneeze.

Ashford, slightly taken aback, managed to cover a laugh with an almost-convincing cough. Eyes glinting with humor, he turned to her. "Ah, well. That explains your single state, Miss Letty. Your refined manners mask your tender age." Letty nodded and spooned a massive dollop of jam on another roll. Ashford continued, "But what of Miss Emily? For you are very nearly as handsome as Miss Letty."

Smiling, Emily acknowledged the compliment with a nod. "Thank you, sir, but that is the problem. Every man finds me vastly handsome. But that is mainly because every man finds me vastly handsome after hearing of the fifty thousand pounds. It is not very flattering to see male eyes glint at the prospect of all those pounds. I believe it brings out the worst of your sex, sir." She took a small sip of tea.

"Surely one young man must have a claim on your heart?" Ashford could not help but pursue the matter.

"No. I refuse ever to marry. I am quite comfortable as I am."

Ashford raised his eyebrows. "Indeed? But all of our fondest childhood fables end in marriage, and all end joyfully. They never conclude with the fair princess living happily ever after by herself, rattling about in a lonely old castle."

"Ah-ha." Emily carefully put down her teacup. "They end happily because they conclude with the wedding, not the actual marriage. I would wager that after a couple of years, Cinderella was heartily bored with the prince and their howling babies. Beauty no doubt wished for the return of the beast."

"I am stunned, Miss Fairfax." Ashford leaned back in the chair. "Never have I met a woman who did not wish to be happily married."

"To be frank, sir, I do not believe in marriage."

"Good God, do you not?" Ogilvie cheerfully accepted another helping of eggs from the maid. "But our society demands marriage. It is the only way to preserve domestic bliss, to maintain law and order. Why, marriage is the very bedrock of British society."

"Perhaps for some." Emily ran a finger along

the rim of her teacup. "But I have never seen a truly happy union, a marriage of equals. Some start as such, but end as something very different altogether. And weddings are awful. Wedding dresses are usually dowdy old things no one really wants to wear. I do not actually believe in any of the stuff that brings childhood fables to a happy conclusion."

"Then why do those fables so invariably end with those conclusions?" Ashford was genuinely curious. He was also mesmerized by Emily's intense blue gaze.

"Because the audience demands it. It is what they expect. They wish to see their own hopes and dreams enacted over and over again, but with more pleasing results. We are all perverse gluttons for such punishment."

"How very singular," Ogilvie replied.

"Perhaps. I just know that I will be vastly more content by avoiding the jaws of matrimony."

"The jaws of matrimony?" Ashford repeated slowly. An unreadable expression crossed his face. "Interesting notion, the state of marriage seen as a wild, dangerous predator."

Emily laughed. "That's precisely what it is! A threat to a woman's happiness, indeed her very life! But tell me, if marriage brings such boundless joy, why, sir, are you not ensconced in a blissfully wedded state?"

"How do you know I am *not* married?"

"Oh, we know lots about you, Mr. L.A., from—"

"Letty!" Emily snapped, her face flushed. They all turned to her, and calmly, she said, "Dearest, please do not speak with your mouth full."

"But it wasn't full, see?" She opened her mouth and turned to her sister, then to Ogilvie and Ashford, pointing at the blameless, empty and maligned mouth.

"Charming," Ogilvie muttered.

"Well, so you have no wish to become a wife." Ashford was at a complete loss for words. For a moment he just stared at his plate. "What does your brother say of this reluctance to marry?" Ashford asked at last.

"My brother?" Emily was confused. "We have no brother, sir. Only four girls. I am the eldest, Letty is the youngest. My middle two sisters are married and settled in England."

Ashford swallowed a bite of excellent ham. This was indeed a splendid breakfast. "Then who is Edward?"

"Edward?" A slow dawning came over Emily's face. "Edward is the ham. My sister Letty has a rather unpleasant habit of naming the livestock. Daisy, for your enlightenment, was the former owner of the delicious kidneys."

Ogilvie rose hastily from the table, pointing at his now-empty plate. "Excuse—" was all he was able to mumble before dashing from the room. Letty grinned and followed him. "I'll fetch Williams," she said with glee.

* * *

"Miss Fairfax," Ashford said after the sound of footsteps subsided. "Please forgive my friend Lord Ogilvie. I fear he is suffering from a rather delicate stomach this morning." They were alone in the breakfast room.

"I understand, sir. On occasion my own father has suffered from just such an ailment." She smiled.

"So tell me," he said easily. "Just how came you to represent the playwright Edgar St. John?"

"Excuse me?"

"I am just curious as to how you became his delegate at the duel. It is a most unusual situation, you must own."

She hadn't expected to be asked such a direct question.

"Well, you see," she stammered. "How it happened, indeed. It was quite amusing, actually."

"Yes?"

"More ham?"

"No, thank you. Is Mr. St. John a neighbor? Perhaps he is a friend of your father?"

"No, he is not a neighbor nor is he a friend, exactly." She paused. "Did you hear that?"

"Hear what?"

"A noise. A very loud noise."

"I heard nothing, Miss Fairfax. Is the playwright one of your many suitors?"

"I did hear a noise. Someone may have taken a tumble. Perhaps I should investigate."

"The only noise I heard was the distinct sound of

you avoiding my very simple question. Who is Mr. Edgar St. John?"

Emily looked over at Ashford. This was not what she had anticipated in her imagination. Never had she envisioned her own Mr. L.A. being so inquisitive, or so very persistent.

This was not going as planned.

"May I venture a theory?" He focused on her with uncomfortable intensity.

"Of course." She hoped he would offer a happy, viable explanation for the entire situation. And if so, she would simply play along.

"Is it possible, just possible, that you, Miss Emily Fairfax, are in fact Mr. Edgar St. John?"

"Mr. Ashford!" she exclaimed, stunned. Immediately she stood up, as if to flee the table. He also rose, in a most gentlemanly fashion, and then she sat back down. After a brief pause, he, too, settled back in the chair.

"Come, come, Miss Fairfax," he said at last. "Pray do not sport with me. And do not underestimate me."

"Sir, I know not how to respond."

"Please do me the honor of responding with the truth."

"Sir," she said softly, searching for an answer, any answer that would placate the man.

"If I give you my word, as a gentleman, to keep your secret, will you tell me?"

At first she did not answer, and while she hesitated, he prodded. "Please let us end this charade. I know you must write as Edgar St. John. I have pieced together all I am able since the moment we met on that hill this morning. This is the only logical solution I can conclude. You also used the phrase 'the jaws of matrimony,' which, if I am not mistaken, is a direct quote from the St. John play *He Begs to Differ*. Now, quoting a play is by no means proof of authorship, otherwise we would all be Shakespeare. But the simple fact that 'the jaws of matrimony' so perfectly summarizes your own rather unique opinion is rather revealing."

She began to speak, and he held up a hand for silence. "Furthermore, I presume your sister knows of your secret identity, and no one else. Otherwise it would be sheer foolishness to bring your young sister to a remote field to meet a pair of strange, possibly dangerous men. The only reason I can fathom is that Letty knew of the meeting, and would not allow you to go without her."

Now Emily took a deep breath. Just the hint of a smile was beginning to form.

He, too, began to grin. "So tell me, how did your illustrious writing career begin?"

There was no point in denying the truth any longer. And with a strangely liberating sense of relief, she stared at him for a long moment.

And then, beaming, she leaned forward. "It all began as a lark, sir. I had not the smallest notion that anything would come of it. But it began years ago, when we were all small children. We used to write our own plays for amusement. Poor Letty was usually forced to take on the role of the lapdog or pet monkey. My other sisters were the fair maidens."

"And you, Miss Fairfax?"

"I was always the hero," she said with a small dash of pride.

"Interesting casting."

"Isn't it, though?" she agreed. "So once, several years ago, I devised a story, wrote it up as a play, and sent it off to Mr. Giles, the theatrical agent. I picked the name from my father's papers simply because it was the first name I came across in that issue. After sending it to London, the entire thing was forgotten."

"Forgotten? I find that hard to believe."

"Forgotten is the wrong word. I pretended to forget, did my best to ignore the embarrassment of a manuscript I had so impetuously sent to a busy London theatrical agent. I promptly put it out of my mind, otherwise I would go mad dwelling on the sheer folly of it all. And then, a little over a month later, I received a letter saying the play was to be produced."

"You must have been delighted," he said warmly.

"Shocked, astonished, and then, finally, delighted. But please tell me, sir, do you attend the theater in London often?"

"Not frequently, I confess. But I did see Mr. Edmund Kean as Shylock."

"Did you really! How wonderful! How I envy you!"

"And I did see Mr. Edgar St. John's latest play with Lord Ogilvie."

Emily could barely contain her curiosity. "Did you like it? Was it well attended? And well performed? What were the costumes like—good? I do hope. And—"

"Miss Fairfax, please!" He smiled. "I went with Lord Ogilvie to ascertain if your words had cast aspersions upon the good name of my friend."

"Oh. Of course." She was able to remain silent for only a few brief moments. "Still, did you enjoy it?"

"Yes, I did. The characters are marvelous, especially Oswald—the audience roared every time he enters. I enjoyed your play very much, although it was most unfortunate that your Lord Oswald was so similar to my friend. He took great offense, as you know."

"I had no idea such a man could really exist," she admitted. "In all honesty it was a coincidence, pure and simple."

"In that case I am glad indeed your words did not result in the spilling of blood, Miss Fairfax. And again, you have my solemn word that I will never reveal your identity. Even to Lord Ogilvie."

"If you do, sir, I may be forced to call you out."

"Very well. And I vow to meet you on just such a field of honor should I betray your trust."

Smiling, she looked down at her plate. After a small silence she spoke. "Sir," she began. "I have answered your question. May I now ask you one in return?"

"In point of fact," he arched an eyebrow, "I *guessed* at your answers. I suspect you would have never answered the question willingly."

With a gracious nod she acknowledged the truth of his statement.

"Of course, Miss Fairfax, I will answer any question you may possibly have."

"Thank you, sir." She glanced down, searching for a way to phrase a most difficult, personal question. Then she looked up, directly into his face. For a moment she was once again taken aback by how very handsome he was, by his strong, regular features. There was just the vague hint of lines bracketing his mouth, and he cocked his head, prompting her to continue.

"I confess I have read about you in all of my father's gazettes and newspapers. So my question is this: Why are you a second at so many duels? Yet I cannot recall ever reading of you engaging in one yourself. Why is that?"

"Duels are foolish," he stated with perfect reason.

"In truth they may seem so if viewed with a rational, unemotional mind. Yet anyone with spirit must admire such daring. And one must admit, pure logic does not stop most men who move about society and the world to engage in duels, who rise to the brilliant challenge they pose. And recall Mr. Burr and Mr. Hamilton several years since, sir. Even Americans duel in their newfound democracy."

"And do you recall what that duel was about?"

"Well, no sir. I do not. But the main point is that the duel took place. It was allowed to come to a most natural and magnificent conclusion."

"I try to prevent duels. They are a waste. Nobody ever wins, and nobody ever remembers what the duels were about. I try to be a cooler prevailing head."

Emily continued as if he had not just spoken. Her voice rose in rhapsody. "I do believe there is nothing more manly, more glorious, than two men meeting on a field of honor with the sun rising just beyond. That is the way to settle an argument, if one has courage of his convictions. If one is brave and good and true."

Ashford's voice remained calm. "I do my best to prevent duels, no matter what convictions brought the parties to such a place."

"What on earth for? You are only interfering, sir. You are preventing gallant men from protecting their honor. From stating their beliefs and then standing up for those beliefs in the most extraordinary fashion possible. By stopping such events you are rendering their beliefs, their very souls, useless, devoid of substance. You are coming between—"

"I am coming between Miss Emily Fairfax and her love of a good story," he interrupted. "You are piqued that my interference prevents needless bloodshed. And further annoyed that the scandalous details are not rendered in the next week's papers for your secondhand titillation."

"Not at all." Emily lowered her voice. "It is simply that you are preventing a natural resolution. It is as if you are stopping a flower from blooming, or a waterfall from flowing. Perhaps a volcano from erupting."

"Have you ever seen a duel, Miss Fairfax?"

"Well, no. Of course not. Yet still . . ."

"They cause the destruction of entire families. I have seen slow, agonizing deaths from lingering wounds—the so-called winners often die as well, Miss Fairfax. The winner's death is every bit as hideous as that of the vanquished. What know you of blood and violence, you cloistered here in Ireland?"

"I have heard and read—"

"You have heard? You have *read?*" Tossing his linen napkin aside, he leaned forward urgently. "I have seen. I have lived. And it is not glorious. It is not ennobling. It is sickening and ugly. It is the putrid stench of death, no matter who is right or wrong. And after all is done, believe me on this, Miss Fairfax—no one remembers what caused the original dispute. Winner or loser, the words spoken with such heat the night before ring hollow and meaningless in the barbaric face of death. It is a tragic waste of all lives concerned. Any why, pray tell, do you suppose so many gentlemen wish me to be their second?"

"I know not," she breathed.

"Because they can escape death thus without losing their precious reputations. Because they know I will do my best to stop every duel I come across. Because they can resolve their issues and live to see another sunrise. That is why. And never once has a single gentleman refused to meet on a field of so-called honor when they have heard I am to be a second. Indeed, I have been asked on many an occasion to serve as a second to both parties."

"Sir, I am sorry to have offended you."

A sinking sense of disappointment washed over her. Although his appearance was even more splendid than she had ever imagined her own Mr. L.A's. could possibly be, his attitude and beliefs were far from heroic. The real Ashford was a glorious physical specimen of manhood with a dull, retiring soul.

He seemed to relax just slightly. "Forgive me. There are several topics about which I become passionate, and dueling is one. Again, forgive me, Miss Fairfax."

Although she nodded politely, she was bitterly disappointed. Oh how she wished she had never met the real Mr. L.A.! Or if she had met him, if she could have only seen him without hearing his milksop opinions! Then her fantasy could continue, untarnished.

Now things would never be the same. Never.

Suddenly there was a commotion outside of the breakfast room. Williams, the somber butler, entered and bowed. Visible from behind his back was a butterfly net.

"Begging your pardon, Miss Fairfax, but it appears the butterflies Miss Letty introduced into

the household are causing something of an uprising
in the kitchen. Cook is terrified of insects, miss,
owing to the incident last summer with Miss Letty's
bee farm. So if you please, Miss Fairfax, any suggestion you can offer would be most welcome indeed."

A distant shriek of "Not in my batter!" pierced
the air, followed by the distinctive sound of shattering crockery.

"Thank you, Williams. I will be there directly."

Williams backed elegantly out of the doorway.

Ashford smiled. "It seems you are urgently
required elsewhere. I shall locate Lord Ogilvie, and
will no longer impose on your hospitality. Thank
you so very much for—"

"No, please! I will return in a moment." Emily
rose to her feet, as did Ashford. "I fear such emer-
gencies occur with frightful regularity in this
household."

"Miss Fairfax, unfortunately we must return to
England. I have pressing business there. But I will
recall this morning as a most interesting event."

"Perhaps you may . . ." she began.

"Miss Fairfax, I . . ." he said simultaneously.

They both smiled, their eyes meeting for a
moment. Ashford cleared his throat. "May I have
permission to write you?"

Ah, she thought. *The fifty thousand pounds once
again works magic on yet another bachelor gentleman.*

"Yes, of course," she replied mechanically. "I
would be pleased to correspond with you, sir."

Letty dashed into the room, her face aglow with

excitement. "Oh, Emily! You must see what has happened in the kitchen! And Mr. Ashford? I fear your friend Lord Ogilvie is most indisposed and . . . goodness!" Letty gazed curiously at Ashford and her sister. "Have I missed something interesting?"

Emily shook her head, but Letty would not be silenced. "I should never have left the room. Please, do tell me what I missed!"

"Forgive me," Ashford smoothly interjected. "But where is Lord Ogilvie?"

"Oh, he is outside. You two gentlemen are to borrow one of our carriages and a driver to go back to your lodgings in town. Father says it is fine, but requests that you do not transport chickens in the carriage as their feathers make him sneeze. And Lord Ogilvie sends his thanks for breakfast, and sends Emily his best compliments." Letty took a few steps closer to her sister. "Emily, you do look quite pale."

"I am fine, Letty." Her voice was a bare whisper.

Outside they could hear Ogilvie climbing into the carriage as cries of pursuit could be heard from the kitchen.

"Well, then," Ashford began. "Miss Letty? Thank you for a most unusual morning."

"You are welcome, sir." Letty stepped forward and shook his hand. "And may I add you are the finest second I have ever had the pleasure of enjoying in an almost duel."

"I return the compliment," Ashford bowed. "Good-bye, Miss Fairfax, Miss Letty."

"Good-bye, Mr. Ashford," Emily responded softly.

And then, hat and gloves in hand, he took his leave.

Emily stared out of the window through the lace curtain panel and saw the carriage roll down the drive, swerving to avoid Cook as she dashed across the yard. A wistful smile played upon her lips. And she wondered, as the sight of the carriage grew ever more distant and she prepared to quell the riot in the kitchen, if she would ever again meet a man who could compare to the spectacular Mr. L.A. of her own imagination.

Chapter Three

～❧～

Bond Street, London
23 April 1814

My Dear Miss Fairfax,

I do hope this letter finds you in good health, and that both Miss Letty and your father have recovered from the butterfly invasion that overtook your household last week.

Our crossing was uneventful, although poor Ogilvie seemed rather distressed by the choppy seas. Or perhaps his distress was prompted by my uttering of two names, Edward and Daisy. As he has barely spoken to me since, I cannot fathom the reason for his discomfort.

I do not wish to lecture you, but I do hope you have reflected upon our discussion of duels. Perhaps you may one day understand my feelings concerning the entire hateful topic. In any case, Miss Fairfax, I wish to thank you once again for your warm hospitality. And I do hope that soon you will visit London, and I can show you Parliament. We are out until October, at which time I will present my maiden speech. Hopefully my powers of persuasion will be more finely honed than they have been of late.

With sincere admiration, L.A.

Fairfax Castle, Ireland
30 April 1814

Dear Mr. Ashford,
Thank you so very much for your letter of 23 inst. I confess, your views on dueling did, indeed, both startle and perplex me, as they do still. You are correct. I was not perusaded by your arguments. Perhaps it is simply the male race in general that renders me bewildered. Women, I believe, have a more passionate nature as a whole. But most females of my acquaintance are intrigued and captivated by gentlemen moved by passion to act so bravely as they do in a duel. Enough, for I feel we will never agree on this topic. I understand the London season is in full flower now. Tell me, is the infamous Lady Jersey still terrorizing the ballrooms of London? And have any new dandies come to rescue (or ruin) this season's crop of fresh debutantes?
I am indeed glad to hear that you and Lord Ogilvie had a fairly easy crossing, although I believe your friend would have found it easier still without the mention of Letty's dearly departed livestock. You were more than welcome to visit, sir, and any hospitality on our part was given with much delight.

Your friend,
E. Fairfax

Lucius Ashford stared down at the papers stacked upon his desk. There were newspapers, Parliamentary pamphlets, hastily scribbled notes from his tours of some of the poorer neighborhoods, and memoranda to himself on national reform. It was a rather stuffy room, with leather-bound books thick with dust, but he found it a comfortable if cramped place in which to work.

And on the top of all those dry, dull papers was the crisp letter from Miss Emily Fairfax, written in her bold yet decidedly feminine hand.

Outside, the chaotic bustle of London City passed beneath his office window, the shouts and calls, the clip-clop of horse hooves, the grating, metallic roll of carriages and carts. Occasionally he would hear a burst of ill-played music from a traveling show, or the high barks of a lady's lapdog. Several young men staggered zigzag through the street, all three dressed in evening clothes from the previous night, all three singing a bawdy rhyme about a bit of muslin named Gwen with an unfortunate fondness for gin.

But in his mind he was in a more bucolic place, of pastoral green hills, soft breezes, birds chirping and gentle peace. And then, upon further reflection on the image in question, he grinned.

Peaceful? Gentle? Perhaps the countryside of Ireland could be described thusly, but most certainly not when the images of Miss Emily Fairfax and her young sister Letty were added to the visual painting. No. They who had so perfectly destroyed the calm of Ireland would stand London, perhaps all of England, on its side.

It was an appealing thought.

Selecting a quill from his pottery jar, a lopsided

gift from one of his grateful constituents, he shaved the point with his penknife and contemplated what he would say to her in this next letter. It would, he hoped, further a friendship. And he would write simply, without flourish, from one friend to another. He could send her tidbits of London life for use in her plays, observations she could not get from other sources.

In the days since his last letter, he had carefully collected the images to send. There were the hundreds of vessels jostling for room in the Thames, with passenger ships attempting to nudge merchant ships for the precious dock space. Or of the comment he heard uttered by a fellow MP, that all of London seemed to have been out of town. He attended assemblies and noted the absurd behavior of people of rank, the odd gestures, the ridiculous new dance steps, the most recent gossip. A group of young men had begun to sport purple-and-orange silk waistcoats trimmed in wool tartan, halting the bold fashion only after more than one lovely young lady doubled over in laughter at the sight of the garment. And a new bow had recently come into vogue, employed by self-conscious dandies and accompanied by a peculiar hesitation every third word. His only hope was that this silly trend would be of a mercifully short duration.

He would describe to her the commotion when he was visiting the tailors Schweitzer & Davidson on Cook Street, and in strolled the Prince Regent himself with his toadies, his artificial whiskers quite apparent without the aid of artificial lighting.

All this he would tell her, and more.

Then he stopped. What if she took his continued correspondence as an insult of the most impudent kind? He would be sure to add the usual formal flourishes so that even a maiden aunt could not object to the letter.

Indeed, he realized, Miss Emily Fairfax was herself a maiden aunt.

However, he also would enjoy the chance to challenge her overly romantic view of duels. If he could convince her of their brutality without being forced to reveal the real reason for his attitude, then he could convince his political opponents of anything. She could be his test subject.

He had work to complete. Parliament would be called in October. Soon he would be making his first speech in the House. He needed to concentrate on that, to form words of such eloquence that true reform could take place. He had waited for this chance. He had studied the conditions of poverty that most MPs so studiously ignored.

The smile gradually left his face. It would not do to insult Miss Emily Fairfax. Nor would it do to neglect his primary duty.

He had whittled his quill down to splinters, nothing but the feather stripped of its point waving in his hand. With an impatient sweep he cleared his desk of the shavings and selected another quill.

He would not write to her now. His emotions were too close to the surface—it would not do. Not at all. Perhaps later, after his speech was composed. Maybe after his speech had been delivered. For the moment he could not let his thoughts wander too far from the vital task at hand.

The useless feather floated to the ground.

The bright feather touched Emily's nose, as Letty waved it playfully before her face.

They sat in the parlor, trimmings and ribbons and brightly colored bits of silk strewn about. Several chip bonnets, naked of adornment, one painted white, were lined up on one of their father's old wig stands.

In Letty's hand was a purple ribbon she had folded into a buglike shape, with garrish red feathers and gold springs bursting from the center.

"Letty, dearest," Emily said slowly, for what seemed to be the hundredth time. "I assure you, in Paris they are not featuring millinery of such exotic design. Here," she again pointed to the tinted etching of French fashions, the elegant, subdued women looking wan, underfed and bored. "See how delicate the bonnets are? This one has only a simple blue ribbon around the crown, this other has nothing but satin ties. This is the current fashion in Paris." She checked the date of the gazette. "Well, two months ago, at any rate."

"But we are not in Paris. We are in Ireland."

"Precisely my point." Emily smiled. "Because if we were to appear in London in such a fashion, we would be labeled instantly as Irish."

"I'm proud to be Irish," Letty exclaimed, straightening her posture.

"So am I, my dear. But it is never in the best of taste to be, well, so very obvious."

"Gentlemen of the military are," Letty replied with perfect reasoning, holding her creation aloft to admire it from all angles. "They wear uniforms. And you have always said that military men are vastly fashionable."

"They are. But their uniforms also proclaim them clear targets for the enemy."

"Like Lord Nelson!" Letty grinned, thinking of the fallen naval hero who wore the full splendor of his many decorations into battle, and was promptly killed by the French.

"Precisely. If we wear such a hat in London society, we will be shot at once. Most likely by one of our own sisters." Then Emily smiled gently at her youngest sister's crestfallen expression. Poor Letty should not be forced to suffer merely because Emily was in a dilemma over what to do about Mr. Lucius Ashford. "Oh, Letty. Forgive me. Your designs are brilliant. Trim your bonnet in any way you desire. Perhaps such a hat suits you best."

"Do you think it is beautiful?"

"Of course! And upon second thought, it is the most beautiful and loveliest hat I have ever seen. Here, let me help you fasten it properly. The wax will not hold."

Letty blew upon the red feathers and the gold springs, delighting in the way they danced and bounced with the movement. Then she strung bright beads on silver string, tying them to the brim to dangle freely.

Emily reached for her sewing box, and again her thoughts traveled to several weeks before, when Mr. Lucius Ashford had come to Fairfax Castle. She had hoped he would write her a fascinating letter. Instead, he had sent her a perfectly polite note, one even the most severe of chaperones could not possibly fault.

Once again, he had disappointed her. It was not his failing, not really. Perhaps she expected too much. Maybe that was her problem, one of her many problems.

She wondered if she should be brazen enough to write a second letter before he wrote her again. How would she begin such a letter? Perhaps with a comment about the weather, or a mention of the newest additions to their livestock, the calves and the kids and the chicks. Now *that* would be subtle.

Dear Mr. Ashford,

You will be happy to know that Mildred, the sister of the late Edward the Hog, of Bacon fame, has safely delivered of five piglets. All are suckling well. Enclosed is a fair rendering of the recent blessed event. . . .

Letty was saying something, but Emily was not listening. "Yes, dearest. Of course," she replied automatically, smiling to herself at what his reaction would be to such a missive. Whatever Letty had said, Emily's response pleased her greatly.

No, she could not write to Mr. Ashford. Even if she asked to inquire if he had left an umbrella at Fairfax Castle—an idea she had thought up the previous night—her motives would be all too transparent. Inconveniently, the day of his visit had been unusually, vexingly fine.

How peculiar, Emily mused. Never before had she given a straw for what others thought of her. But now she wanted most desperately for one man, Mr. Lucius Ashford, to think well of her. The very notion that he would think her rash or uncouth was intolerable.

Why on earth should she care what one dull, passionless man thought of her?

Then a thought struck her.

What if he had merely pretended to be a dull, passionless man? Of course! It would have been the height of poor taste to display one's more ardent side to a young lady, especially given the circumstances of their meeting. There had been no formal introduction, no chaperone. Indeed, the more she thought of it, the more she appreciated his sense of propriety.

It was up to her, the female, to take the lead. She would reveal her own emotions, and wait to see his response. Should his response disappoint, she could simply dismiss him from her mind. There was very little to lose by making the effort, and potentially a great deal to lose by not.

Perhaps he was the dashing Mr. L.A. she had been dreaming of, after all.

"Letty!" She stood up, ignoring the bits of ribbon and the small scissors that tumbled from her lap. "I have a letter to write!"

"Really? Then may I trim all of your hats as well?"

"Yes, of course dearest. . . ."

Ideas were already spilling into Emily's mind. This would be a test, the ultimate test for Mr. Ashford. She would shock him, startle him, provoke him. His response would determine their fate.

But it was up to her to set the scene.

Whatever happened next, her letter was sure to inspire quite a reaction from Mr. Lucius Ashford!

Fairfax Castle, Ireland
8 May 1814

Dear Mr. Ashford,
It is a most glorious spring day, the first warmth of the season is just beginning its gentle chore of coaxing the chill from the countryside. To celebrate, I visited a nearby pond, and although the water was yet brisk from winter's final breath, I removed my clothing and plunged headfirst into the icy pool. I imagined myself an ancient sea nymph, with all trappings of our impure world cast aside on the soft, moss-kissed shore. It was utterly invigorating. Or, as Lord Byron would say . . . "For me, degenerate modern wretch,/ Though in the genial month of May,/ My dripping limbs I faintly sketch,/ And think I've done a feat today."

Are you an admirer of Lord Byron? I do think he is the most captivating of poets, and one cannot help but admire his wonderfully natural passions. He allows them to unfold gracefully, as passions were meant to flow. Pray do reveal your innermost thoughts on poetry, Sir, as I do have a desire to know.

Your affectionate friend,
Emily Fairfax

Lucius Ashford read, reread, and once again read the letter from Miss Emily Fairfax.

"Good God," he murmured.

The afternoon post had just arrived. He had planned to stop by Gentleman Jackson's boxing rooms, and then head back to his offices. But the letter had so surprised him, so entirely thrown him off balance, that all thoughts of engaging in physical activity had been removed from his mind.

For once he was relieved his manservant kept irregular hours, and had not yet arrived for the day. He needed to be alone, to compose his thoughts.

What he needed was a stiff drink of brandy.

Without hesitation he walked over to the sideboard and poured himself a drink. After a quick sip, he glanced at the letter once more, and added another hefty splash.

What had been her meaning in posting such a letter? She touched on poetry, passion, and—if he was not gravely mistaken (and her words left precious little room for doubt)—bathing without apparel in open waters.

"Good God."

He could, of course, answer her letter briefly with a few simple lines. *"Am fond of spring, ponds in general and of bare bathing in particular. Dislike Byron intensely. Find both his poetry and his character too calculating for my taste. Sincerely, L.A."*

But that would not please Miss Fairfax. She wished him to reveal himself, to be spontaneous. Most of his life he had been doing quite the opposite, revealing as little of himself as possible. Controlling his emotions. Only Ogilvie truly knew him, and that had been more a consequence of their long acquaintance than any deliberate effort at divulging private mysteries.

He swallowed another sip and determined he would indeed write her a letter. This time he would not mince words, he would tell her all—the reasons for his actions and beliefs, the genesis of the man he had become.

Never before had he dreamed of doing such a thing, of setting down on paper his agonizing journey, much less sharing it with a virtual stranger. Yet somehow it felt right. Instead of analyzing his response, he would for once allow instinct to unfold as naturally as even Miss Fairfax could wish. And perhaps in doing such a thing, he would learn more about himself.

Then he allowed himself a smile. She would certainly not expect this.

"Well, Miss Fairfax,"—he put down the empty glass and turned toward his desk—"you are not the only one who can shock and surprise."

With that he began the letter. And after nearly two hours it was completed and sealed, just in time for the last post of the day.

The young man on the stage of the Olympic Theatre on the west end of Wyth Street was not happy.

Unlike the other actors milling about, all attired in costumes of a more subdued nature, Henry Hughes was dressed in the multicolored cloth of motley. The billowing sleeves of his jacket ballooned comically with every gesture, as did his matching pantaloons—complete with a vivid green and gold insert at the crotch. He kept his movements to a minimum, not wishing to draw additional attention to his ridiculous outfit. Upon his head was a tightly fitted motley bonnet, tied in a huge bow at his jutting chin, with small brass bells tinkling merrily from the points of the cap.

"Mr. Elliston," he said clearly to the man before him. The manager of the theater, himself a part player three times a week at the famed Drury Lane, did not respond. He was coaching a child tumbler on the fine art of a somersault.

"Very fine, Master Howard!" Elliston the manager enthused to the youngster, knowing very well that Henry Hughes was glaring from beneath his colorful jingling bells. "Excellent! Upon my word, you will be the next Master Betty," Elliston clapped, referring to the boy who took the London theatrical world by storm several seasons earlier with his recitations of Shakespeare. In truth, the lad had been a full half-dozen years older than he had claimed—closer to twenty than to the eleven he willingly admitted—yet he had caused a sensation. And he was still touring the provinces with some success.

"Mr. Elliston," Henry Hughes repeated. "I beg of you, do not force me to play the role of Harlequin tonight. I am a man of great passions! I am a tragedian. I deserve to play the great tragic roles. I am Othello and Romeo and Hamlet and—"

"But sir," Elliston replied to the actor, his deep voice saturated with utter reason. "You are a perfect fool."

Henry Hughes paused for a moment, wondering whether he had just been insulted or complimented.

Robert William Elliston, a large, loquacious man who had once been intended for the church, pursed his thick lips with satisfaction. He had taken over management of the Olympic the previous year, even as he continued his successful management of the Surrey and the Theatre Royal in Birmingham. He was a difficult master, wringing every pence from every actor. Indeed, his players worked double, forcing them to scramble between the Surrey across the Thames to the Olympic and back again in full paint and costume to make their cues.

Six months earlier he had secured an unknown provincial actor by the name of Edmund Kean to play his Harlequin and whatever else the Olympic required. But Kean had bolted to the Drury Lane, where he was now the rage of London with his brilliant portrayals of Shylock and Richard. Elliston, not a man to be betrayed on any level, was still furious with Kean. Upstart guttersnipe! To add to the humiliation, he'd been forced to placate the Drury Lane in order to maintain his own position there— his one jot of respectability and legitimacy in the unsavory world of theater.

This nobody Henry Hughes reminded him all too much of Kean—the same burning eyes, the same strange intensity. Even his size and build, rather short and slight, was similar to Kean's. He could not punish Kean at the moment. But he could punish Hughes in his stead.

"Mr. Hughes," he said in his oiliest tone. "Perhaps you were not informed of this in the provinces, but we are not living in an age of great drama. Poetry, yes. Science, but of course. But drama? No. So we must make do with what we have, and leave the great tragedies to the great theaters. Run round to the Drury Lane or Covent Garden, lad, if you wish to wrest tears from the audience."

Elliston made the suggestions in the greatest of confidence, knowing full well that Hughes had all but camped out at both locations, unable to even secure an audition. The young actor's face reddened for a moment before he spoke.

"But there must be a decent play someplace!" Hughes stamped his foot, which had the unfortunate result of causing his bells to jingle. "A new one, with a role that will best display my talents."

"One can only have patience, Mr. Hughes. And

in the meantime, practice your juggling and tumbling, for tonight you are to be Harlequin. Oh, and I have procured for you a most amusing device. As you tumble it will produce a series of gratuitously offensive sounds. The audience is sure to assume that you, sir, have the considerable skill required to to render those sounds with your very own body."

"I . . . I . . ."

"Good evening, Mr. Hughes. And do have care—I understand that cloth of motley sets aflame with great ease. Beware the footlights. We would not wish you to become a human torch." With that Elliston bowed, and returned to the young acrobat.

Henry Hughes stood for a moment in sputtering fury, and then went below to the green room, where he knew Snife, the double-jointed toe dancer, was sure to have a bottle or two or brandy.

Someday, he vowed to himself, he would be the most magnificent actor in the history of the London stage.

Someday soon.

Emily Fairfax was vexed.

Pacing in the large, marble-floored hallway of Fairfax Castle, her gaze kept returning to the table where Williams had placed the day's mail.

And once again, there was nothing from Lucius Ashford.

By now he must have had her letter for over two weeks. There had been more than enough time for some sort of response to her letter, some sort of acknowledgment.

And he had seen fit to respond with thudding silence.

All she could do was cringe when she thought of what she had shared with him, the content of her letter, how she had exposed herself.

How he must have roared with laughter at her naïveté! Had he shared her foolishness with anyone else? Ogilvie? Other Members of Parliament? The entire population of London?

"Good God," she moaned to the guilty pile of letters, bills and gazettes. "I even quoted Byron!"

The thought was too much to bear.

So much for disregarding the man, for ignoring how it felt if he did not write.

If only she could undo it, make it all go away. If only she hadn't been so impulsive as to send the insipid Mr. Ashford the cursed letter about swimming naked in a pond.

"Good God," she cried, louder than she had intended.

"Miss?" Williams stepped into the hallway. "Do you require anything?"

She paused, several answers on her tongue. Yes, she required a letter she so foolishly posted to be retrieved. Yes, she required the addressee of that letter to be marched off a short plank. Yes, she . . .

"Miss?" He asked again.

"No thank you, Williams." She smiled and clenched her fists. The servant bowed and made a swift exit.

And Emily's thoughts returned to Ashford and her letter.

Then a thought came to her, a wonderful, blessed, and entirely rational thought: she would show him.

Perhaps revenge was not the prettiest of emotions, but it would have to be better than helpless, stinging, simpering shame.

She took the stairs two steps at a time to her room, sweeping past the new underhouse maid who pressed herself against the wall in surprise. "Miss," she nodded.

"Oh, hello," Emily smiled over her shoulder.

In a moment she was at her desk, tapping the quill against the crystal ink bottle. This was the one place she felt sure of herself, the one world she could control. And then, for the first time in what seemed like ages, she relaxed.

And she promptly wrote the first scene of a new comedy. Her latest lead character was a pompous, duel-stopping, stammering MP by the name of Sir Luscious Ash-Heap. Lost in her words, chuckling at some of the more ridiculous scenes, she was completely unaware of the hours passing. By the time she looked up from her work, her hands were aching and spotted with ink, several hours had passed, and she felt an enormous sense of relief. Just writing those words, making sport of a man who had hurt her so very deeply, seemed to give her back a sense of herself.

As she stared at the pages she had just written,

she made a decision to do two things. One, she would never allow this libelous play to ever see the light of day. It was for herself alone, for her own amusement and to console her wounded pride. And two, she would never examine her deeper emotions concerning the whole matter. After all, it was done. Over. Well regulated to the past, along with childhood illnesses, the death of a favorite pet, and other painful memories. Thus there was no reason whatsoever to explore just why Mr. Lucius Ashford had managed to so completely discomfort her. It was simply time to get on with her life.

All Letty needed was a few bits of lace to decorate the stage curtain for her puppet show, and to provide a veil for the bride puppet.

"Emily?" She put down her scissors and wandered to the hallway.

"Miss Letty," a young maid not much older than Letty herself curtseyed, careful not to drop her stack of fresh linens. "I believe Miss Fairfax has just gone on rounds to visit the tenants. She said she will be back before dark."

"Oh," Letty replied. "Thank you."

The problem was, she really, really needed the lace now. Everything else was all set, all ready to go. Well, excepting, of course, that she had no audience at the moment. And no real story, just a general idea about a beautiful bride, a dreadful pirate, and a handsome prince.

What she really needed was a little lace.

Then a thought occurred to her. Didn't Emily have some lace trim from last year's petticoats? Yes! She recalled it exactly, the lace did not suit the skirts, for it was too bulky, but would be perfect for a veil and a little embellishment for the curtain, to keep the audience from becoming too terrified by the dreadful pirate.

She knew she should not go into Emily's room without permission, but she also knew, absolutely knew, that Emily would not mind. Not for a project of this importance.

Still she crept into Emily's room furtively, employing all the stealth of an accomplished fiend of the worst sort. Glancing behind her, she slipped over to the large highboy, the one with all the secret drawers and the pineapples carved on the top. Slowly, gently, she opened the last drawer, where Emily usually put leftover bits of ribbon and lace and velvet. And there it was, right on the top—the lace she had been hoping to find.

But it wasn't quite as wide as she remembered. While it would do perfectly well for the curtains, it would not do at all for the veil. Taking out some pieces large enough for the curtain, she reached deeper into the drawer, until her fingers bumped into something that was most definitely not cloth.

Curious, she pulled it out, a lump of something wrapped in old muslin. Dividing the muslin, she saw the title *The Reluctant Rogue* in Emily's distinctive hand.

"What could this be?" she mumbled. Why, it was

a play—a secret play that Emily hadn't told her about!

Why had she kept this a secret from Letty?

Hurt, she began to read, realizing that this was what Emily had been doing in her room for the past fortnight. This is why she had been having her meals sent upstairs, and using up all those candles at night.

But as she read, the mild hurt left her, and soon she began to giggle, her hand over her mouth to muffle the sounds. Why, this was the best thing Emily had ever written!

Then another thought crossed Letty's mind. Maybe Emily had been so sad lately because she didn't realize just how wonderful this new play was.

"Of course!" she exclaimed, then clamped her hand over her mouth again.

But it was true! Poor Emily was hiding this wonderful new play because she did not know how wonderful it was.

What she needed was a little help. Her chin set, Letty closed up the drawer, remembering to bring her lace. Then she stopped.

If Emily saw the lace, she would know she had been in that drawer.

Instead she replaced the lace, and then, looking around the room, found an oversized, leather-bound atlas of the world. It was about the same weight, same dimensions as the manuscript.

Carefully, she wrapped the atlas in the muslin and put it exactly where the manuscript had been.

Nothing seemed disturbed, and Letty skipped from the room, the play beneath her arms.

She would send it off to Mr. Giles in London directly. Soon, Emily would know how perfectly wonderful her new play was. And so would the whole world!

Mr. Edward Giles could not help but smile when he had finished reading the new play by Mr. Edgar St. John.

Although Mr. St. John was certainly no genius (Giles felt that only Shakespeare and himself could be placed safely into that category), he did have a certain gift for light comedy. And this most recent one, *The Reluctant Rogue,* was delightful. Indeed, it reminded him of something Sheridan might have done, or one of the lesser-known Restoration dramatists who occasionally enjoyed renewed popularity these days.

Now Giles was most pleased that St. John had not been killed in that duel earlier in the spring. He had forwarded the challange to his mysterious playwright with some misgiving, for had he been killed in Ireland, the plays would, of course, stop coming. On the other hand, the excitement stirred by the author's sudden and perhaps untimely death would have prompted a box office frenzy.

Well, perhaps if Edward Giles's luck held, the author would write several more plays, and *then* meet a bloody end. One could always hope.

Giles patted the manuscript with affection. In

truth, the main character of Sir Luscious Ash-Heap was absurd, but hilarious. In the right hands, with the right actor, it could be one of those plays that creates a sensation.

He had heard that Elliston over at the Olympic had a Harlequin of some promise. A young man new to London, who had even tackled the difficult role of Shylock with rather unexpected success. Giles tugged at one of his bushy brows for a moment, recalling Elliston's sporadically bizarre behavior. There were rumors that his drinking was once again beyond contol, and that he had been spied having an animated conversation with the roof of a carriage. By candlelight. On another occasion he had confused his mistress with his wife and, in an example of supreme befuddlement, with an actress of great reknown, insulting all three beyond repair.

Well, Giles mused, he supposed it could happen to anyone.

In the world of London theater, Robert William Elliston was considered ever so slightly mad.

Giles amended the thought. He knew for a fact the entire city considered Elliston as mad as a March hare. Yet he was also an innovator, able to discern great talent as well as make all connected with him a great deal of money.

He would send it at once over to Elliston at the Olympic, and hope for the best.

Chapter Four

‎❧

Emily stared out of her bedroom window, making sure her form was well hidden in the shadows as she watched one of the undergardeners flirt shamelessly with the new housemaid. Once again she was engaged in one of her favorite pastimes: observing others without their knowledge. It was a pleasant enough diversion, usually harmless and always vastly more satisfying than attending to the more tiresome household duties.

The maid outside, just arrived from County Clare and whose given name of Emily had been changed to Mary to prevent confusion in the household, tilted her head as she listened to the gardener's words. Whatever he said pleased her vastly, and she laughed and turned away, swaying her hips as she walked without a backward glance at the admiring gardener. He leaned on the hoe, shook his head in appreciation as she turned the corner, and returned reluctantly to his work.

"Nicely played, Mary," she whispered. How satisfying it must be to have such freedom, to be allowed to flirt and sway her hips and know a gentleman is watching. Clearly the only possible reason to sway in such a precarious manner is for the entertainment of the opposite sex. And from the expression on the young gardener's face and the enthusiastic way he continued to watch the maid, he was indeed greatly entertained.

Why couldn't Emily be so natural, so open with men?

And how surprised Mr. Ashford would be to observe her perform just such a trick!

Of course she knew the very barest rudiments of the fine art of flirting. But like an audience at an exotic circus, she also knew that the easier a trick appeared, the more difficult the trick must be to perform. She would probably have more success riding an elephant or taming a lion than she would in attracting the opposite sex. Unless, of course, she posted her dowry upon her forehead, with the anticipated annual income just below in smaller, more subtle print.

She closed her eyes. How absurd to feel such envy for a housemaid. Yet in many ways, Mary was lucky. She was engaged by a generous employer, on an obscure yet profitable estate. She was pretty, young, and all of the male members of the staff— even old Williams—followed her with distinct enjoyment glinting in their eyes. Mary knew how to flirt—a talent that had to be learned—and she knew how to garner the most pleasure from those universal masculine glints.

Mary knew she was appreciated for her own charms, not for her social position or her income.

How pure and intoxicating such knowledge must be!

But Emily Fairfax was not a housemaid. Instead, she was a young woman with huge responsibilities. Since her mother's death she had been forced into the unwelcome position of being mother to her three younger sisters as well as running the household of Fairfax Castle. Besides her immediate family, her dependents included the servants, the tenants, and to a lesser extent other inhabitants of the area around Fairfax Castle. She alone was the overseer. Her father had all but abdicated his responsibilities as she proved herself increasingly able.

In this she was alone. At times she wondered what it would be like to have someone to shoulder the responsibilities with her, preferably someone with strong, broad shoulders. What a comfort that would be, what wonderful solace to have someone upon whom she could depend.

Of course an assortment of men had been paraded before her as potential suitors over the years. There were old men in padded hose and stiff wigs, young men with overly eager grins and solicitous manners. There were titled gentlemen with flagging fortunes and impetuous bucks with gambling debts. At times she felt she had taken tea and danced country reels with every unattached man in Ireland, England and Scotland, as well as a few from the Continent and a Greek diplomat. She was astonished by the lengths to which a man was willing to travel in hopes of a few thousand pounds.

None of them had interested her in the least. And none of them would have been interested in her had she been forced to rely on her charms. And that never bothered her, the knowledge that these men were only entranced by her family wealth.

Not until Mr. Lucius Ashford came into her life.

He was the one man who had arrived at Fairfax Castle determined not to flatter, woo or even impress her. Perhaps that is why she could not get him out of her mind.

Writing the silly, ridiculous play had been something of a help. It had purged her of some of her more romantic, unrealistic notions by making him seem absurd. But even as she wrote, part of her understood this was her own fiction, not reality. She was making up a character for him simply because he had not allowed her to know his real character.

Why would he wish to pursue a friendship with a provincial Irish spinster? Hardly the sort of female to inspire interest in such a worldly man, even one with such erroneous opinions.

Slowly she left her place by the window, stepping over the soft Persian carpet to her desk. There she paused over the unopened letters that had just arrived in the post. And again there was nothing there from Ashford. Not that she had expected to hear from him by now. But part of her felt a quiver of anticipation as Williams brought in the mail, a quiver that quickly vanished with the first glance at the bills and two letters from her sister Caroline, one from an aunt in Dublin and one from Mr. Giles in London.

Why couldn't she flirt and bat her eyelashes like a normal female?

Because it had been drained from her bit by bit during the past dozen years. Because every time she felt that old girlish dream of romance begin to rouse within her, something would quell it, either a family crisis, or a neighborhood dispute, or—most often—Emily herself.

She was unable to play the coquette because she had not the practice or experience in that realm. And also because she had never encountered a man such as Lucius Ashford. The more she thought about him, the words they exchanged, the way his expression darkened while they argued, the more confused she grew about their actual meeting. Did she miss something, forget a vital moment? Had she ignored a gesture full of significance, with a deeper meaning than she had been aware of at the time?

In hindsight—and rather embarrassing truth— she realized this was a man with whom she did indeed long to tease and flirt and perhaps even be wooed by. This was a man she was unable to erase from her thoughts, even as the days of their meeting slipped into weeks. She had attempted to flirt, and had failed. She had sent him a provocative letter that failed to provoke.

With a sigh she turned her attention back to the stack of letters, opening the one from Mr. Giles in London first.

Perhaps he was with a woman at that very moment, some bit of social fluff who could sway her hips as easily as Mary, who made him laugh and—

Then she stopped, certain she had misread the letter.

" . . . *and of course we will rush* The Reluctant Rogue *into immediate production, as you so very compellingly requested. And might I add, my dear Mr. St. John, that you may rest assured we all anticipate the revenue from this play should more than compensate the losses you suffered during your recent and most tragic flood . . .*"

"Tragic flood? What on earth . . . ," she whispered, stunned. For a long moment she simply stood in mind-numbing confusion, then threw the letter down and ran across the room to the bottom drawer of the chest. Pulling it open with more force than she intended, the entire drawer slid out and fell to her feet.

Bits of unfinished sleeves, trimmings, and small squares of brightly patterned fabric fluttered to the floor. Hands trembling, she thrust them into the main lump of cloth, feeling blindly for the large square object wrapped in yet more cloth. Then she felt it—solid, square and reassuring. For an instant her panic subsided.

Until she unwrapped the cloth. There, in green leather binding and gold-edged type, was a copy of *Mr. Cooke's Atlas of the World.*

"The play, the play," she mumbled as she frantically searched the drawer, scattering the remaining contents over her shoulders in her quest. But even then she knew it was gone, vanished, the play that had been intended to simply soothe her wounded pride. The play that had felt so exhilarating to write, but only because she had been confident that no one else would ever see the stinging words. The play that had never been meant to see the light of day.

"No!" Emily said aloud, stumbling back and reaching for the wadded up letter.

Mr. Giles further announced that the Olympic Theatre was already well along in her new play's production. As it would soon be summer, and the patent houses of Drury Lane and Covent Garden would be closed until autumn (thus allowing the other theaters a chance to garner large audiences). It provided an excellent opportunity to debut *The Reluctant Rogue*. He added that the character of Sir Luscious Ash-Heap was her very best comical creation to date.

How could this have happened? How could her hidden manuscript have found its way to London, to Mr. Giles? It was a veritable nightmare come to life. What diabolical force of nature could have conspired to so do such a hideous thing?

Then she stopped, struck by the one simple, obvious answer to the question.

"Letty," she said softly. And, with the letter balled in her fist, she ran into the hallway.

"Letty," she repeated in a slightly louder tone,

but with the murderous, underlying threat usually reserved for an accusation of high treason.

There was only one person on this earth capable of destroying her sense of well-being with such deft and utterly natural genius, only a single soul who possessed the unequaled talent necessary to ruin the most carefully laid plans.

She no longer cared how shrill and unseemly her voice became. In the echoing Great Hall of Fairfax Castle came one great, unladylike bellow.

"Letty!"

Letty's sobs were becoming ever more ragged, pitiable and above all, deafening.

"For God's sake, Letty," Emily snapped, pacing the floor of her room and trying very hard not to wrap her fingers around the soft, pinkish and all-too inviting throat of her youngest sister. "Please tell me exactly what you did."

Letty hesitated and blew her nose into one of Emily's very best French handkerchiefs. Her eyes remined wide and liquid and fixed on Emily, warily following her while she paced back and forth, as if her sister would attempt a sneak attack if given a chance.

On this point Letty was quite on the mark.

"I repeat my question. What precisely did you do?"

"I thought . . . lace . . . for my puppets," Letty gasped. "That you felt sad because maybe you thought your play was not good . . ." She paused again to blow her nose with a theatrical flourish. "So you see," she swallowed, and then offered a watery smile. "I did it all for you."

"Did *what* all for me?"

"Sent your manuscript off to Mr. Giles with a most wonderful letter begging him, absolutely *begging* him to produce the play immediately. I mentioned some rather dire financial circumstances to hurry the matter."

"A flood, perhaps?" Emily offered between clenched teeth.

"Exactly! Wasn't that an excellent touch, Emily? Poor Mr. St. John had most of his livestock and his very favorite footman washed away in one magnificent flood. His name was Bert, short for Albert."

"Bert?"

"Oh, poor Mr. St. John. You see, he had been such dear friends with the noble Bert for all of his life. Raised as brothers, they were, even in spite of their vastly different circumstances. So when Bert saw the rushing wall of water—those are the exact words I used—coming toward Mr. St. John's property, well. Bert, being Bert, could not help but save whatever small, timid animals he could."

"Bert! My God, Letty, I don't give a damn about your fictitious Bert. Do you realize you—"

"Well, you should care, Em. You really should." Letty straightened, offering an admonishing glare. "After all, he was *your* fictitious Mr. St. John's dearest friend in this world. How could you be so cruel.

And using the 'd' word was quite unnecessary and even harmful to my ears."

Emily stared in astonishment, her entire body beginning to tremble with fury. "Letty, I know not what to say."

Then Letty smiled her most beatific smile. "I understand, Em. And I do forgive you, as I am sure Bert would. He was a most forgiving soul."

"Leave this room at once."

"Pardon me?" Letty blinked.

"I am just beginning to realize how very wrong I have been to give you such a free rein. Please leave at once. I must prepare to leave for London to undo as much of the damage as possible. I will address you later, Letty. But I urge you to leave at once."

But Letty had only heard one word. "London? Can I go?"

"Can you go?" Emily repeated in stupefaction. "Of course you cannot go! My God, Letty, you are the reason I must make this journey! Do you realize that—"

"Oh, how I long to see Caroline and Fanny! And the Gardens," she clapped. "We can go to the Gardens!"

"No we cannot! Letty, are you listening to me? You are to stay here. Father and the others will watch you, and I will give you lessons to complete."

"You mean I cannot go to London? But I was only trying to help you."

Emily pressed her palms to her temples, willing

them to stop throbbing. "Letty, please understand that—"

"That was the only reason I sent the manuscript. Really it was." Letty stared evenly at her sister, and then feigned great interest in the corners of the lace handkerchief. "I hope your journey is not terribly long. You know how very bored I tend to get when left to my own devices. Then I am forced to entertain myself."

Emily's hands dropped down to her sides. "Is my little sister threatening me?"

Shrugging with the innocence of a kitten, Letty was unable to contain a slight smile. "No, Em. I am just stating the truth, that I have a most wretched propensity for mischief, and cannot be held responsible if left to my own devices."

Emily searched for an answer, but there was none, for Letty was correct. It was marginally better to take her to London and keep her heavily guarded than to leave her behind and worry about what that devilishly creative mind would concoct.

"You must promise to behave in London," she warned. "You must absolutely do as you are told, and at all times."

Letty nodded eagerly.

"You will be watched constantly," she continued. "And do not forget: the Tower of London will be close by, and I hear they are looking for some new guests."

Letty's eyes widened for just a moment, then narrowed. "Of course," she said sweetly before she turned to leave.

"And Letty."

"Yes?"

"We're not finished with this yet. I will lecture you all the way to London about privacy, and the consequences of your rash behavior."

Letty waved over her shoulder as she skipped from the room, and Emily sighed in momentary resignation. She had much to do to prepare for their journey. Then she remembered the letter from her sister Caroline.

But the news from Caroline in London was not good.

Fanny, their other sister, was in a very bad way. She had grown ever more reclusive in the few years since her marriage, and Caroline attributed Fanny's decline to her apparent inability to have children.

Caroline's letter quickly became more typical, cataloguing her own husband George's business triumphs, the budding brilliance of her small boys, the staggering beauty of their infant daughter, and the recent improvements in their town house. Chintz, Caroline assured Emily, was now the fabric of favor for the most elegant parlors.

Emily refolded the letter. When was the last time she herself heard from Fanny?

It had been months.

Perhaps she should write to Fanny, a gentle letter of vague support. But then maybe Fanny would not welcome such a letter. She might think it intrusive, or impudent that Caroline had so clearly alerted her of the problems.

Perhaps it was just a squabble between Caroline and Fanny, like so many others that had happened with such regularity in the nursery.

But that was unlikely.

How could she tell from the one-sided versions she received from Caroline? Without seeing Fanny for herself, it was all but impossible to determine the seriousness of the situation.

Perhaps it was just as well that Letty had forced this trip. She was long overdue for a visit to London, to see her dear sisters, to find out how Fanny was faring. To stop her play from being performed. She would immediately send a letter to Mr. Giles, urging him to remove the play from production. There was so very much to do once she arrived.

Including, maybe, just maybe, a visit with Mr. Lucius Ashford.

Within a week she was stepping into the entrance hall of Caroline's town house in Mayfair. Letty had been as excited about traveling to London as their father had been thrilled at being able to remain in Ireland. He had no desire to journey there, calling it a place of "vile scents and even more vile personages." His daughters aside, he mentioned. Then, after a slight pause, he added his sons-in-law and perhaps his grandsons. As he had not yet had the pleasure of meeting his infant granddaughter, he withheld comment concerning her.

Yet he did send Emily off with a list of new clothing to order from his favorite tailor on Bond Street (who was the only man, her father declared, able to re-create the most popular fashions from 1785, the last year of truly handsome menswear as well as the last year of truly handsome men) along with an extensive list of books and gazettes.

Exhausted and windblown from the journey, Emily was nonetheless delighted to have arrived at her sister's elegant Grosvenor Street home.

Handing her pale blue pelisse to the butler, she began to untie her bonnet and pull out the pearl-tipped hat pin.

"Oh, Caroline! How very wonderful it is to—" Emily's words were cut off by her two small nephews, ages six and four, who barreled into her knees with the force of Wellington's cannon fire.

Caroline immediately burst into tears. Always the family crier, she had been known to sob when both overjoyed or melancholy, if the weather were rainy or fine, and whether the heroine of a story lived happily or died tragically. No extreme emotion coursed through her without proclaiming itself with tears. With her lace handkerchief pressed lightly to her round face, she allowed herself to weep freely.

"Emily, my dearest sister!"

But the dearest sister was unable to reply, for her nephews were busy at once pulling her down to their level and attempting to scurry up her legs. Upstairs the baby was shrieking with most unlady-like vigor.

Emily attempted to redirect the boys' plump hands from her clothing. "Why are children always so sticky," she murmured to no one in particular, glancing down. There were purplish outlines of four small, eager hands all over the front and sides of her new dotted muslin gown.

"Someone here had raspberry jam with tea," she whispered.

The boys squealed in delight. "And strawberry as well!" Charles held up a hand with a redder shade of jam for her inspection. Their faces, too, wore double smiles of jam, and Thomas had some in his wispy brown hair.

Caroline smiled gently at the scene. "I do believe they remember their aunt Emily," she said, in a voice muffled by her delicate handkerchief. "It's been almost a year since we were last home at Fairfax Castle, yet still they remember their dear, sweet auntie. Do you not think that is especially clever of them?"

Laughing, Emily kissed each one atop their sticky heads. "Of course it is. They are nothing short of brilliant, these two rascals. Charles! Tom! Are the two of you absolutely bent on knocking me over?" The boys paused to exchange looks with each other before continuing their onslaught with renewed giggles.

"How beautiful you look," choked Caroline as she watched her sister struggle to remain upright, her bonnet tumbling to the marble floor.

Although Emily never acknowledged it, she was

considered by her sisters to be the loveliest one in the family. They had always envied her features, especially her small nose and blue eyes that sometimes appeared greenish and sometimes gray, depending on her mood. And they also envied her lack of attention to her looks, that she always managed to look fashionable without putting any effort into the process.

She routinely shrugged off their admiration, assuming the compliments were due solely to her position as the eldest sister. Of course her little sisters would think well of her looks, she would smile to herself. For a great portion of their lives, she was the tallest of the four, and therefore best able to strong-arm praise, deserving or not. For years Emily had ruled supreme in the nursery, and still assumed any words of esteem concerning her appearance were merely remnants of childhood habit.

Standing in the hall, with the early June sun streaming behind her, she had not the faintest notion of her own beauty. The butler swept her bonnet from the immediate danger of trampling, and she thanked him softly. A few errant golden curls tossed across her cheek as her face beamed.

Caroline, although pleasant-looking and amiable, was already growing into her solidly matronlike stance. Even the stiff bone corsets she employed were powerless against the steady spread of her hips and waist. Her lace cap and lace neckerchief proclaimed her the matriarch of the house. Gone was the comely thing who married well at seventeen and blushed prettily at her groom. But she did not miss that girl in the least.

Now she was a self-assured member of the ton, her position in society every bit as secure as her domestic life. They were subscribers at Almack's, regular partakers of dry cakes, bread spread with inferior butter, and famously flavorless nonalcoholic punches. Once they even took tea at the Prince Regent's Carlton House. And her husband, George, routinely had his port at White's, sometimes seated in the new bay window.

Caroline was very content indeed.

Emily, by contrast, seemed to be an unfixed, ethereal creature, her slender figure outlined beneath airy muslin, the joy on her face as natural as the children's. It both vexed and confused her sister that Emily had no desire to experience the normal things in life, such as marriage and children. Then, naturally, becoming a member of all the best clubs, maintaining an enviable social position, and discovering the subtle thrill of delivering the cut direct on a crowded dance floor. Above all, it seemed impossible that Emily was almost two years older than Caroline, and Caroline had adopted the airs and dress of a woman over twice her age.

How fortunate she was! And how dreadful life must be for poor Emily!

A fresh wave of emotion swept over Caroline. Emily glanced up and, observing the pained expression on her sister's face, allowed Charles to seize her reticule, which naturally forced Tom to make a valiant attempt at pulling it away from his brother. At last, with the boys occupied, she could speak to her sister.

"Oh, Caro," Emily sighed. "How good it is to be here. And how wonderful it is to see you."

Caroline dabbed her eyes as she folded her into an embrace. She looked over Emily's shoulder to the street outside. "Where in heaven's name are Letty and George?"

The footmen nodded as they brushed past the women with Emily and Letty's luggage.

"Your husband took her over to Gunter's for some marzipan," Emily replied. Then she smiled when she caught sight of the old woman coming down the steps. "Nanny Goose!"

"Miss Fairfax!" She kept hold of the banister as she descended. Emily recognized her former nanny's gown as one of her mother's, in a fashion that had been the rage sometime before the turn of the century. "Miss Caroline, there is no need to cry. You will muss your collar and redden your nose, and it is a shameful example for the boys."

"Yes, Nanny," Caroline replied. "I do believe the boys are in need of supper."

"They are in need of a great deal more than supper, Miss Caroline. Such as discipline and a sound swat." The children stopped their tug-of-war and dutifully handed the reticule back to Emily.

"Thank you," she said politely.

The both bowed from the waist, then looked up at their nanny for approval. When she nodded and pointed to the stairs, they marched solemnly up to the nursery for their suppers. Once they rounded the first curve of the staircase, their feet thumped at double pace.

"Gentlemen!" Nanny said in a conversational tone. Immediately the thundering slowed to a more manageable trot.

"Now let me look at you, Miss Fairfax."

Emily brushed her hair from her face and curtseyed. "Do I meet with your approval, Nanny Goose?"

"My dear," she held her arms open for her former charge. "You always did." There was an unaccustomed break in her voice before she stepped back and appraised Emily more thoroughly. "So why are you not married yet, Missy?"

"Oh, Nanny. Not you, too," Emily sighed. "I thought that in visiting London, I would be free of that eternal question for at least an hour."

"Ha! Not here, Em. Oh, Nanny—is the baby asleep?"

"Asleep, and as good as gold."

"I had so wanted Emily to see her before it gets dark."

"Miss Fairfax may view the baby when she awakes from her nap, Miss Caroline. Now, Missy, where has Miss Letty gone?"

"For marzipan with her uncle George." Emily tilted her head. "He really is a brother-in-law, but Letty insists that 'uncle' is more appropriate, considering their age differences. Oh, Nanny, Caro," she sighed. "How very good it is to be here."

"Will you be standing in the hallway for the next fortnight?" Nanny asked pointedly.

"Of course not! Forgive me, Em. I've already ordered tea. . . ." Caroline lead the way to the parlor.

"I'd best go up and watch those boys. No telling what mischief the scamps will find," Nanny said briskly.

"I'll be up later, Nanny Goose," Emily called.

Nanny chuckled softly as she followed the boys.

"She looks exactly the same as always," Emily marveled. "Does she sleep in some sort of pickling compound to preserve herself?"

Caroline proudly led the way to the second floor salon, which was clearly designed to impress. And it did.

"Here, Em. Take this chair. Do you like the new sofa and wallpaper? And the carpet—it's from Persia. The urn over there is a genuine replica of a Greek-inspired design."

"Oh, Caro," Emily lowered herself gratefully into the comfortable wing chair. "This entire room is just beautiful. George must be doing very well indeed."

"He is! Is Nanny gone?"

"I just heard her close the nursery door upstairs. Why?

"Do you know that you're the only one she lets call her 'Nanny Goose?' I do believe you are still her favorite."

"How is she holding up with the boys and new baby?"

"Better than I am," Caroline confessed, pouring her sister tea and adding the two spoons of sugar Emily always enjoyed. The tea service was an elegant sterling silver set with ivory knobs, the cups and saucers the finest paper-thin china. "She suffers a little rheumatism when the weather is damp. Here." She handed Emily the cup.

"Thank you." Emily took a sip. "How I've needed this." Then she put the cup down. "Tell me, how is Fanny? And have you discussed this with her husband, Robert? I was most alarmed by your last letter. Indeed, it is one of the main reasons for my visit."

Caroline shook her head at the mention of their other sister. "I cannot tell, Em. George sometimes sees Robert at the club, but I do believe he is as affected as Fanny. George does not say much about him, always changing the topic. They no longer speak of children. I know it pains her to see my boys. When the baby was born, she didn't visit for over two months. She claimed she was unwell, and did not wish to bring illness to either me or the baby. Still, I knew the real reason why she had no desire to coo over an infant. And when I saw her at last, her eyes were puffy. She wore long sleeves when everyone knows short sleeves were in fashion that month."

"Poor Fan. What of Robert? Does he seem to blame her? I know his family must be quite upset.

Only son, married for almost three years with no heir on the way."

"I hear from Lady Duff there is talk of rewriting the will."

"No!" Emily was genuinely shocked. "I do hope Fan doesn't hear of this. She would be devastated. And it is only three years, after all. We will visit her as soon as possible."

Caroline nodded, a tear rolling down her cheek.

Before Emily could say anything else, the front door flew open with a crash. "Caro? Em?" They heard a girl's voice call from downstairs.

"Letty! We're upstairs!" There was a racket as Letty took the staircase three steps at a time, then Caroline stood up as her little sister ran into her arms. "Oh, my little Letty! How you have grown!"

"So have you, Caro! You must be as big as—"

"Letty," Emily warned.

But Caroline just laughed and untied her sister's bonnet. "My, what fascinating trimmings on your hat." She examined the bonnet more closely. "What are these, silk insects?"

"Yes. Isn't it a wonderful design? I made it myself."

"Did you?" Caroline winked at Emily. "I thought this must be the latest fashion from a Parisian milliner."

"No, I made it! Well, I decorated it, anyway. The straw part was already made. I did one for Emily as well, but she said it was too fine to risk ruining on the trip. But I brought it for her anyway. Oh, and I almost forgot!"

Her energy was so infectious, Emily began to laugh.

"What's so funny, Em? Anyway, I brought a surprise for each of you. Here, Caro." With that she presented her sister with a small wrapped package that had been bunched in her fist. "It's marzipan! Just for you." The sides were dotted with stains of an unknown origin.

"How thoughtful, dearest." She kissed her little sister's head with tenderness.

"Don't cry, Caro. It's only candy, and Uncle George paid for it. And he ate most of it on the way home. That's why the biggest piece has a bite taken out of it. If you don't believe me you can match it with his front teeth. It's a perfect fit."

Caroline sniffed in gratitude. "And where is your uncle?"

"Your husband"—Letty clapped with delight—"is with my big surprise for Emily. That is where your husband is. Hear that, Emily? Caroline has a husband. We should do something about that while we're here in London."

"Letty." Emily raised her eyebrows. "I do not trust you. What's going on in that terrifying little head of yours?"

"Nothing. Not a thing. Caroline, do you not think Emily should be married by now? She is the eldest of the Fairfax women. At this rate I'll be married well before she is. Shouldn't Emily be married?"

Caroline nodded as she took a bite of marzipan. "Indeed. I am hoping to have her settled by the end of this trip."

"Oh no, you don't. You know how I feel on the subject." Emily sighed as she closed her eyes and leaned her head against the edge of the wing chair. "Honestly, if I were placed any more firmly on the shelf than I am now, I would have nails in my feet."

No one responded. There was a peculiar silence in the parlor, broken only by a shuffling of feet, and Emily opened her eyes. "What is—" she began.

Then she saw her brother-in-law, a big grin on his face. "George!" She jumped out of the chair. "How wonderful to—"

He simply continued grinning and looked at her feet.

"What are you staring at?"

George, like his wife, had grown comfortably stout, and it suited him well. The prosperity of his thriving shipping business was evident in every item of clothing, from his vivid white and absurdly starched and tied neckcloth to his brilliantly polished boots. Even his stance proclaimed success, an impossible-to-ignore delight with himself, his situation and his surroundings.

His sparse hair was combed in the new upswept style, with carefully placed curls framing his face as he seemed to peer more intently at the hem of her gown. "My dear Emily, I am merely searching for the nails on your feet to affix you to the shelf. How about over there on the mantel, next to the Staffordshire dogs?" He stepped over and kissed her gently on her cheek, holding both of her hands as he pulled her out of the chair. "How beautiful you are, dear sister."

Letty tugged at his jacket. "Can I bring in my surprise now?"

"Yes you may, Letty," George said. "Good Lord, Em, what happened to your gown? I do hope those appalling handprints are not the work of my sons."

"They are," she confirmed. "I hadn't realized how—"

"Here it is!" Letty chimed. "Surprise!"

Emily glanced over to Letty, prepared to face a pony, or a troupe of roaming acrobats, or anything else Letty would deem a surprise.

Instead, she looked directly into the deep brown eyes of Lucius Ashford, standing hat in hands in the parlor.

"Oh!" Emily gasped, and felt her cheeks burn with both surprise and humiliation. This was the very man who had refused to acknowledge her letters, the man about whom she had written a wretched, quite possibly scandalous play. At once she was unable to catch her breath and could not in a million years think of a sensible word to say.

"Well, she sure looks surprised. I told you she would be surprised," Letty announced with confidence.

Ashford smiled and bowed. "Miss Fairfax," he began, then turned to Caroline. "And Mrs. Edgeworth. How delightful it is to see you both."

But Emily interrupted. "How?" was all she could manage.

"I saw him from the window of Gunter's when Uncle George was buying sweets."

"Indeed, she was gone like a flash," George agreed. "Imagine my surprise when I realized that our Letty was acquainted with Ashford!"

"You know each other?" Emily was beginning to feel weak in the knees.

"Everyone knows Ashford. He's by far the most popular Whig in London. We even let him into the clubs and tolerate his political views in moderation."

"Are we Whigs or Tories?" Letty asked.

"Tories, of course, dear," George answered. "We all take great delight in attempting to convert our friend Ashford. I believe he, too, enjoys the sport. But we had no idea he was acquainted with Letty and Emily and your father."

"You know our father, Mr. Ashford?" Caroline asked. "Heavens, how on earth did—"

"Mr. Ashford came to Ireland to watch his friend shoot Emily and—"

Emily shook her head at Letty as Ashford outspoke her. "Mrs. Edgeworth, I was in Ireland on business with a friend, and we happened upon your sisters. They very graciously invited us to breakfast at Fairfax Castle, where we made the acquaintance of your father."

"Oh, I see," Caroline replied, although it was very clear by her confusion that she did not. She recovered herself quickly. "Well, Letty. Would you like to come round to the stables to see the new colt?"

"In a little while. First I would like to visit with Mr. Ashford."

Emily realized Caroline planned to leave her alone with Ashford, the man who had determined she was not a worthy correspondent. Not only that, but he no doubt had possession still of the most imprudent words she had ever written. Other than her latest play, of course.

"I will take Letty," Emily offered cheerfully as she began to exit the room, reaching for her sister. "I am sure Mr. Ashford and my brother-in-law must wish to discuss all sorts of masculine topics. So sirs, I will take my leave—"

"Not at all," chirped George. "Ashford and I have had our fill of all things masculine, have we not?"

"Well, I . . ." Ashford began. Emily suddenly realized that he did not wish to remain alone with her any more than she did.

Coward, she thought to herself, even as a fresh sting of mortification prickled her consciousness.

"Come, Letty," George said, offering her his arm. "We'll let you name it. Caroline?"

"Why would you name a colt 'Caroline'?" Letty asked. "That's a wretched name for a colt."

"No, I mean," George began. Then laughed. "Never mind! Would you like to join us, Caro?"

His wife shook her head. "Pray excuse me, I'm going upstairs to check on the baby and the boys.

Em, there's an extra setting on the sideboard. Do pour Mr. Ashford a cup, and offer the spice cakes from the tray."

"I love spice cakes!" exclaimed Letty, turning on her heels to grab a cake.

"Caroline! Please stay!" Emily all but shouted. There was a strained silence as everyone glanced at her in curiosity. She could swear she saw a slight smile on Ashford's lips, and she could see the open door beckoning her from the torment of the parlor. "I mean, you must hear Mr. Ashford's views on so many things. He is most informed, most informed indeed."

Caroline looked at Emily with an expression that clearly indicated she thought her older sister had lost her mind. "Well, at another time I would dearly love to hear Mr. Ashford's informed, eh, information. But right now, pray excuse me. George?"

George said nothing, but with a pleasant and unchanging expression on his face he clamped his hand on Letty's shoulder and pulled her from the parlor even as her hands flayed for a spice cake. Caroline smiled, and with a beatific nod she glided out of the room, leaving Ashford and Emily alone.

At first he said nothing and watched her every movement with unwavering interest. Now she had a chance to truly observe him, to take in the very fact that he was there, in her sister's parlor. He was every bit as handsome as she recalled from April, perhaps even more so. His coat was a deep brown, almost the same shade as his eyes but without the same depth or brilliance, and his trousers were of a buff-beige, as was his waistcoat.

Unlike her brother-in-law, there was an air of casual, unstudied elegance about him. There was no sense that he spent hours before his mirror arranging his curls just so (as was the case with George), or that he employed a team of servants for the sole task of keeping his linens a blinding shade of white. Instead, Ashford was perfectly natural, every bit at ease in the self-consciously refined parlor as he was in the hills of Ireland.

He was, she decided, the most splendid-looking man she had ever seen. And he was also a living, breathing symbol of her every humiliation.

"Did you hear someone at the door?" she asked cheerfully. "Perhaps I should go see if someone is downstairs."

"Ah," he tilted his head slightly. "I hear a servant answering."

She had the distinct impression he was enjoying her discomfort. Straightening her back, she offered a tight smile.

"Would you like some tea, Mr. Ashford?" Her voice was clipped. Hopefully he would bolt, the sooner the better.

"No, Miss Fairfax. I have no wish to intrude on your privacy. You must be fatigued from your journey." He glanced at her, and then quickly looked away, as if embarrassed by even being in the same room with her.

Of course he was, she thought. How he must disdain her for the letter she had sent. Searching for something, anything to relieve the awkwardness of the situation, she gestured for him to sit down. He shook his head and remained standing, top hat and gloves still at his side.

Although he stood several paces from her, she could almost feel the vibration of his scorn from that distance. The room all but trembled, and for long ticks of the fine mantel clock they stood in uncomfortable silence.

"Sir, I must ask you—" she began.

"Miss Farifax," he said simultaneously. "Forgive me. Please continue."

"I was curious, sir, did you receive my letter?"

"Yes, indeed, and I thank you. Did you receive mine?"

"Of course," she attempted a smile, recalling his polite but cold note, the simple thank-you for breakfast. Absolutely correct, and absolutely soulless. "The mail is quite regular, even in the remote wilds of Ireland."

"Ah, well . . ." He cleared his throat. "Very good. Excellent."

She waited for him to say something else, to make a single comment on the nature of her second letter. But he did not. "I must be gone," he said at last. "I am late for an appointment. I will find my own way, Miss Fairfax. Thank you."

"Sir."

He paused, as if he would say something.

"Do you wish to say anything, Mr. Ashford?"

"No. No, of course not, Miss Fairfax. Nothing to say, nothing at all." He offered a crisp smile and left the parlor.

She followed him down the staircase to the door, where the butler bowed and opened it for him. Once outside, he put on his top hat and gloves.

He glanced away from her, and when his dark gaze returned it was pleasant, yet somehow detached. "Please convey my regards to your sisters and Mr. Edgeworth. Good afternoon." With a nod he was gone.

Emily watched him retreat until he was lost in the crowds on the street. A strange feeling passed over her, as if she knew this man less now than she had in Ireland.

Of course he lied.

There was no prior engagement, at least not for over an hour. And it was nearby, on St. James.

But he had to leave, to get out of that home. It wasn't the house itself, which was carefully furnished in this season's most fashionable style. The place was agreeable enough, even enjoyable.

It was Emily Fairfax he had to escape.

She had made no comment, none at all on the eight page letter he had sent. How foolish he had been to reveal so much to a woman he barely knew.

How she must detest him!

"Pardon me," he mumbled as he bumped into a gentleman's shoulder. The man nodded in irritated acknowledgment of the encounter, and both kept on walking.

Ashford had been genuinely delighted to see Letty when she called out to him on the street. A smile crossed his face at the remembrance. And then to discover that George Edgeworth was married to their sister. How many times had he supped with George, and never a mention of his wife's family?

Emily.

He took a deep breath and exhaled slowly as if to steady himself.

Was it possible that she was even more lovely than she had been in April? He had somehow comforted himself with the notion that her beauty had been culled from her surroundings, that an Emily plucked from her familiar and exquisite home would be less charming, less lovely.

Less able to wake him from the soundest of slumbers with an aching sense of something vague yet powerful, something unfamiliar and familiar at the same time.

But it wasn't so.

The initial sight of Emily with her hair tangled and her dress covered with small handprints, had moved him as had nothing else. Then the expression on her face when she saw him. Was she happy? Shocked? Disappointed?

His own emotions had been so powerful, he was unable to rationally judge her response.

And when her family left them alone, he had an

absurd desire to ask her directly what she had thought of receiving such a lengthy missive. She had smiled with distant politeness at him, with her slightly crooked smile, and he felt as if he had been slammed against a brick wall.

It was childish to have such a physical reaction to a female, even one with such an admittedly lovely face. He was behaving like a besotted schoolboy, as if he had been so serious all of his life, only to make up for lost time now, when he could least afford the luxury.

That is why he had to leave. His political career depended upon it. His speech was coming up, the most important moment of his life, and he could not be distracted. Must not be distracted.

There was a thin gold chain about her neck with a small cross. When she offered him the spice cakes, all he had wanted was to touch that chain, to feel the warmth infused into the metal from her body. And to savor that gentle heat, to claim it somehow as his own.

"Absurd," he said aloud, and a woman gave him a wary look as he allowed her to pass.

But it was absurd.

Of course it was.

In a couple of months his speech would be over, the bill offered and either passed or not. Then, perhaps, he could see Miss Fairfax again, determine if her effect on him was genuine or the product of an overworked mind.

Miss Fairfax. Miss Emily Fairfax.

He allowed himself one more thought.

Emily.

Then he straightened and walked briskly to his meeting. He would be a little early, but could employ the time to straighten his thoughts, to organize his ideas, to solidify his arguments, and above all, to push the young woman with the uneven smile from his mind.

And he was so consumed with his thoughts, he did not see the man in the shadows, the man in the dark cloak who followed several silent paces behind his prey. But the man saw Ashford. He had been watching him for weeks now, and soon it would be time.

It would be easier than he ever imagined to eliminate Lucius Ashford from the face of the earth, to blot him like the troublesome speck he had become. Easier, and vastly more satisfying than he had ever imagined.

Chapter Five

The actor with the unnaturally bright eyes performed the gesticulating sequence once again, wagging a finger at the charming rear of a retreating lady as he reached for a prop sword with the other hand.

Robert William Elliston, who was directing the new production, pressed his fleshy lips together. His shadow of dark whiskers was more pronounced than usual, and his attire was even more unkempt. There was a distinct custard stain on his lapel, and the edge of his cravat was lined with gray grime. But his own appearance was of no consequence to him at the moment.

Instead, his powers of concentration were focused on his young actor, Henry Hughes. More precisely, he was fully committed to keeping the actor in the dark about how very perfect his performance was. Elliston had learned long ago that it was never wise to let a performer become aware of his skills before opening night. Too much aplomb also caused an actor to believe he was deserving of a raise in pay. No, it was always wise to keep an actor uncertain and humble. Let him believe he may soon be tossed out on the streets, that the unknown person watching the next rehearsal might very well be his replacement.

Elliston knew this was going to be a triumph in every way. He knew it in his bones. This production would be the next rage of London, perhaps all of Europe.

The moment he read the script, he knew this was what he had been looking for and secured the rights from Giles at an absurdly reasonable rate. The playwright, Edgar St. John, had desired the play be produced as soon as possible. Giles was delighted with Elliston's terms, but not nearly as delighted as Elliston himself was.

The play, *The Reluctant Rogue,* was new and fresh and perhaps even a little daring. The lines were sharp, movement and staging limited only by a director's imagination. And that absurd little actor was perfect for the lead role. It would make them all rich and famous.

Elliston had feared in losing Edmund Kean to the Drury Lane, he had lost his solitary chance of a lifetime. Now, out of the blue it seemed, he had been given a second chance of a lifetime.

And this time, he would make the best of it.

"Sir?" A woman addressed him, but he was so lost in his thoughts, he didn't hear her approach. "Mr. Elliston?"

"Yes." He turned and faced the speaker. She was young and lovely and very clearly well raised. And of course he knew what she desired. "My dear, you are not fit for this profession. Go back to your parents at once."

The young woman laughed. "No, sir. I'm afraid you misunderstand."

Elliston peered more closely. Perhaps he should revise his original estimation. She was more than just pretty, she was quite beautiful. And fresh, bright as a new spring day. No pox marks, no squinty eye, tall and straight with a clear voice and just a touch of something else. Stroking his chin, he stared at her with professional interest. "Irish?"

She was clearly surprised. "Why, yes, sir. Did my country airs give me away?"

"Not at all!" Elliston allowed a dash of excitement to grow. What a refreshing Juliette she would be! Perhaps he should start her as Ophelia. Yes, that would do. Next season, Juliette, with Hughes as Romeo. "I will offer you six pence a week, no more. That is the best I can do."

At first perplexed, she then smiled, a charming dimple on her cheek. "No, sir. I fear you misunderstand. I have a play for you."

Only then did he notice the bundle she held in her hands.

Damnation, he thought to himself. Spare me from society ladies and their attempts at playwrighting.

"Forgive me, miss. But we are already engaged in a production. Perhaps—"

"Yes, sir. I see. But this is a new version of *The Reluctant Rogue*."

"Who sent you?" Elliston snapped. "Giles? Worthington at the Drury?"

Emily Fairfax blinked. "Why no, sir. I was sent by Mr. Edgar St. John. He is a neighbor of ours in Ireland, and wished you to have this excellent revision at once."

"Revision?" Without asking he took the manuscript. "You say it is better?"

"Indeed, sir. Mr. St. John assures me it is far better than the first." Relief began to flood through her.

"Thank you, miss," he said, already looking over the pages.

"Yes, well. Good day, sir." She was barely able to keep the joy from her voice.

He waved her away distractedly, his bushy brows furrowed in concentration.

She watched him for a few moments before she left the theater, satisfied that her mission had been a success.

It had been worth it, then, the past few nights penning the new play. Whatever Mr. Ashford's faults, and there were many of them, he most certainly did not deserve to have his reputation shredded in public.

She grinned. Perhaps she could do that in private.

Her last sight of Mr. Elliston was a rewarding one. He was sinking into a uncomfortable-looking chair, flipping through her pages. The last few were still damp from her pen.

And so she left, satisfied.

A few moments later, Elliston looked up to return the manuscript.

"This is no good, it has none of the flavor, none of the—" The young lady was gone.

Elliston shrugged and tossed the manuscript to the floor. He would indeed save it, but only as scrap paper. Good quality stock such as this was devilishly hard to come by.

The three sisters stepped from the carriage onto the pavement in front of Fanny's town house, straw scattered in heavy clumps upon the stones.

"Oh, look!" Letty exclaimed. "Straw! There must be a circus nearby."

Caroline and Emily exchanged glances. "Well, dearest," Emily began gingerly. "I believe the straw is here because some lady on the street will soon have a baby."

"Really? How interesting. Caroline, did straw grow in the street when you had your babies?"

Caroline blushed to the very roots of her carefully arranged curls. "Letty, one musn't say such things. It's not polite."

"Whyever not?" Letty blinked up at Emily, the large rim of her hat shading her face. "I don't understand what's not polite about straw. But why does it grow when someone has a baby?"

"Well, it doesn't grow. The straw is placed upon the pavement to muffle the sounds of carriages and horses," Emily explained. "That way the lady of the house, and later her baby, are not disturbed by all that clattering."

"That's so nice," Letty concluded with satisfaction. Then she gasped and rose upon the tiptoes of her slippers. "Maybe it's for Fanny! Maybe she's having a baby this very morning! That's why she was too busy to answer all of my letters, or to invite us over the moment she knew we were coming to London."

"Oh, Emily," Caroline looked at her older sister helplessly, tears already brimming in her eyes.

"That's a lovely thought," Emily assured Letty. "The loveliest of thoughts. But not this time, sweet. Not this time."

The three of them stared up at the house before them, Letty still slightly perplexed, Caroline dabbing her nose with a handkerchief that had been tucked into the sleeve of her green spencer.

The house was perfectly respectable, although not nearly as grand as Caroline's residence, and certainly a far cry from the lavish estate of Fairfax Castle. This more modest house was still within the realm of fashionable elegance, if on the slightly battered fringe.

Emily took a deep breath. "The shades are drawn," she remarked.

"They always are, or at least they have been for these past ten months or more. So very gloomy." Caroline tried to shift the mood, and with an artificially bright smile she turned to Letty. "My dear, once again you have a most lovely hat. Why, should any members of society catch a glimpse of your caps, I daresay they will become all the rage."

Letty glanced up at Caroline, then back at the house. "I don't like this place. It's not a very friendly sort of house, is it?"

Emily patted her youngest sister's shoulder. "Well, silly—how on earth can a house be friendly? It can't very well step up to us and offer a hand, can it? Or ask us in for tea and muffins." But even as she spoke she knew precisely what Letty meant. She was right. It was not a very pleasant or welcoming house, with the beginnings of a very obvious crack forming beneath a window, or a large discolored splotch emerging from a corner gutter. And as much as the place had lacked warmth in the past, now it seemed completely devoid of all charm.

"I sent round several notes informing her of our visit this morning," Caroline said quietly. "She did not respond in any manner, but then she hasn't responded to my notes for quite some time."

"Well," Emily said with sharp resolution, "we will not be deterred. Come, Little Hens."

Caroline smiled, remembering that her oldest sister always used to refer to them as her Little Hens. Letty still gazed at the house with undisguised misgiving as they climbed the six steps to the front door and knocked. After what seemed like a very long time the door opened, and Fanny herself stood before them.

"Fanny!" Letty exclaimed, stepping forward. Then she recoiled. "Fan, you look awful!"

And it was true. Emily did her best to hide her profound shock at how very altered her sister's appearance had become.

Once she had been considered something of a beauty, more due to sheer vivacity than to any striking comeliness of her features. She had been a laughing child who became a mirthful young woman—at least until she married. Then she became almost solemn, a change Caroline saw as welcome maturity, but Emily viewed with growing concern.

But one look at Fanny caused her to realize that something was very wrong. More than wrong. This was not simple maturity. Fanny appeared pale, perhaps ill. And her manner, even on a first glance, was furtive. She remained behind the door, opened only a sliver, to expose a shoulder and part of a thin, drawn face.

"Oh, Fan," Emily said warmly, reaching out. But Fanny just looked down at Emily's open palms until they dropped to her side. "How wonderful it is to see you!"

Fanny blinked, a curiously delayed action, as if just realizing there was company. "Good heavens. Emily and Caroline. And Letty. Why on earth did you not tell me you were coming to town?"

"Why, Fan, I sent you no less than three notes," Caroline cried. "Our footman assured me you received them."

Fanny chewed her lower lip, as if weighing the words.

"May we come in, Fan?" Emily asked gently. "We so long to visit."

"Today is not a good day," Fanny said at last. "Perhaps next week. Yes. Next week would be far better."

"But we are your sisters! There is no need to stand on ceremony with us," Emily assured.

"I . . . really." She looked nervously over her shoulder. "I must get back inside."

A man's voice called from within, and Fanny began to close the door. But Emily quickly placed her foot across the threshold. "Please, Fan. Is that Robert? I would so love to see him. Maybe—"

"Please, Emily. I must go inside. Please let me go!"

"Fan, what's wrong?"

For an instant she looked directly into Emily's eyes, and Em all but gasped with alarm. The expression reflected in her gaze was wide-eyed, almost feral terror. It was the unmistakable look of a cornered animal.

"I must . . . really . . ." Her voice wavered. Behind her the masculine voice bellowed louder, and Fanny jumped as if she had been struck. With tremendous force the door slammed shut. At the last possible instant Emily pulled her foot back, although the corner of her hem was momentarily trapped. As she worked the fabric free, the heavy sounds of locks and chains sliding into place were audible on the other side of the door.

Dumbfounded, Emily, Caroline and Letty stood helplessly on the steps.

"Well, that wasn't very nice," Letty said in a small voice.

"I didn't have a chance to ask if she was attending Lady Duff's party," Caroline said distractedly, trying to make sense of what had happened. "Emily? What think you?"

She smiled down at Letty and gave her shoulder a reassuring pat before answering. "I am very worried, Caro," she said softly. "Very worried indeed."

The two older sisters simply exchanged nods, not wanting to continue the conversation in front of Letty.

"Letty?" Caroline said brightly. "Have you ever tasted coconut?"

Letty smiled. "No, but I have always longed to go to a tropical place and live on nothing but coconuts." Thus the three sisters went in search of tea and sweets before deciding what to wear to Lady Duff's famous annual party.

But all Emily could think of were her sister's frightened eyes.

Caroline made a valiant attempt at keeping her face pleasantly blank.

"Emily, dearest," she began gently. "Must you really wear that hat to Lady Duff's?"

Emily winced as she looked at her own reflection. "There is no way out of it, I fear. I told Letty how very proud I would be to wear it, that it pained me to recall in my haste to pack and settle affairs at Fairfax Castle, it was sadly left behind. I knew not she had taken the liberty of packing it for me. I had assumed it was back in Ireland, where it could do no harm." Again, she met her own eyes in the mirror. "Clearly I was mistaken."

"But really, it is quite absurd. This is Lady Duff's first big tea of the season. She has hired the finest musicians. The food will be beyond anything you have ever encountered, Em. Quite stupendous. But your hat, my dear, is likely to put people off their appetite. I daresay I feel quite ill just looking at it."

"I believe that was the effect Letty was striving to achieve."

"Emily, please listen to me. All of society fortunate enough to garner an invitation will be present. There will be eligible men at this gathering. Men of consequence, and ladies of vital importance in society. But when they see Miss Fairfax in her beetle-infested fashions, well, I cannot say it will do either of us any good."

Emily tilted her head and watched with dismay as a silk spider began to swing from beneath the rim of the bonnet, and a purple flower bounced madly from tiny wire springs at the crown. Two large May bugs were attached to the tips of the green satin ties. When fastened into a bow under her chin, the flies appeared to be chasing each other. "Letty worked very hard on this."

"Yes, she did," Caroline agreed.

"We already have one unhappy sister. We cannot risk having two." Emily glanced about the room to be sure they were alone, then lowered her voice. "Caroline, what are we to do about Fanny?"

"I do not know." Caroline's rounded shoulders slumped forward. "But she is far worse than she was last month. And I'm beginning to fear there is something much worse than a lack of children in that household."

"I agree. Do you think there is the smallest chance she will be at Lady Duff's?"

"I know not."

Emily swallowed. "Poor Fan," she whispered. And then, with determination, she took a deep breath. "Perhaps we can find out something at Lady Duff's party. There are bound to be those who know Robert and Fanny there, even if they do not attend." Then she allowed herself a small smile. "Tell me, how is the lighting at Lady Duff's house?"

With relief Caroline returned the smile. "It is said the Duffs buy more wax candles than anyone in London. They are more illuminated than most theaters. Indeed, the manager of Vauxhall Gardens recently inquired how the Duffs achieve such brilliant, precise lighting."

"Are there any dim corners?"

"Lord Duff has just installed gas lamps throughout the entire estate. He is one of the first in London to do so. But that doesn't signify much, as it is to be a lawn party, mostly. The weather is fine and bright. When dusk comes they have dozens of lanterns to hang from every branch and bough.

There will be no dim corners. There are barely any shadows on their grounds."

"How wonderful for them, to have such weather, such an ample supply of candles," Emily said sadly.

"You really don't have to wear this." Caroline stood behind her sister, observing her own reflection in the process, and unable to avoid feeling rather self-satisfied with her own new hat. It was simple and elegant, and the ties were broad enough to very nearly abolish her double chin. With the fringed crimson silk wrap about her shoulders—which added a touch of color as well as concealing the plumpness of her upper arms—she was every inch the well-dressed society matron.

Movement of her sister's hat trimmings drew her eyes back to Emily. How exquisite she was, natural and unaffected. Caroline often envied the arch of her brow, graceful as the wing of a dove, and her nose. It was just right, straight and well proportioned. Her lips were lamentably mobile, not the thin, fixed lips of other noted beauties. She was too prone to smiling and giving away her feelings with her expressions. Yet she had to admit, her sister was so very lovely!

But with that horrid head wear, all anyone at the Duffs' would see are insects and spiderwebs. "I have an idea," she began excitedly. "You can wear it as far as the carriage. That will satisfy Letty, and then we can change hats en route. I have a beautiful one with that pale shade of blue that is so flattering to your complexion—so new I haven't even worn it myself. It will be our little piece of innocent sub-terfuge. I will smuggle it under my shawl. Then, upon our return, we will replace the hat."

"What are you two talking about?" Letty asked, entering Caroline's dressing room. She, too, was wearing a new hat—this one with small mammals perched in various poses along the edge. There was a carefully cut hole on the left side of the brim with the distinct face of a ferret poking through. It's nose was made of a red glass bead, and it's eyes of jet. On closer inspection, the ferret had some unidentifi-able crumpled object clenched in its teeth.

"Nothing, Letty. We were simply discussing who will be at the Duffs'," Caroline smiled. Then her smile wavered a bit. "Why are you dressed in your new frock?"

"Uncle George said I can go to Lady Duff's with you. It seems that even though I'm years away from being officially 'out,' Lady Duff likes to appraise future brides early. Uncle George said it was sort of like examining a colt to see what kind of horse it would become, or something. Anyway, the boys and the baby are out with Nanny. There's nothing to do here, especially since you won't let me play with the guns or the knives from America. Uncle George said I can do less damage at Lady Duff's than here." Then she brightened. "Emily, the hat is even better than I ever imagined on you!"

"George said you may come with us? *My* hus-band George?" Caroline said with dismay.

"No, George the King of England. He came by

and told me to come. Of course I mean your husband George." Letty allowed her eyes to roll back in a most unattractive manner.

"Letty, believe me when I tell you that you will be bored to tears. Truly. There is to be no entertainment, no music. No food. Not even a watered-down punch. And don't you have that lovely coconut cake! How lucky you are! It will probably rain. I hear Lady Duff has asked the dullest vicar in England to practice his longest sermons. The guests will be made to sit in the most uncomfortable chairs imaginable. And only the most unpleasant, wretched sorts of people will be in attendance."

"Then why are you and Emily going?"

"Because, dearest, sometimes people who move about in society must frequent tiresome events. That way we may attend more pleasurable amusements without guilt."

"That doesn't make any sense," Letty concluded. "Besides, I'm already bored to tears. I might as well be bored to tears at Lady Duff's. Em, do you think Mr. Ashford will be there?"

"Ashford?" Emily swallowed. Would he be there to see her in the ludicrous hat?

"I doubt it very much," Caroline concluded. "I hear he is busy with governmental issues. Something about a bill or a law, I believe. Or a speech."

Emily was both relieved and dismayed. Indeed, when she thought the matter over thoroughly, she realized that the only way she had seen Mr. Ashford was under extreme duress, either on account of a pending duel or when he had been literally snatched from the streets by Letty.

It was becoming painfully clear that Mr. Lucius Ashford would not come willingly to Emily, nor did he wish to correspond in any manner.

Not that it mattered, not really. She would rectify the situation with the play, assist Fanny in any way possible, and then return to Ireland. And that would conclude any chance of ever seeing Lucius Ashford ever again.

Letty and Caroline were still arguing about whether Letty should attend Lady Duff's party.

"Oh, Caro. I think George is right—we should just take Letty. It cannot possibly hurt, and she was invited."

"Was I? Then it would be rude for me to disappoint them, would it not?"

"Very well," Caroline said without enthusiasm. Then she adopted the tone of mother hen. "But you cannot wear that hat, Emily. Tell Letty exactly what we think of it. She has to know. It is kindest for us to tell her."

The smile dissolved from Letty's face. "What do you mean?"

"The bonnet is not flattering to Emily. There. That is the truth, plain and simple." Caroline folded her arms and nodded once, relieved for having been so very honest.

For a long moment Letty said nothing. Then, very slowly, she untied her own bonnet. "I understand," she said softly. "It's not pretty. And Emily was just pretending to like it all along. Pretending just to be nice, as she always does." She allowed the hat to tumble to the carpet, kicking it once with the toe of her shoe.

"Oh, Letty," Emily began.

Then she looked up from her hat on the floor. "Sometimes I forget." Her voice was a mere whisper. "I forget that I am just a child, and how tiresome that must be for everyone. You are grown ladies." She looked at Caroline, her large blue eyes already filling with tears. "Grand ladies. And Emily should be a grand lady, too. It is only because of me, because of me and Papa that she has had to stay at home. But I forget, Em, because you help me to forget. You listen to me and play with me. You helped me with the bee farm even though you thought they were ugly and one stung your nose."

"Letty," Emily felt her own eyes prickle with tears.

"You helped me make a village out of smelly mushroom tops, and let me sleep with the puppies when Papa said I could not," she continued. "You told me my story about the peg-legged pirate was fine, even though I know the part about eating the whale from the inside out was revolting. You passed up the fish course for months. So when you said you liked my hats, I believed you. Because I forgot."

By now Caroline was sniffing. But Emily spoke first. "My dear Letty," she said matter-of-factly. "You are quite correct. I do not like your hats."

"Emily!" Caroline cried, wrapping a protective arm around her youngest sister. "How can you say that? I never thought of you as cruel. Never! Do not listen to her, Letty. I like your hats. Very much indeed!"

"Please do not interrupt me, Caro. What I was saying, before you jumped in like an eager mouse pouncing on cheese, was that I *love* your hats. I adore them. 'Like' is not a sufficient enough word. And it is with absolute pride that I will wear this bonnet into Lady Duff's dull affair. I can only hope that you will come with us and wear your own hat with just as much pride. Why, we will be the envy of the bon ton."

Letty raised her chin, her cheeks damp with tears and her freckles splotched with red, which happened whenever she was upset. She looked at Caroline, then at Emily. "Really?"

"Of course," Emily looked at herself closely in the mirror. "I only wish the rest of my attire could match my bonnet for fineness."

Letty's lips gradually spread into a smile, and her tears quickly converted to the more customary sparkle. Emily bent down and handed Letty the fallen hat. With a grin she replaced it on her head, tying a big bow at her chin. "Maybe we will even be mentioned in the society gazettes! Fancy Papa reading about us back home."

Caroline glanced from one sister to the other. "You two look so lovely! Just like a picture. I am quite jealous that I do not have a hat to match yours. Quite envious indeed. Positively green with it."

"But I do have one for you, Caro," Letty said ecstatically. "It was to be a surprise! Yours is the best, the very best one I ever made. I'm sorry, Em, but it is so. It is a huge picture hat, not just a little bonnet. So there is much more room for my decorations. This one had birds in a nest, with the mama bird feeding worms to the baby birds. And every time you walk, their beaks open. I'll fetch it now!" she exclaimed, and ran from the room.

The second she was gone, Caroline paled. "Emily! What shall we do?"

"We shall wear the bonnets, of course. Otherwise we will break her heart, and that cannot be allowed." Finally Emily smiled at her sister, who wore the expression of a condemned prisoner. "It doesn't really matter. Nobody will notice. And even if they do, I reckon they won't give a fig."

"But Emily, really. Lady Duff's? And in full daylight?"

"And what alternative do we have?" Emily asked cheerfully.

After a short struggle, Caroline shrugged. "None. None at all."

"Oh, honestly, no one will notice. And do trust me, as I just said, no one will give a fig."

Ashford held up the invitation to Lady Duff's party. It was of the very finest paper stock, thick and luxurious, with the feel of satin. A folded invitation would make a decent sole of a shoe. Two invitations connected would bind a family Bible. He supposed that some people would no doubt prize the invitation to such an extent that they would become family heirlooms, precious mementos to be cherished and stroked reverently for generations to come.

Who would even care about this absurd party in a week's time? But he knew that answer very well: everyone who did not have at invitation at this very moment.

The cost of one round of these mailings could supply his office and his own paper needs for at least a year. And Lady Duff was not forced to pay postage for her invitations, for her servants hand delivered them. Even if she had sent them through the post, her husband's position in the House of Lords would allow the invitations to be franked.

He did not have the time or inclination to attend, but he had already returned his acceptance weeks ago. At the time he had assumed the gathering would help him politically, that perhaps he could convince some of the more rigid Tories that passing a bill to aid the poor, especially children, would eventually benefit everyone in the entire nation.

Soon after he accepted the invitation, he learned the party was to be nothing short of a marriage mart. Even Lord Duff had made arrangements well in advance to be away from town on the date. Thus he had made up his mind to write the hostess a suitably appeasing note, claiming a sudden attack of some health calamity, or perhaps pressing personal business. It mattered not what he wrote, for as soon as Lady Duff conveyed the unexpected nature of his absence to the other guests (and he knew, from previous experience, that she would), the gossips would formulate a much more fascinating account. No doubt it would involve a duel, perhaps bloodshed and death. No one in London who happened to be absent from the party would be omitted from the speculation, including Lord Duff himself.

The night before, however, he had encountered George Edgeworth at Brooks's. And Edgeworth had mentioned casually that his wife and sister-in-law would be going to Lady Duff's party, although he had managed to wiggle out of it by claiming business with an out-of-town customer.

"I find the Duffs insufferable," Edgeworth had said as he lit his pipe and nodded to the serving man for another brandy. "But Caroline is bent on becoming a member of society's first circle. Good Lord, you should see her bills, Ashford. She spends more on a single gown than I pay for three well-made suits of my own. And she must be seen at all of the great events. We even have prime tickets to that new play opening next week at the Olympic. Not that she cares for plays, mind you. But the thing is to be seen in the best seats at those plays. The play itself is all but pointless."

"What play is that?" Ashford asked, only half listening. Another gentleman seated in a leather wing chair just behind Edgeworth had been most attentive to their conversation. Edgeworth had spoken in a louder voice than he had realized, and no doubt the interloper had been delighted with the information that George Edgeworth found the Duffs intolerable. Although everyone felt the same sentiments, no one dared to pronounce them aloud. The man turned and Ashford could see him in profile. It was, indeed, Nicholas "Fidgey" Malcome, the biggest gossip in London besides Lady Duff and the Prince Regent.

"So of course we will go. I saw his last and it was most amusing."

"Yes," Ashford frowned. He genuinely liked Edgeworth, and knew adverse prattle could harm his emerging position.

"Did you see it, Ashford?" Edgeworth asked.

"Which one was that?"

"I haven't the faintest notion of the title of the thing. But St. John always manages to amuse."

Now Ashford was fully attentive. "Edgar St. John? The playwright?"

Edgeworth laughed. "Of course. Did you not just hear me? The new St. John play is opening Wednesday next."

"The new St. John play." He took a sip of brandy, enjoying the pleasantly warm path it made down his throat. "I would be most interested in seeing it."

"You? Why, I never thought of you as a man with a bent for amusements. You strike me as too serious by half to find enjoyment in playgoing and whatnot. But if you like, you may join us in our box. I believe Caroline's sisters from Ireland are coming. They get precious little amusement in there, I would imagine."

"Thank you, Edgeworth. I daresay I'll take you up on that. And perhaps we should attend Lady Duff's affair—"

"I would rather be eaten by—"

Before George Edgeworth could continue, Ashford jotted down a few sentences in pencil and handed it to him.

He raised his eyebrows in acknowledgment. "Yes, I do believe I will attend. I would rather be there to eat the magnificent assortment of foods and savor the company of so many delightful people. I will send a note directly that my plans have been altered." Then he mouthed to Ashford, "Thank you," with a wink.

A slightly disappointed Fidgey Malcome left the club, Edgeworth stood Ashford for a second brandy, and social disaster had been averted.

Mr. Edward Giles could only shake his head over the note from Edgar St. John requesting that he withdraw the newest play in favor of a revision. Even had it been within the realm of possibility (which it was not) it would have been all but impossible at this late date.

"Playwrights," he mumbled to himself, reading the note once again. "They all belong in Bedlam."

Of course, this was the same man who had written an impassioned letter about his livestock and a flood. Granted, he had also written a play sure to be a financial success.

So in deference to the later accomplishment, Giles chose to ignore this latest bit of madness. And he determined that should the excitable Mr. St. John find time to write another such note between his various duels, watery catastrophes and unusual attachment to his four-legged friends, he would ignore that one as well.

After all, it would be the polite thing to do.

Chapter Six

The man was grateful for the darkness of the rooms, for the shadows that enfolded his home even in the brightness of midday. That was the singular advantage of having to do without most of the servants he had formerly employed, not to mention the candles and lamp oil. He found the gloom a comfort, almost a friend.

For he was aware he had precious few friends in the world at that moment.

His wife opened the door and greeted the visitors wordlessly. She had done everything wordlessly of late, and for that he was also grateful. The last thing he needed was a harpy nagging him. Thank God that had stopped.

Thank God he had stopped it.

He stood when the three men entered the parlor. "Good day," he mumbled. They did not reply. He gestured to an uncomfortable-looking chair and settee, but they ignored his thin veneer of hospitality.

"So have you been watching him?" the Major said.

"Yes, of course. I have done exactly as you instructed."

"Are you aware that a groundswell of support is beginning for Ashford's reforms?" As usual the Major did not attempt any flowery language.

"That has nothing to do with me," he said defensively, wiping a hand over his mouth.

"Ah, but it does," the Major replied. He couldn't be sure, but there seemed to be a grin behind his gruff voice. His features were bathed in darkness. "I have been told that it is possible, just possible, some of your debts may be forgiven if you agree to go one step further to help us out. Lend a hand to some old friends, so to speak."

"I am listening."

"Should Ashford's reforms pass, and there is a good chance they will, what with his growing popularity in the House, much of our organization will be held under close scrutiny. Some of the factories up north would be forced to pay higher wages, thus cutting into our profits. And in particular he wishes to assist some of our female workers, the charming ladies in our employ. Now, they need no help. We provide the guidance they need. I am sure you would not like to see that part of our business suffer, would you?"

"No, no. Of course not. But I fail to see how I can be of help. I am not politically connected. Barely know the man, even socially."

"Ah, yes. But you see, you do. You are more connected than you realize to Lucius Ashford, MP. Are you aware that George Edgeworth has been seen at the club, enjoying brandy with Ashford?"

"Well, I was aware of their friendship. But it is most casual. Just as I used to enjoy something of a friendship with George Edgeworth. Used to have brandy at the club. It means nothing." He attempted, without success, to keep the bitterness from his voice. "I was asked to leave the club some months ago, and have therefore not been aware of my esteemed brother-in-law's social activities."

"And were you aware that your sister-in-law, the Irish spinster, also claims a connection to Ashford?"

"Emily?" Robert blinked, genuinely surprised. "No, of course not. I saw Edgeworth and Ashford with the youngest sister, then Ashford leave the Edgeworth house. But a connection with Emily? I can't imagine."

"Yes. Use those connections, sir. Use them, make the most of any contact you may have with Ashford."

"Major, I doubt if I could possibly influence the man. I hear he is stubborn. Nothing I could say would cause him to withdraw his reform bill."

"Idiot. Of course nothing you could say would alter his course. We are not asking you to have a pleasant chat with the man."

"I know. You wish me to harm him so he is unable to present his bill. It should not be difficult. He frequently travels without company, and—"

"That has changed. We have decided to ensure continued success, and have come up with another plan."

He hesitated. "Then what do you want of me now?"

"We want you to eliminate him."

"Eliminate?"

"Eliminate. Exterminate. Eradicate. Use whatever word you wish. Just rid him from our path as soon as possible."

"That is murder!"

"Yes, it is. But do you have a choice, sir? Do you wish your activities of these past several years to be revealed to all? Then you will face certain prison, possible death. But if you perform this particular favor, you have a chance to rise again. So your choice is murder, or suicide. Which shall it be?"

Robert swallowed. "How shall I do this thing?"

"We do not care. We do not wish to know. I would say that in your position, I would feel more comfortable hiring roughs to complete the deed. Pay them a small sum. It matters not. Just do it, and soon. If you do not move forward, we most certainly will move to destroy you."

"This is no choice. You are offering me no alternative. Perhaps I can change his mind through other ways. I could attempt—"

"There is no time for that. The decision has been made. You know us well enough to believe we will indeed carry out our end of the bargain should you fail in yours. Do you understand?"

He nodded in the darkness.

Without a good-bye, the three men left as quickly as they arrived.

And Robert was left with the disturbing task of determining how a man would die.

Everyone agreed that Lady Duff had outdone even herself with her Afternoon in Spring Fete, as she had so whimsically titled her party.

And for Lady Duff to outdo herself was no simple matter. Every year, the former Harriet Johnson—rumored to be the illegitimate daughter of either an Italian prince or a distant cousin of King George—launched her own official season with a spectacular social event. Lady Duff was in reality the very legitimate daughter of a Glasgow blacksmith. She spread the rumors herself, after long ago deciding that a noble birth on the wrong side of the sheets was far more elegant than her own perfectly drab beginning.

Last year's prettily designed La Belle Soiree was an elegant affair with, as its name indicated, a French theme. Never mind all the unpleasantness with Napoleon. Those in society ignored politics and even patriotism when it concerned the really important elements in life, such as wine and food and a ripping good party. The French were the only ones who truly understood fashion as well as the proper employment of excess. And the French nobility were just like the British, except the women wore more perfume and the men wore more lace. True, those who had actually mingled with the French aristocrats were occasionally taken aback by some small, unimportant details, such as their apparent aversion to using forks (they complained that the prongs pierced their cheeks) and a distinct reluctance to bathe (more noticeable now that Mr. Brummell dictated cleanliness over heavy floral scents). Nevertheless, that party was still talked about after twelve months. Lady Duff was clearly doing something right to remain a topic of conversation amongst so much competition.

Duff's End, the family seat for the past three generations, was a large, violently unattractive pile of stones located in a fortuitously fashionable part of town. The earlier Duffs, who had money at the time but unfortunately not taste or a title, built their home in an area of town that was almost out of town back then. Now town had come to the Duffs. One needn't even bring out the coach to attend one of the Duff's parites or balls, although even their nearest neighbors would rather harness the four or six or eight horses and the best carriage and dress their men in the finest livery than be seen walking the few hundred paces to the affair.

And what an affair it was!

The Afternoon in Spring Fete was an open invitation for the best and most amusing members of the ton to present themselves at their best and most amusing. Lady Duff prided herself on her ability to prompt brilliant conversation, and never did one of her parties pass without at least several small events or uttered witticisms become the latest bon mots of society. There were delightfully awkward meetings of ex-lovers, uncomfortable encounters with political opponents, and long pauses over course after course of exquisitely displayed, frequently inedible food.

Because of the elaborate plans she invariably carried out, there was something sinisterly artificial about her gatherings. The French theme was achieved by hiring a seamstress from Paris to help her servants with their accents, although a French accent mingled with the pronounced Cockney of some of the underhouse maids was somewhat disconcerting. Owing to the difficulties in obtaining genuine French items during that time, Stilton cheese had to do for Bleu, and some other dreadful substitutions were necessary. But it was an impressive display of wealth, which was much of the point. Perhaps it was vulgar. Maybe ostentatious. Everyone agreed it was oh-so-common, even as they enjoyed the fruits of the commonness.

And this year was no exception. Lady Duff had rented beasts from a half dozen private zoos to mingle with the guests and to decorate Duff's End both inside the house as well as without. At first she was determined to allow the beasts to run free, just as in nature, although in nature the animals were not rented by the hour and were usually not dressed in jingling collars with embroidered shoes covering their hooves and paws to protect the floors.

They were to be the centerpiece of her springtime theme, the cunning, entirely natural frolicking animals. Why, the entire front lawn would resemble a charming painting! When several concerned zoo workers explained that the beasts were not meant to mingle together on her lawn or any other lawn, she scoffed—until she was offered a very vivid description of the larger animals attacking the smaller ones, and all of the animals attacking the guests, and she reluctantly agreed to keeping the more exotic beasts caged.

Another signature of the Duffs' events was the timing. Lady Duff delighted in scheduling her levees at unconventional times, so that virtually everyone was inconvenienced by the date as well as the hours. Supper, tea and dinner were melded into one long stretch. Gentlemen involved in business or politics invariably missed vital meetings. Those dabbling in the arts knew the day would be an utter loss. Newspapermen worked overtime, bribing the servants and coachmen for details on clothing and the happenings within the party itself.

Ladies with children were the least affected, for as usual the servants would perform all parenting duties, insuring yet another generation of distant, emotionally brittle offspring to run the nation.

At the appointed time of three o'clock in the afternoon, Lady Duff checked herself in the mirror one last time, pleased with what she saw. Although she was on the other side of fifty, her real age—like the other details of her birth—remained shrouded in mystery. Even her husband was uncertain of her genuine birthday, and absolutely ignorant of her first marriage to a Swiss clockmaker, which ended to everyone's satisfaction (except that of the law) when he moved to America.

Lady Duff and all of London were ready for the Afternoon in Spring Fete to begin.

Caroline kept her gaze cautiously straight ahead, not even glancing out the carriage windows on either side. She sat stiffly in the center of the seat, her hands folded in her lap. Her expression was one of studied distress, as if any crack in her flimsy composure would completely undo her.

"Oh, look, Caro!" Letty exclaimed, bouncing on the leather seat opposite, the springs creaking with her movement. "Did you see that man on the corner? He was wearing bright red shoes! Where do you suppose one gets bright red shoes?"

"Mayhaps he has a twelve-year-old sister," muttered Caroline.

Emily patted Letty on the shoulder and did her best to control the urge to laugh. "Come, Letty. Do not hang out of the carriage so." Letty pulled in her arm, but continued to announce all of the fascinating sights they passed on the way to Lady Duff's.

"That man is walking a funny little dog. What kind of dog is it? A confectioner's shop. I wonder if they have marzipan there. Are those the new gas lamps? No, they are just plain ones. What a strange carriage! Did you see that? I think it had three wheels!"

Caroline remained stiff and unyielding, her large hat taking up most of the seat. The other two sisters sat across from her, riding backward, granting the married Caroline the honor of traveling forward with her own expanse of seat.

Not that Caroline noticed that particular honor at the moment. The size of her hat would in fact prohibit another passenger from taking a place on her side anyway. Indeed, the brim alone came close to bumping Emily's forehead every time they rode over a loose cobblestone or turned a corner.

"Please, Letty," Caroline urged between clenched teeth. "My nerves. Have a care. My nerves cannot take this."

Letty grinned. "I do not know why you are so very grumpy. You have the best hat by far."

"She is right, you know," Emily confirmed. "I envy you that hat. It is an absolute marvel of design and construction. Honestly, how did you fit so many creatures on the brim?"

Letty grew very somber. "It was not easy."

"Please, let us discuss something else." Caroline closed her eyes as if to eliminate the immediate world.

Letty looked at both of her sisters. "Hum," she said critically. "I believe we have made a grave error."

"Have we?" Emily smiled. Looking at Caroline's hat, it was difficult not to smile, for the thing was the most astonishing creation she had ever seen. It was draped in a unique shade of purple, a fabric Letty had found in a trunk in the massive Fairfax Castle attic. Her father had said it was no doubt left over from an ancestor who was either a disgraced member of the church or color-blind. Upon the purple satin were dozens of colorful animals, including a large bird with feathers of dyed chicken plumes on its tail and a mouse made of some sort of fur. She had even fashioned special hat pins; a half dozen were required. The hat pins were linked by an intricate system of thread and string to create a fence so the smaller animals were not threatened by the larger ones.

"Otherwise, I do think people would become uneasy when they look at the hat," Letty had explained.

"They still will," Caroline had said to herself.

"Are we almost there? I thought you said they lived nearby," Letty asked.

"They do live nearby. I instructed the driver to take the longest route possible. The fresh air should do us good," Caroline said miserably.

"Do we have time to change our hats?" Letty said.

"Excuse me?" For the first time in an hour, there was hope in Caroline's voice.

"I said do we have time to change our hats. Yours is all wrong, Caro. I am sorry to say that your hat doesn't suit your gown. Not at all."

"I disagree," said Emily. "I think her hat is absolutely spectacular."

"I know," agreed Letty. "That is why you should wear it. Caroline, would you be terribly heartbroken if—"

But Caroline was already yanking out the hat pins. "Oh, no! Of course not! How very lucky I have been to wear it as long as I have! What a privilege, a joy!"

"Letty, will you wear it then?" Emily asked.

"No. Unfortunately it's too big for me. But Em, it will be absolutely perfect for you. Don't you think so?"

"Yes, indeed!" Caroline was positively gleeful. "Here, Em. Let me help you."

"But what will you wear, Caroline?" Panic began to rise in Emily as Letty untied her bonnet, which suddenly seemed wondrously elegant.

"I think maybe she should wear the plain hat she had on before, her own one. The colors are all wrong, you see," Letty explained gently. "Should we go back and get it?"

"There is no need!" Caroline all but sang. "I have it above in a box, just in case of rain!"

"You won't mind, Caro, will you? I will make you one for next time." Letty plunged the first of the hat pins into Emily's hair.

"I understand," Caroline said gravely as she tapped on the roof to have her own hat handed down.

"What do you think, Emily?" Letty frowned and readjusted the pin.

"I am so very, very lucky," she replied. "Very lucky indeed."

"Mr. Ashford! How delighted we are that you could come!" Lady Duff crossed the room to reach him.

The "we," he assumed, was the "royal we," since Lord Duff had made it a point to be absent from the day's events. It wasn't that Lord Duff did not support his wife in her social ambitions, for the connections she made or at least solidified were usually helpful to him in areas of his own interest; hunting and—above all else—dog breeding. He was a man far more comfortable around animals than around people. Just as she allowed him time with his precious dogs, he allowed her the means with which to entertain in lavish style. In fact, he was fond of relating that his very favorite bitch had been obtained as a direct result of his wife's last party.

"That would be Mrs. Armstrong," more than one listener would think and occasionally say aloud, referring to Lord Duff's equally dog-loving mistress. Lord Duff, of course, was referring to Millie, his spotted pointer.

Lucius Ashford bowed. "Lady Duff, I do thank you for the invitation."

"Why, of course I would invite you, sir! The most eligible bachelor in London, and the most mysterious. I daresay you shall not remain either a bachelor or mysterious for long, with all of the lovely women in attendance today."

Ashford smiled, knowing exactly what he was expected to reply. One of Lady Duff's genuine talents was to evoke compliments from others. The sincerity of those compliments was always in question to everyone within hearing distance (except, of course, to Lady Duff herself). For one could not escape being seen as a complete cad if one didn't respond correctly to Lady Duff's well-designed comments.

He did what was required of him. "There are indeed lovely women in attendance, Lady Duff. And perhaps our hostess is the loveliest of all."

There. He said it, and not a single thunderbolt crashed from above to disprove his words.

"Oh, Mr. Ashford." Her blush was as famous as it was contrived.

Then, suitably gratified, and well aware that any further conversation would only dilute the flattering effect, she flew off to greet another guest.

And as always at one of these gatherings, he was beginning to regret his decision to come. The regret would either intensify as the minutes ticked by, or it would vanish if he could find someone with whom to speak, someone who could aid in the passing of his bill.

That was the real reason he was there, he told himself. To further the chances of his fair labor proposal that he was to introduce to Parliament, to see it become a law of the land. It had taken years of research and hard work, of managing to get elected during a year of turmoil and war abroad, hoping to focus Parliament's attention if only for a moment on the less glamorous subject of impoverished children and the best ways to give them a chance of a better life—indeed, of any life.

Ashford stood for a moment on the threshold of a grand salon. There was a peculiar odor permeating the air, of foods mingled with something vaguely sour.

It took him only a moment to see the large cage in the corner filled with monkeys.

"Good God," someone murmured behind him. "Are those monkeys?"

It was Sir William Cates, who had been one of the last century's most notorious rakes. As with most formerly notorious rakes, he had matured into a somewhat intolerant prude, frowning on anyone who indulged in the exact same amusements he himself had once celebrated so frequently and so publicly. The previous year he had embarked on a one-man campaign to banish the use of spirits in polite society. When polite society, in turn, banished Sir William—finding his constant rantings on the evils of liquor tiresome—he became less strident, and refrained from pouring out tumblers of alcohol on flower beds and potted plants.

"I believe those are monkeys," Ashford confirmed.

"What do you s'pose Lady Duff intends to do with them?"

Ashford turned to Sir William, who was several inches shorter than himself and wearing his gray hair in an old-fashioned curled cue. The stockings that began where his britches ended, just at his knee, were of white silk, which made the calf pads quite obvious.

"Well, Sir William, they are situated by the buffet. And there is a complete array of cutlery nearby. One can only speculate."

"Good God! You don't s'pose she intends us to eat them, do you?"

"I'm not certain. One can never tell what Lady Duff has planned."

Sir William's eyes widened. One of the monkeys screeched and began to bang on the cage, the screeches building up to a high-pitched crescendo, which prompted the other primates to join in. One of the larger monkeys rocked the cage back and forth, which knocked over a side table. Sir William was forced to shout above the clanging, screaming turmoil. "I am most certain Lord Duff would never approve of his wife serving monkeys to her guests."

"Probably not." Ashford leaned casually against the wall. "But then again, Lord Duff is not present."

Shock and dismay registered on Sir William's face. "I am going outside for some peace and quiet." With one last look over his shoulder, he retreated.

More guests were arriving. He strolled around the lavish rooms of Duff's End, noting that every chamber had a different assortment of caged animals, from parrots to llamas. There seemed to be no design or plan to the animal's placement, other than what Lady Duff thought would be most attractive with the decor of each room. He, too, decided it would be more comfortable outside.

Stepping out through the main entrance, he paused at the large expanse of stone and marble in front of the house. Just beyond the brief stretch of green they called the lawn was an ornate iron gate with the graceful letter "D" displayed repeatedly, in case one was in danger of forgetting who owned the splendor behind the gates. There was an impressive line of carriages pulling up to deposit guests, each conveyance more elegant than the previous one, each guest—mostly female, it seemed—more elaborately gowned than the next.

"Damnation, Ashford, how I hate these things." George Edgeworth nudged his friend. "I'm sure Lady Duff was ecstatic to see you." He grinned, and pulled out a small cigar. "What do you think?"

"Better save it for the club," Ashford replied.

Edgeworth looked longingly before slipping the cigar back into his jacket pocket. "You're right, of course. What the damnation is the theme of this levee? 'Pungent Beasts'?"

Ashford laughed. "Something about springtime, I believe. But I did have sport with Sir William Cates, who is now convinced we'll be dining on wild animals."

"Good! He deserves it. Did you know he once rode through Hyde Park on a camel? Perhaps he's concerned about some massive animal revenge."

Both men chuckled before Edgeworth continued. "Were you here last year, at that New World thing? She had her footmen all dressed up in loincloths. Wait, last year was France or Napoleon or something of the sort. Maybe it was the year before. They all blend together into one prolonged outrage."

"No. I did attend the ancient Greece one, though. Most of the women were draped in tablecloths. One doesn't appreciate a well-done toga until one sees it done badly. I believe they were misled by the urns and romantic poetry." He paused. "Is your wife here yet?"

"I haven't seen Caroline or her sisters, which surprises me. She's usually out before the hostess. Hello," he squinted beyond the gates. "I think I see our carriage."

"Where?"

"Just beyond the fifth 'D' to the left."

"Ah, I see. It may take them a while. Four carriages to go before their turn."

"That can take hours. Shall we go in search of some nonbeast refreshment?"

"Perhaps we should wait for your wife. Or go down to assist them."

Edgeworth grinned. "How solicitous you are, Ashford. I never knew you were such an absolute gentleman. Well, not that you are not a gentleman. I simply never saw you as a conventional one. Although I have heard such from secondary sources."

"Which secondary sources?"

"My sister-in-law."

Ashford looked at him, then glanced away, his expression unreadable.

"I believe she is quite taken with you, sir. You made an impression on her in Ireland."

"I'm certain you are confusing me with Ogilvie."

"Not likely. She said you were the most handsome man she had ever seen, and that one of her primary reasons for visiting London at this time was to renew her acquaintance with you."

"I am sure she has other business here," he said uncomfortably. "Shall we go down and help your wife from her carriage?"

"I prefer to talk with you here. Soon enough we will be surrounded by a press of gaggling females. Yes indeed, Ashford. You are quite the hero to my sister-in-law. And what possible business can she have in London?"

Lucius Ashford heard an animal bark, although it didn't sound like a dog. "Is Duff here with his hounds?"

"No. I believe there are seals or walruses in the fountain in back. I hear they are to be served with the cheese course."

Ashford laughed. In the distance he saw Fidgey Malcome, the gossip from the club. Malcome waved at them, and Edgeworth raised a finger to his top hat in response.

Suddenly there seemed to be dozens of people on the lawn, mostly women, although Ashford recognized several faces from Parliament as well as from Brooks's and White's and Boodle's. There was a fraternal understanding that passed between the men, an unspoken but deeply felt sense of wanting to be somewhere else, but being forced to either accompany a woman or make an appearance for the sake of business.

As for Ashford, he kept an eye toward the gate and the new arrivals even as other women surrounded him.

Had Emily Fairfax really spoken so highly of

him? Although he wanted to believe it, it seemed out of character. That is, what little he knew of her character. Any woman who possessed enough discretion to keep her identity as the famous playwright Edgar St. John from most of her family seemed an unlikely choice to be uttering the praise of an almost unknown man. Not only that, but she had failed to respond to his letter. And then there was their awkward meeting at Edgeworth's town house, which certainly did not point to any affection on her part.

A thought crossed his mind. Perhaps she wished to respond in person rather than on paper. Yet she had been taken off guard by his arrival in the parlor, and had been unable to articulate her thoughts. It was an interesting notion, and a strangely hopeful one.

"George, tell me," he turned to his friend. "What exactly did Miss Fairfax say?"

Edgeworth, who had been in the middle of a conversation with Mrs. Blakestone Evans, a rather plump but very wealthy widow, looked up from admiring her diamond shoe buckles. "Eh?"

"What exactly did Miss Fairfax say?"

"About what?"

"About me."

"Oh, she said many things. So Mrs. Evans, have you ever—"

"Such as?"

Edgeworth stopped. "Such as? I don't know, Ashford. She said you are handsome and she wishes to marry you. Anyway, Mrs. Evans, as I was saying—"

"What was that?"

Visibly annoyed, Edgeworth smiled at Mrs. Evans. "Pardon me. My friend here is most interested in a young lady who wishes to marry him."

"Indeed!" Mrs. Evans's face flushed with excitement. "Do tell! Mr. Ashford, I have long felt you have tarried about enough on the marriage market. It is high time for you to relieve some fortunate family of a sizable dowry and a daughter."

"Well, I—" Lucius began.

"You are right, madam. And I am delighted to announce that Mr. Ashford will one day marry my dear sister-in-law."

"Edgeworth!"

Mrs. Evans ignored him. "But isn't Mrs. Edgeworth's sister Fanny already married? She does not appear much in society, certainly not as much as Caroline. But I did believe her to be married. Am I mistaken?"

"Of course you are not, madam. This is another sister, one who lives in Ireland."

"How delightful! I was there in the seventies, and enjoyed it vastly. So quaint, so very green! My late husband, who always had a way with words and a gift with a phrase, even called it 'The Emerald Isle.' Wasn't that clever of him?"

"Positively brilliant," Ashford said. "But I assure you, Mr. Edgeworth misspeaks. I am not engaged at present."

"But mark my words, he will be," Edgeworth added. "As soon as the young lady reaches a marriageable age, her groom will be waiting."

"Marriageable age?" Ashford took a few moments to compose himself, then he smiled. "Letty."

"Of course, Letty. Who else did you think was—" Then Edgeworth stopped. "Lucius. You don't mean you—"

"No. Of course not."

"My God, you're in love with Emily," he whispered.

"You are mistaken."

"I had no idea."

"Sir, what did you say?" Mrs. Evans said. "That is my bad ear, and with all of these people about I cannot hear well. What did you say?"

"Nothing, Mrs. Evans. It was but a jest." George looked at his friend. "You do not look well."

Mrs. Evans, vexed at not being privy to their conversation, left the two men in search of better prey.

Ashford took a deep breath the moment she was out of earshot. "I am fine."

"Really, I did not know. Oh, Ashford. I am damned sorry. I did not know."

"There is nothing to know."

"Are you aware that she plans never to marry?" He tried to make light of it. "I was after her myself when I first met the family. She sparkles when she enters a room. I even asked her first, but don't tell Caroline." His voice softened. "Emily will never marry. Do you know the offers she has had? The titles and wealth she has turned down? Not recently, though. The offers have stopped now that she is in her late twenties. Indeed, your better bet is to wait for Letty. She has already declared her love for you. Just as much money. Vastly amusing. Sure to buy you candy at every opportunity. I vouch she'll be the family beauty."

"I'm sure she will."

"I am damned sorry, old man," Edgeworth repeated. "You know, I have never seen you so affected by a woman. I do believe you really love her."

"Forget about this," Ashford urged. "For my sake, for everyone's sake. I sent her a letter that was perhaps, well, perhaps imprudent. She did not respond. It is nothing, truly nothing."

"Certainly."

Edgeworth was about to say something else when there was a slow buzz of commotion.

"What on earth?" someone exclaimed.

"In heaven's name, what *is* that?"

"I don't care if she has a million pounds," sniffed Fidgey Malcome. "I wouldn't be seen with her for the Crown Jewels."

Slightly curious, Ashford glanced in the direction of the descending hush. At first he couldn't see what they were pointing to; who had arrived. Then the crowd parted.

The first person he saw was Caroline Edgeworth, looking splendid indeed in a fashionable new gown.

Beside her, with a repressed grin on her face, was Letty, wearing an appalling but absolutely predictable bonnet covered with insects of some sort.

Ashford smiled, and her face reddened with delight when she saw him. She jumped ahead one pace, then restrained her motion at a hissed command from Caroline. She stiffened, walking with deliberation as if the momentary delay in reaching their goal would prove fatal.

Then he looked behind the two. At first he was unable to make out precisely what he saw. There were vast amounts of purple. Was it a turban? Some sort of large seat cushion?

A ripple of giggles rose through the party like a wave. More exclamations, some guffaws, a few outright explosions of laughter.

And then he saw what was under the massive purple cushion.

It was Miss Emily Fairfax.

Ashford felt his heart twist as he saw the expression on her face, a curious combination of mortification and defiance. Without a single instant of hesitation he glanced at George Edgeworth, and together they stepped forward to greet the ladies.

Chapter Seven

Stepping out of the carriage with one of Lady Harriet Duff's servants gaping in undisguised amazement at her hat, Emily realized that she had two choices before her. One, she could die.

Actually, when she saw the dozens, perhaps hundreds, of fashionable members of London society mingling on the lawn she knew death was the best way out. Already she was slated to endure social death. That was obvious. The physical one would be a simple matter indeed.

But she also knew that had she been called to her Great Reward at that very moment, Letty would be sure to bury her in the hat. So there was no way out of it, not even death.

The second choice was to simply pretend this was happening to someone else. In a way it was, for the real Emily Fairfax lived a secluded, comfortable life in Ireland, away from everyone present. This event had no relevance in her real life.

In spite of her growing embarrassment, Emily could not help but see the nearly Homeric comic proportions of this moment. Here she was, about to face the very fabric of London aristocracy, and she was wearing a hat made by a twelve-year-old with a decidedly unique sense of humor.

"Impertinent," Caroline said in response to the dumbfounded servant's expression, although she spoke quietly and without conviction, as if very aware his reaction was but a prelude to what was to come. And also very aware that his expression would be mild compared to that of the ton.

Emily's feet felt as if they were encased in lead shoes as she marched up the lawn. Concentrating on the beautiful embroidery of her slippers, pink and blue silk and paper-thin leather soles, she kept her head down, hoping to go unnoticed. Hoping that no one would see or speak to her, and she could leave quietly at the first possible opportunity. Later, safely behind the solid brick walls of Caroline's town house, she could laugh at the ridiculousness of the afternoon. Until then, she simply wanted to attract as little attention as possible.

Letty had dashed ahead of them at the sight of some animals in the distance. Of that Emily was glad, in case someone made a comment or remark that would sting the milliner.

The brim of the hat was so large, it rendered her all but blind. Her line of vision was restricted to the ground and the lower two thirds of an average-sized adult. Perhaps it was a blessing, she thought, that Letty's design prohibited sight as well as taste.

Of course she could not help but hear a few stray comments.

"Good Lord," exclaimed some woman Emily

could only see from the neck down. "It she supposed to resemble a mushroom?"

"That must be the latest fashion in Ireland," a man whispered in dripping sarcasm.

This was not her home, she reminded herself once again. She could survive this. Her chin held high, she thought of her pride.

"Lord help me," she breathed as her hat tipped up, and she saw the full range of smirking, laughing and just plain stunned people.

There was a rather surprised expression on some of their faces as her direct gaze met theirs. It was as if they were not really expecting a human being to exist beneath the hat.

Now some were growing bold enough to titter. Safe in the collective protection of their fellow partygoers, the isolated comments were becoming a single unified jeer.

But she kept on smiling, as if wearing a beautiful tiara that was inspiring envy. Caroline had stepped to the side, and Emily made no attempt to join her. She could hear her brother-in-law's voice.

"Let me greet Emily," he said with pleasant ignorance.

"George," Caroline's voice smiled as if warmed by the sun.

"My dear." George offered his arm to his wife. "And Emily, how splendid you are in that hat."

Emily could see his legs, but not much more. "Why, thank you, George."

Emily felt a stab of pity for Caroline. How miserable to be ruled by the whims and penchants of others. Caroline's own levee was just weeks away, and it was to be her own launch into society.

For a moment Emily lost her limited sight of her sister and brother-in-law, and so she nodded at a cluster of people, which proved something of a tactical error, as she had not first taken into account the unbalanced nature of her hat. Her entire head threatened to roll forward, but she straightened quickly, with a quick touch of the brim, as if she was greeting them all with a jaunty wave. The perilous hat was righted.

It struck her as absurd that a hat could cause such a commotion, and she allowed herself the pleasure of the thought of working a similar scene into a future play. Unfortunately this was not a play, but real life.

As she walked, the area cleared. She could not be more abandoned if she wore a sign with "I have the plague" stamped upon it in large red letters.

She would walk a few more steps, she decided, and then return slowly to the carriage, claiming a headache. It was almost the truth, as her neck was sore, and her head was indeed beginning to pound. The carriage would no doubt be there, since there were so many jammed into the small cul de sac that no vehicle could possibly escape.

Only a few more steps.

Then, from across a vast expanse of emerald lawn and what seemed to be thin air, came a large, warm hand.

"Miss Fairfax," he pressed her hand to his chest. And for a moment she was utterly confused.

What sort of madman would risk greeting her?

Lucius Ashford stood before her in all of his solid magnificence. She could barely see him because of his height, but knew who it was by his clothing, understated and unadorned, but elegant. The dark green cutaway was made of an incredibly fine wool, and his cravat, from what she could see, was a spotless white.

His hand enveloped hers, and she could feel the roughness there, the strength of his grip.

Emily swallowed. He was, perhaps, the most sought-after man in all of London. She knew that before, of course, when she had simply read of him in the gazettes, before she actually met the man himself.

But the more time she spent in London, the more she really observed the respect he had gained. From what her brother-in-law had said, men craved his company as much as women did.

"Did I tell you what Ashford said," George often opened with as he began a story.

He was always invited to the best of assemblies, asked to join the most exclusive of clubs. And there he was, risking ridicule by standing before everyone of consequence and holding her hand.

"Sir?" was all she could breathe. This was, perhaps, the single kindest gesture anyone had ever made for her.

She raised her chin to see his face. And from

under the most absurd of hats, their eyes met, his rich, deep brown, hers bright bluish-green.

"I had to," she mouthed. "Letty made it."

Even as she said those words, he smiled. "I thought so."

That was all he needed to say. He understood without the need for further explanation.

Without her permission his arm cupped hers. It was almost indecent, certainly bordering on improper. But the display was absolutely unmistakable. Mr. Lucius Ashford not only approved of Miss Emily Fairfax, he had just given her his full support before the entire world.

The entire world that mattered, at any rate.

With Ashford at her side, she was even more of a spectacle than before. But somehow it didn't matter, because she was not alone. And she suddenly felt safe, even content.

At a most difficult time, under the most trying of circumstances, she found herself almost absurdly happy.

"Would you like some tea?" he said conversationally, as if their every movement was not being watched, their every step weighed and noted, their words monitored by anyone close enough to hear. "There is a menagerie just beyond which, I believe, Miss Letty has already discovered." He then lowered his voice. "You will smell the entertainment before you actually see it. Maybe you would enjoy an animal or two. Perhaps a monkey?"

Someone laughed as they passed, and he pressed

her hand gently. She was uncertain if the person was laughing at them, or with them.

"You do have my permission to shoot me, sir," she whispered. "It would be considered a mercy. And I believe some parties, mainly those close relations of mine who are attempting to enter society, would be greatly relieved. You may even collect some sort of reward for the service. Some sort of municipal beautification project, I would imagine."

The smile faded from his face as his voice grew serious for a moment. "No. You are unspeakably beautiful."

She stumbled, and he held her hand tightly. "Steady," he urged. "Here, come this way."

"I am not a horse," she replied, confused by his attention.

"No, you are not." Although she could not see his face, she could hear the smile in his voice. Then he pushed her forward very gently.

"Lady Duff," Ashford said to a woman in an elaborate gown. "May I present Miss Fairfax?"

"Oh, indeed." She extended a limp, gloved hand to Emily. "Pray forgive me. I have guests, and matters that require my most immediate attention."

By the time Emily curtseyed, the hostess had vanished.

"Would that be considered a demonstration of the cut direct?" she asked Ashford.

"Certainly not. The cut direct is what everyone else is demonstrating."

"Thank you for that clarification." Emily

laughed. Then she looked up at him, impossibly handsome in the bright sun. "And thank you for not snubbing me."

"Ah, that I could never do, Miss Fairfax."

There was a sudden disturbance to the left of where they were standing. "What is happening, Mr. Ashford? Has someone else arrived with a hat to rival mine?"

"No. Better than that."

"What could possibly be better than that?"

"The Prince Regent has just arrived."

Emily stiffened. This was not the best way to meet the future King of England. She tried to look up, but the slight rise of the grounds made it all but impossible to see beyond a distance of a few feet. "Is he far away from us?"

"Just on the other side of the lawn. Well, well. Now this should be interesting."

"What should be interesting?"

"He's being accosted by a young lady."

"Thank goodness! Now he'll not notice me or the hat. Everything will be forgotten except for the scandal of this assault."

"I'm afraid that's not the case."

"What do you mean?"

"The young lady accosting him is Miss Letty."

"No!"

"She is not allowing Lady Duff any access to the Prince. He's listening to your sister now, and seems confused."

"I can only imagine," she moaned.

"Poor Lady Duff is looking rather annoyed. She's attempting to get the Prince's attention, but Letty must be at her most charming, for he seems to be ignoring everyone else."

"Oh no," Emily cried. "Please, what's happening now?

"Interesting. I never thought I would see this."

"What?!"

"The Prince is leaning down toward Letty. His corset must be loose this afternoon—bending is usually difficult for him. He is examining her hat."

"What is his face like?"

"Rather plump."

"No, his expression. Is he angry?"

"I wouldn't say that."

"Is he happy?"

"I wouldn't say that either."

"Then what would you say?"

Ashford was silent for a few moments. Then he cleared his throat. "Miss Fairfax, I believe—"

"I repeat, does the Prince look happy or sad, sir. I am sorry his corset is too tight and that his face is plump. Still, I do wish to—"

Suddenly Emily was slammed on the left side by what seemed like a large projectile. "Sorry," Letty said excitedly. "But guess what? The Prince likes my hat!"

"How lovely." Emily couldn't help but smile at her little sister's beaming face. Somehow Letty, with her fresh and natural charm, could more than get away with wearing such a hat. "Then he must be a Prince of the most exquisite discernment."

Beside Letty were two highly polished black leather boots, rather smallish, with tassels on the sides.

"Thank you, madam. I take that as high praise indeed, coming from a woman beneath such a fetching hat," replied the male voice.

She raised her head and looked directly into the face of the future King.

He was the most instantly recognizable man in the British Isles, even more so than his father, the King, whose image was increasingly regulated to old etchings and paintings from the seventeen eighties. The Prince was the very essence of style, the personification of all that was great about the upper classes in England.

Unfortunately he was also the distillation of everything that was wrong as well.

His appreciation and support of culture, his splendid education, his gentle manners and innate kindness were all entwined with a deep fascination of life's rougher side. Although he had given up his patronage of prizefighting, he still loved to gamble at the card table, or on anything, for that matter. He adored fine wines in vast quantities and the best foods in even greater quantities, and those two particular weaknesses were evident in his face, which was indeed plump and rather flushed, and his form, which was clearly trussed into a parody of youth.

But it was overall a pleasant face, one that had

been a paragon of male beauty in decades past, but was now a rather muzzy version of the dashing buck.

"Oh, Your Highness," she began to curtsey.

"Ashford! Good-looking jacket, that. What would one call that shade?"

"Green, Your Highness. May I present the Misses Emily and Letty Fairfax?"

"Ah yes. Miss Letty is already a dear companion of these past several minutes, at least. And Miss Fairfax, you are not required to remain in that low bow."

"Thank you, Your Majesty," she replied, her voice muffled. "But a pin has caught by my ear, and I fear I cannot raise my head without considerable injury."

"Indeed! Here, Ashford, give me a hand, will you?"

Lucius leaned over her bent form. "Your left ear or right?"

"Left," her voice was strained.

"Emily, you look as if you're about to perform a somersault," Letty said in a loud enough voice for everyone to hear.

If she had been the focus of attention before, now she was the entertainment.

"The pin with the little crow on the end?" the Prince asked, picking through the top of the hat.

"No, I believe it's the other one, sire. The small slingshot just beyond."

"I have it," Lucius announced. "Hold still." Very

carefully, he pulled out the pin, and the entire hat fell forward and onto the grass.

"Just like a guillotine!" Letty announced with pure delight.

"Yes, indeed," the Prince agreed. "But fortunately for us, the lovely lady has suffered no permanent damage. Are you quite sound, Miss Fairfax?"

She felt as if a large boulder had just been lifted from her head. "Thank you, Your Majesty."

The Prince began to lean over to pick up the hat, when he stopped suddenly, as if unable to make the reach. "Ashford," he said at last. Then he flicked a finger, and Lucius, trying very hard not to smile, handed Emily her hat.

"May I see it, please?" the Prince asked.

"Of course, Your Highness."

Emily watched his expression as he studied the hat. The rest of the party stood just beyond, at a respectable distance. But they were all chattering quietly, some eyebrows arched as if awaiting the verdict of a judge.

"Splendid!" the Prince pronounced after he had examined every pin, fold and bit of netting, as well as each tiny animal. "Miss Letty, did you really create this by yourself?"

She nodded. "Yes, Your Majesty. And that is real fur on the bunny over there."

"Indeed, I see it. Absolutely splendid." Then he looked at Emily for the first time. "Charming," he said. Then he tilted his head slightly. "As magnificent as the hat is, I fear it hides true beauty." With a grin he leaned forward. "Pity more of these ladies do not have access to a hat with such a broad brim. We would all benefit, what?"

Ashford laughed, and Emily—quite unexpectedly—liked the Prince Regent a great deal.

Then his smile faded a bit. "This is the sort of hat the Duchess of Devonshire would have worn. Ashford, I don't believe you knew her before her final illness, but by God, she was a beauty. And once she wore her hair piled high, powered with huge sailing ships—a positive armada, it was. It suited Georgiana, though. Suited her as this hat suits you ladies."

"Ships in her hair?" Letty repeated.

"Forgive me," the Prince said somberly to Emily. "I fear we have given her ideas."

"Trust me, Your Highness," Ashford assured him. "There is nothing of which Miss Letty has not already thought."

The Prince frowned for a moment. "I would very much like to have a similar hat for my daughter Charlotte. She is presently at a most difficult age, and I believe this would please her vastly. Do you suppose you could fashion one for me, Miss Letty?"

The expression on Letty's face was pure and sublime delight. "It would be my supreme honor and most patriotic duty," she vowed.

"Splendid! Splendid!" He gave the hat to Letty. "Now I'd best go off. Did I hear there are pineapple preserves and clotted cream?" He began to walk away, and Letty and Emily curtseyed; Ashford bowed. Then the Prince paused. "Miss Fairfax? I believe there is to be dancing later. Would you save one or two for me?"

Stunned, Emily looked up, as if half convinced there had been some sort of mistake, or a prankster had managed to throw a Princelike voice in order to trick her.

But it had been the Prince, and she had seen his lips move with the precise words she had just heard. This was no joke.

The Prince Regent had stood before the entire, gaping throng and—in a clear and deliberate voice—requested a dance.

"It would be my honor, Your Highness," she replied in a voice that seemed to come from someplace else.

"How delightful," he said to the man next to him. "I am to be honored by both of the charming Fairfax sisters this day." And then he went off in search of pineapple preserves.

"I believe you have just made a conquest," Lucius said.

Emily blinked. "Did that just happen?"

He laughed with a rich, warm tone. "You should not be so surprised, Miss Fairfax. This cannot be as extraordinary as meeting for a duel."

But before they could continue speaking, some of the most distant clusters of people had begun to seek her out.

"Miss Fairfax! How delighted I am to meet you . . ."

"Oh, is that Miss Emily Fairfax? I did not see her when she arrived, how very foolish of me. It would be remiss of me not to say how very . . ."

"Why, I did not see them enter. I must have been round back, with the highland sheep . . ."

Soon she was surrounded with a crush of smiling faces, damp hands, invitations for tea and rides in Hyde Park, and promises to come calling within the next few days.

Later, as she danced with the Prince Regent, she realized that she owed it all to Mr. Lucius Ashford. Without him, she would have retreated back to the carriage. He risked ridicule and his own considerable reputation to stand by her, at a time when her own sister Caroline found that doing so was too much to bear. She was well aware that the Prince Regent would never have noticed her had it not been for Ashford.

He was the one who made the afternoon such a remarkable, head-spinning success.

And while she did not particularly care about what society thought about her, she knew how very important it was to Caroline that she not be a complete disgrace. There was Fanny, too, although they had yet to determine the cause of her difficulties. At least having a sister who is a social disaster would not be one of them.

Then there was Letty. In a very few short years it would be her turn to come out, to face society not as a little girl but as a young woman ready to meet a husband, ready to make a new life for herself. This could pave the way for her, smooth the road to adulthood in a manner that was not possible for the older sisters.

Perhaps this one afternoon would prove vital to all of her family.

There was but one person to thank for this happy outcome. So when the Prince Regent, puffing after their final dance, happily accepted a beaker of punch and made his way off the floor, Emily did not accept the many offers of another dance partner. Instead she went in search of Ashford.

"Pardon me," she said to Lady Duff. "Is Mr. Ashford still in attendance?"

"Oh, my dear," Lady Duff clasped her hand warmly. "I do believe I saw him by the kangaroos just moments ago. Are you enjoying yourself? I do hope my modest little affair is amusing to you, Miss Fairfax."

"Yes, indeed," Emily replied. Was this the same woman who had dismissed her so completely when she had first arrived? "It is quite marvelous."

"Wonderful!" Lady Duff enthused. "Is not the Prince the most perfect of partners on the dance floor? Why, the way he executes the steps so neatly and nimbly, it is an utter joy to behold. Tell me of Fairfax Castle, my dear. How charming it sounds! And what a pity your Irish accent is not as pronounced as it might be."

Just then Emily caught a glimpse of Ashford attempting, it appeared, to make an escape from a circle of comely young women. Two of the ladies were dressed in the military style that was just becoming fashionable, and indeed Emily wondered if they could be pressed into service. One of them even wore false yet glittering medals, as if she had been a hero against Napoleon.

Ashford was nodding and smiling, stepping backward as he spoke. But the women stepped forward with every pace. Instead of exiting the party, he was in danger of taking a good portion of it with him.

"Thank you, Lady Duff." Emily withdrew her hand from the hostess's iron grip. "Again, this is marvelous, just marvelous," she said distractedly. "Thank you ever so much."

And with a hurried curtsey she left Lady Duff. "Interesting," she said to herself as she watched Emily glide toward Ashford. Tapping her fan, her eyes narrowed. "Very interesting indeed."

As Emily approached Ashford, two things came to mind. One, that he must be quite accustomed to being surrounded by women at such events. And two, the women in question were not as comely nor as young as she had originally thought. That second discovery filled her with an unexpected sense of relief.

"Mr. Ashford," she said in a low conversational tone after she had reached the outer circle of his admirers.

"Miss Fairfax!" The delight on his face was as unmistakable as it was genuine. The other women took one glance at Emily and, realizing she was the very same creature who had the entire assemblage abuzz with her charms—especially the Prince Regent—they scattered in glum, silent defeat.

"Now it is I who must thank *you*," Ashford grinned when they were out of earshot.

"How very ungallant of you, sir." The brilliant sun bathed her face in its warmth, as she carried the hat beside her. "Besides, you did not seem to mind the company of those ladies overmuch."

"As charming as they were, I much prefer smaller gatherings. To speak to people rather than talking at people. Besides," he grinned, glancing at her as they walked in no particular direction, "there is something terrifying about being a single man surrounded by a pack of single women."

"You sound as if they were the predators and you were the prey."

"That is precisely how I felt, Miss Fairfax."

"I'm quite surprised," she said lightly. Together they strolled toward the welcoming shade of a tree.

"Surprised that women travel in packs and frighten unwitting men?"

"No. I am rather surprised to hear you spout in such a self-satisfied manner. It is most unbecoming."

"I assure you, it is not vanity speaking," he laughed. "Had I bandy legs and a hump, the same scene would occur. I do not claim advantage over other men, save two."

"Two?" Now Emily laughed. "Only two? How very humble you are, sir."

Ashford paused, then bowed deeply. "I thank you."

"Please enlighten me. What are those two such marvelous traits you say separate you from the less fortunate of your sex?"

"They are simple. One, I am a single, unattached man. That is reckoned as something of a rarity and very desirable trait."

"Very well. That fact I will concede," she acknowledged graciously. "There is a dreadful shortage of single men, what with war and marriage."

"So war and marriage often produce the same results?"

"When it comes to the shortage of men, sir, and the abundance of single women, war and marriage are very much the same. Now, what is the second reason you have so many women encircling you?"

Emily looked up at him as he chuckled, and she was again taken aback by how very handsome he was. There was the faintest of darkening around his strongly defined jawline, where late afternoon whiskers were just emerging. His eyes were focused straight ahead, his lashes incongruously lush on such a very masculine face. In profile his nose was straight and well formed but just large enough to be utterly masculine. And under his left eye was a slight crescent shaped scar she had not noticed before. Very faint, as if it had occurred in childhood, an incident long forgotten.

"Miss Fairfax?"

"Oh, yes?" He had startled her.

"I asked if you would like to sit down under the tree."

"Yes, please. That is, if Lady Duff would not find it objectionable in any way."

"With wild animals and nature being today's theme, she could hardly object to guests being inspired to become one with the earth, could she?"

Removing his jacket, he spread it out over a soft spot in the grass and held her hand as she lowered herself to the makeshift seat. Even through her gloves she could feel the warmth of his hands, the gentle roughness of his skin.

"No, I don't supose she could." Emily adjusted her skirts and Ashford sat beside her on the grass. "But you have not answered my question."

"Refresh my memory, please. What was the question?"

"Why do so many woman find you so devilishly attractive?"

"Ah, yes indeed. That is simple. Mothers love me."

"Oh," she replied uncertainly. "How lucky you are."

"Yes. It usually stands me in good stead, and at the very least I am frequently assured extra large helpings of sweetmeats."

Emily smiled and closed her eyes for a moment, suddenly very tired, and suddenly having a memory of her own mother. How odd to have such a thought, of her sisters and herself as small children.

Letty as a baby, Caroline and Fanny tagging behind, Fanny always smiling, laughing.

What could be wrong with Fan? Was she ill, or desperately unhappy over her apparent inability to have children? Perhaps something could be done. There must be a physician, someone who could help.

"Are you feeling ill, Miss Fairfax?"

"I am well, thank you. Just fatigued, sir."

"Are you certain? Your mood seemed to alter rather swiftly. Is something amiss?"

"Nothing." A feeling approaching panic began to rise in her throat. And she knew, without a doubt, that Fanny was in danger of some sort.

How could she be lounging on a lawn when her sister was suffering not two miles away?

"Miss Fairfax, please tell me. You have gone quite pale."

"It's simply that I am worried about something, someone," she swallowed.

"Is there anything I can do to help?" Gone was the bantering tone of a few minutes earlier. Now he was all sincerity, all seriousness.

"Thank you, but no, I don't believe so." Even as she spoke she wondered if he could, in fact, be of help. Perhaps he has heard something at the clubs, noticed any peculiar changes in Robert Aubridge, if not Fanny herself.

But she doubted they even knew each other. And what was the nature of Fanny's problems? It would be indiscreet at best to reveal her concerns to Ashford. And at worst, it could compound the difficulty. No, she should not share her fears, certainly not with Ashford.

After all, she was still piqued that he did not respond, nor even mention, the humiliating letter she had sent.

"I must leave, Mr. Ashford," she said, gathering her hat and gloves.

"Have I said anything to offend you? Perhaps my comment that mothers love me was a bit excessive. Or—"

"No, not at all, sir. I fear a headache is coming on, and I would rather depart before it settles in full."

"Of course." He helped her to her feet, eyeing her with subtle attention.

Their faces were but inches apart. And without further words, he leaned even closer to her and gently, very gently, he kissed her on the lips.

It was so unexpected, that after the first surprise she did the most natural thing of all. Her eyes closed, and she returned the kiss. It was sweet and tender, but a current of sudden energy coursed through them both. He raised his hand to her cheek, touching her silken skin. Then slowly, he pulled back.

"Sir," she whispered. It was a small word, but full of meaning, of far more than could be expressed there, at that moment.

"Emily." His voice was thick. Then he straightened, and once again was the correct gentleman.

"Should you need anything, Miss Fairfax, please do not hesitate to call on me." But there was a distinct sparkle in his eyes.

"Thank you," she said distractedly, unable to look away. "I must leave now." Then she smiled. "Really, I must."

"I will tell your sisters you have left." He offered his arm, and she slipped her hand through the crook. They said nothing as he escorted her to the carriage.

There was no need for words.

Caroline made the peculiar squealing sound she used to make when she triumphed at blindman's Buff as a child. Her three children, the two boys and the baby girl, all commenced an eerily accurate imitation of her squeal in slightly higher pitches.

"Children! Cease that horrid noise at once," she cried, but it was not in anger or even annoyance, but sung in a tone of pure delight. "Nanny will be with you in a moment."

"Is anything wrong, Mama?" the eldest boy asked. Then, with a strangely mature, somber tone, "Is it Grandpapa in Ireland?"

"No! No indeed, my darling little dumpling. Things could not be more splendid. Oh, Nanny!"

The older woman entered at her own casual, easy pace, her lace mobcap slightly askew, giving her employer a mildly disapproving look.

"Please could you watch the children? I must see Emily and Letty!"

Nanny suddenly looked concerned. "Not bad news? Oh Lordy, is it your father?"

"No, not at all. Oh, Nanny, our Emily is the triumph of the season! Look here, all the gazettes from Thursday's party! All they do is speak of her, and mention me as well! And Letty and her hat designs are all the rage! Lady Conyngham is begging her dressmaker to find one such hat, as is Lady Jersey and even Princess Charlotte. But Letty alone knows how to make them! They call Letty a charming addition to any party, a most cunning child, I believe it says. I was so worried about Letty not behaving, but she did wonderfully well."

"Of course she did," Nanny said indignantly. "Why, Miss Fairfax and me, we raised her. She knows her manners, she does."

"Very well," Caroline brushed Nanny's comment aside. "But Emily, they just loved her! She has absolutely conquered London. She is called . . . let me see the exact quote. Yes, here it is. 'Miss E. F. now holds London in the palm of her fair hand. Roundly toasted on from all quarters, those who were graced with her smiles will not soon forget the thrill. The Prince Regent has called her the loveliest flower of the season, and all who see her are compelled to agree.' That's what it says! Right here in black and white. Emily is the rage of society!"

Nanny smiled. "Our Miss Emily. I always knew she was special, I did." She wiped her reddened hands on her apron. "May I take a look, Mum?"

"Yes, of course." Caroline handed her the gazette and realized this was the first time Nanny had called her "Mum."

Caroline had a feeling this was the beginning of her very own launch in society.

Emily entered the parlor, unaware she was society's new rage. Nanny and Caroline peered at her over the gazette.

"Is anything wrong?" Emily asked. "I heard your dreadful cries from above. Is it Father?"

"No, no! He is well! Emily—look at this! You are a success! You and Letty are a success!"

"Oh," Emily smiled, pleased by the happy expression on her sister's face. "Is breakfast ready?"

"Do you not wish to read the glorious words of praise?"

"After breakfast. In truth, I am famished."

Nanny curtseyed, giving Emily a special grin, and left the room with both children. "Up to the nursery with you young rascals," she clicked.

"Emily, this is marvelous. Just marvelous."

"Lady Duff's party was certainly an adventure," she admitted.

Caroline looked up at her sister. "Why, Emily. You are blushing to the very roots of your hair!"

"I am doing no such thing." But she felt her face flame even further.

"Emily?"

"Nothing is wrong."

"I never said it was," Caroline teased. "Indeed, from my oldest sister's expression, I would reckon everything is quite, quite right. And how, pray, is our dear friend Mr. Ashford?"

"He, well. I assume he is well. He was in quite fine spirits yesterday and . . . Oh, Caroline!"

Both sisters began to laugh. Then Caroline grew only slightly more serious. "How do you feel about Mr. Ashford?"

Emily looked at Caroline, suddenly so mature, as if their places were reversed. "I know not, Caro. But never have I felt anything like this, never. It is so very strange."

"Is it a pleasant strange?"

"Yes," she warmed. "Very pleasant. But somewhat, well. Rather . . ."

"Unsettling?"

"Yes! That's it precisely. It is most unsettling."

Caroline grew even more somber. "Emily, I do hope he plays you fair. He has quite a reputation, you know."

"I know. And he has told me." For a moment they just looked at each other. "I am famished," Emily repeated.

And she was. Caroline smiled gently. "I will think only good thoughts for you." Emily leaned over and hugged her. "Thank you, dear Caro."

Then she left Caroline to the rest of the papers, and descended the stairs, thinking a jumble of thoughts. Of course there was Ashford.

And then there was Fanny.

Emily had discovered several facts about Fanny. In recent months she had become increasingly reclusive, first not showing up, then not even responding to invitations for social events. By questioning George, she learned that something was amiss with Robert's business affairs. Seriously amiss. Indeed, there were rumors that he would soon be asked to give up his membership at the club for economic reasons.

Now she needed to see Fanny alone, and that she would do directly after breakfast.

Letty was already settled at the table when there was another of Caroline's joyful screams from above.

"Oh good." Letty helped herself to a muffin. Then, pausing, she took another. "If Caroline keeps herself busy shouting upstairs, she can't possibly eat all the food. Have you noticed how she always eats all of the muffins before I even have a chance to have a single one?"

"Now Letty. We are enjoying Caroline and George's hospitality, are we not?" Emily looked at the mantel clock, wondering when would be the best time to appear unannounced at Fanny's.

"Yes, but not as much as we were enjoying Lady Duff's. I do wish we were there when the animals escaped. Did you hear that some of them ate each other? And bigger ones went after some of the guests. It will take days and days to clean up the mess, and I hear Lady Duff has taken to her room and will not emerge until they find the last few snakes."

"Well," Emily smiled, attempting to mask her

distraction. The last thing she needed was Letty's well-meaning help. "I do believe some of the guests deserved to have a chimpanzee ride on their backs, do you not?"

"I do." Letty looked up at her older sister, watching the way she poured the tea, the way the light streamed through the window and touched her hair with glimmers of gold, as if she were some sort of magical fairy.

Someone at Lady Duff's had exclaimed that Emily must have her portrait done, as all of the great beauties do. She had seen some of those famous beauties at Lady Duff's, and Letty realized what liberties artists such as Gainsborough or Reynolds or Lawrence had taken with their subjects. Most of them were not pretty in the least, certainly not young, and would seem very out of place under a bent-bough arch or on a blossom-covered swing.

But Emily would look right at home in such a setting.

"Are you going to eat that most coveted of muffins?"

Letty realized the muffin had been in her hand for quite some time. Then she heard footsteps.

"Caroline's coming! Hurry up and eat!" Letty urged.

"Don't gobble. I am sure the muffin will not be plucked from your hand."

At that the door to the breakfast room flew open. "Letty! Put that down!" Caroline tapped her hand, forcing the muffin to fall onto the table in a scattering of crumbs. "Come, we don't have time. Callers have already arrived."

"Callers?" Emily and Letty said simultaneously.

"Of course callers." She pinched Letty's cheeks. "There's some color. You may want to do something about your hair, dearest. Well, come on."

"Callers at this hour? Caro, it is not past eight-thirty. This is unspeakably rude," Emily said. How could she escape if trapped by callers? "I have never received visitors before ten in my life, and those who arrived at that time were usually blood relatives dwelling under the same roof."

"That's not true, Em. Remember when Ashford and Ogilvie came just at dawn back home?"

Emily gave her a pointed "hush" stare, but Caroline was beyond hearing anything Letty would have to say.

"This is London. It is a sign of honor." Caroline parted the curtains and peered out on the street. "Oh! It's Lady Harriet Duff! My word, what an honor—Lady Duff's carriage has just pulled up!"

"Does that mean they found the snakes?" Letty asked reasonably.

"Come at once! We will eat later."

There was no way out of the situation. All Emily could do is suffer through the visits. But they couldn't possibly last long. And maybe Fanny would be more likely to receive her at a later hour.

"Perhaps she has brought the snake with her as an escort," Emily suggested. Letty gazed regretfully over her shoulder as the maid cleared away the muffins and Caroline pushed her through the door.

The callers kept up at a steady pace throughout the day.

Every time they thought they had a brief respite, another carriage would pull up, another well-gowned lady or highly-polished gentleman would be announced, and they would begin a fresh quarter hour of meaningless conversation and benign comments about the weather.

Letty was dismissed when her company manners abandoned her during the overlong visit of Mrs. Jennings and her unmarried daughter Isabelle. Emily envied Letty, for she, too, would have very much enjoyed leaving the overly warm drawing room to play spillikins in the nursery with the boys or to satisfy her concern for Fanny.

Even the Prince Regent arrived by afternoon, with a cluster of friends including the famous Mr. Brummell. This was the ultimate feather in Caroline's cap, although the visit was very brief and the Prince was on his way to another engagement. Still, he was there, in the Edgeworth salon, and Caroline could only be pleased that the new chairs looked so well with the recovered fire screen.

Emily was diverted for the moment in watching Brummell's movements and comments, his posture and posing. Everything he did was carefully plotted for effect, every comment cobbled and shaped before it was ever uttered. Every gesture practiced before his well-employed mirror. This was the man who all but dictated what was done in society, what was acceptable to eat and drink and what was considered vulgar.

While Caroline was beside herself with utter rapture at having Beau Brummell approve of her silver tea set, Emily was more impressed by the unnatural gloss of his fingernails and the scent of starch from his neckcloth. He struck her as a rather fussy little man who seemed to spend the better part of his day in the arduous task of appearing casual and spontaneous.

Even his famous witticisms failed to strike Emily as particularly witty. Instead, they seemed more cruel than clever, more the naughty schoolboy with a mean streak than the sophisticated gentleman. Most of his more biting comments were turned on another individual's lack of taste or failure to measure up to his own peculiar, exacting standards. Women were a particular target, their looks and weight and the status of their romantic affairs.

What an odd little man, Emily sighed to herself. And what on earth will he do should he ever fall out of favor with the very society he had so firmly ruled, or find himself breaking the stringent rules he had so capriciously established.

Finally, later in the afternoon, the steady stream of callers slowed to a mercifully thin trickle. Even Caroline seemed to be losing her zest for hospitality, and her cheerful features were becoming increasingly strained into an imitation of a smile.

"Caro, may I have the carriage?" Emily asked when the last of the visitors left.

Caroline was too exhausted to express much surprise. "Of course. But where on earth are you going? Why, it's very nearly evening."

She almost admitted her nagging fears about Fanny, but instead said she simply wished to go outside after being indoors all day. That did nicely, and even Letty failed to demonstrate much interest in her oldest sister's outing.

And then, just as she began to ready herself for the trip to Fanny's house, a final, unexpected caller arrived. It was none other than Fanny herself.

Chapter Eight

"Fanny!" Emily exclaimed when her sister entered the parlor. "How good to see you! Indeed, I was just on my way for a visit."

"Oh, were you?" Fanny smiled vaguely and glanced about at the sumptuous furnishings, tugging her gloves off one finger at a time.

Caroline was for the briefest of moments all but speechless at the sudden and unexpected sight of her reclusive sister, but with the emerging grace of an aspiring celebrated hostess, recovered quickly. "Fan, do come here and sit with me on the sofa. We have tea and cakes." She shot a glance at Emily, who offered a small nod of encouragement. "Here, let me take your umbrella. You'll be much more comfortable without it, and I doubt very much we'll be rained upon indoors."

But Fanny would not release the umbrella. Instead she kept it held tight in her grip, her knuckles whitening, as she stood firmly in the center of the room. She blinked, taking in the details of the parlor. "It is lovely, Caro. Really, how very exquisite the room is. You have worked wonders."

"Dearest, would you partake of some tea?" Caroline gestured with a sweeping, and she hoped elegant, wave of her hand toward the newly replenished tray.

"No, thank you," Fanny replied. "The refreshments look positively delicious. And so artfully arranged."

Although her words were polite and correct, there was something utterly wrong. The quality of her tone was distant and flat, emotionally removed. She spoke the trite conversation of a new acquaintance.

Emily pretended not to notice. She kept her own voice light, as if they were having the most pleasant and routine of visits.

"Come," she grasped Fanny's hand. "Please sit on the sofa. It is most remarkably comfortable." With only a little pull, she led her sister to the couch.

Caroline quickly fluffed a small pillow on the sofa before stepping to a side chair and allowing her two sisters to pass. "There! All settled," she concluded when Fanny sat stiff-backed on the edge of the couch.

For an instant Caroline's and Emily's eyes met, each wondering what to do next. Emily spoke first. "Oh, Fan. How very wonderful you are looking." Even as she attempted conversation, she could not help but notice how alarmingly thin Fan had become, with the hollows of her cheeks deeply sunken and her light brown hair hanging lank and lifeless beneath her bonnet. Emily recognized the hat as one she had given her several years ago, and it was sadly worn. There seemed to be a faded marking on her left cheek, covered less than effectively with a limp swirl of hair.

"I am not looking wonderful," Fan said at last. There was no self-pity in her voice, only a statement of fact. Caroline looked at her, then swiftly looked away. Fanny smiled at last. "How is dear little Letty?"

"She is just upstairs with the boys, no doubt filling their heads with all sorts of corrupt notions. Shall we fetch her?" Emily asked.

"No, no. Please. Not yet. I, well . . ." She turned the handle of the umbrella. "I would like to visit with the pair of you first," Fanny said softly. "And how is Father?"

"He is just the same," Emily smiled. "Always with his nose in the gazettes or his precious books. He sent some pleasantries for you and Robert, but I haven't unpacked them yet."

Again there was an uncomfortable lag in the conversation. Caroline cleared her throat. "I do hope you and Robert will be able to attend our levee." Then she paused. "How is Robert? I don't suppose George sees him as much as he used to, for he never mentions him."

"He is quite consumed with business," Fanny said. "Quite consumed indeed." Glancing around the room, she remarked on a porcelain vase here or a newly cut silhouette of the boys there. "So tell me," she said slowly. "Have you met any new people in town?"

Caroline began to explain the afternoon's visits, the many callers, the people who attended Lady Duff's party and what they wore and who they were with.

"Do you know of a Mr. Ashford?"

Startled, both Caroline and Emily were momentarily taken aback. "Yes, we do," Caro replied. "He is a friend of George's, and indeed is also acquainted with both Emily and Letty. Why do you ask?"

"Does he visit here frequently?"

Although Emily thought Fanny's interest in Lucius odd, she was glad to have a coherent conversation in progress. "Well, he was here yesterday, I believe. We met him in Ireland."

"Did you?"

"He was there on business and we had him for breakfast at Fairfax Castle," Emily answered.

"I would like to meet him. Pray, let me know well in advance whenever he visits."

"Yes, of course," Emily looked over at Caro, who raised her eyebrows and shrugged with as much curiosity as Emily was feeling.

But something felt wrong, and clearly Fanny herself was uncomfortable with the subject, twisting the umbrella in her hand and shifting her position on the couch.

"Caroline, do tell us about the plans you have for the levee," Emily began brightly.

"Yes, please do," Fanny nodded as if eager to steer away from the previous topic.

"Well," Caroline pursed her lips. "It is very trying. Very difficult. Far more difficult than one could possibly imagine." She sighed, warming to her topic. "We are trying to establish ourselves," she explained. "George needs to secure certain connections for business. And while we have attended many notable functions, and George routinely spends afternoons at the clubs on St. James's, this dinner is to be our launch into real society, real fashion. It is our turn to shine. We have sent out the invitations, but the verdict is still out as to who will actually come. We sent them to everyone, simply everyone. And since no one has yet declined, we have to plan for a great number of guests. And the expense—already this has cost us many hundreds of pounds. I daresay it will be into the thousands by the time the event arrives." Caroline's eyes welled with tears, and she dabbed gently with the corner of a lace handkerchief.

"How dreadful!" Fanny exclaimed. "Is there no way to simply serve tea, or perhaps plan the event at an inconvenient hour so that nobody can come?"

"Oh, how I have longed for just such a solution," Caroline all but sobbed. "And besides that, I despair of ever finding Emily a husband. At least I did, until the very gentleman you mentioned—"

"Now really," Emily interrupted, not wishing her sister to continue on that thought, but encouraged to see Fanny emerge ever so slightly from her shell. She was far from pleased with the turn the conversation had taken. Still, she couldn't help but notice the barest suggestion of a sparkle in Fanny's eyes. Emily crossed her arms. There was no choice. She had to continue the distasteful conversation. "This is beyond silly. We are entering the realm of the absurd. I do not wish to discuss the marriage mart. Let us return to Caroline's levee. Tell me, Caro, have you selected a theme? Or any sort of—"

"She has never really had a chance," Fanny added, ignoring Emily. Her voice seemed to be growing surer, stronger. "After all, this is only her third time out of Ireland. She has her own little provincial world with Papa and Letty. But one day Letty will marry, and she will be all alone in that big castle, rattling about with the servants and handing out mince pies to the tenants at Christmastime."

"I'm trying to find her a husband, Fan." Caroline looked directly at Fanny. "But she won't have one. She has just scored a social coup, yet she will not press her advantage. Isn't that odd? However, as I was saying, I do harbor some hopes that Mr—"

"Caro!" Emily all but shouted.

Caroline pressed her lips together in an obvious, yet painful attempt at discretion.

Fanny did not seem to notice, wrapped in her own memory.

"Do you remember that gentleman who used to call on her back home?" Fanny placed the umbrella against the leg of a side table and leaned forward eagerly. "He was a handsome young man.

The one with the thing on his lip. What was his name?"

"I do not recall. But he never came back after the second time."

"That is because the two of you ambushed him with arrows from above. You were both going through your archery phase," Emily tried to explain reasonably. "The man almost lost an eye."

"None of them ever did return," Fanny nodded. "When I first came to London, everyone was so surprised that she was not yet claimed. People asked about her. She is undoubtedly a beauty. It's just that . . . well, they still do ask about her. But it is most peculiar."

"What on earth is *that* supposed to mean?" Emily asked.

"Just that you don't seem to require the things most normal women require. It is as if you have been formed of a different sort of clay. Isn't that so, Caro?"

"Indeed. I couldn't phrase it better myself."

Color had returned to Fanny's cheeks. She was beginning to look positively healthy. "Thank you. Now, pray tell me of your gathering."

Caroline then began to discuss some of the plans for the party. "We are serving no less than five different wines."

"Five!"

"Two of them French. And at present I have approved fifteen meat dishes, six soups including, of course, turtle."

"Of course! I have a wonderful turtle soup recipe. It's from Lady Craven, I believe . . ."

Emily leaned back into the sofa, satisfied for the moment to see the lines of worry ease on Fanny's face.

But how very odd that Fanny had pressed so on the issue of Lucius Ashford. How very odd indeed. Perhaps she, too, followed the gazettes, or had heard some gossip or rumor.

Emily's two sisters were now head-to-head, discussing the upcoming party with the same passion they had once used at play, and later to plan their own weddings.

And as usual, Emily smiled, grateful to see them so happy, yet somehow feeling apart.

Later she could find out what was bothering Fanny. At the moment it was more important for the recently strained bonds of family to be restored.

And Emily, taking a deep breath, hoped she could somehow make it right again for Fanny, to make her happy. That had always been her role, really.

What did they really know of her, her sisters? Very little, she supposed.

It didn't matter, she reflected. After all, this was a time of drawn-out war and sudden peace, of rapid transformations in all aspects of society, of revolutionary politics and brilliant literature. Caroline grew serious as she offered a provocative inquiry.

"What do you think of pork, Fanny? I hear some of the better homes are serving it."

"Pork? Never! Why, next you'll be telling me the better establishments serve oysters or fish eggs!"

"Fish eggs! What a comical thought. Tiny things, one would imagine. On toast points, I presume."

"Of course!" The two sisters scooted closer and leaned their heads together, intent on the urgent question of menus, which soon evolved into a discussion of fashion.

Fashion, Emily thought.

She wasn't oblivious to it, although Caroline accused her of just that very offense.

How very little those two knew her. How stunned they would be if they ever discovered that Emily was the playwright Edgar St. John. That she did, indeed, desire the things that other women want. But over the years she had changed. Rather, she had been forced to change.

Their mother had died when she was but sixteen. Yet she was the eldest, having reached that magical age that seemed to separate childhood from adulthood. Everyone turned to her in the confusion, from her father to the servants. She just did what was required of her without having a chance to think.

The reality was that she had been every bit as frightened and bewildered as the other girls when their mother died. More so, perhaps, because just before her mother's death, on that special sixteenth birthday, she had shared a special tea with her mother.

Her mother's confinement had been drawing

near, and Mama—while as beautiful as always—was uncomfortable in any position. A large pillow was propped in the small of her back, and sometimes her complexion grew pale. Emily felt occasional stabs of concern. She had overheard someone say that Mama was too old to be having another child, although to Emily she looked as young as she always had. And sometimes a faraway look would cross her mother's features, and she would linger on the sight of the girls, or of her husband. Such a strange, wistful expression.

Still, it had been such an afternoon! For the first time, Mama had spoken to her truly as an adult. Tea had been set up outdoors, with the first flowers of spring and the constant music of birds chirping. Emily poured the tea, her mother nodding in approval, as if training her eldest daughter to take on the role of adult, of hostess.

They had discussed the future that day, Emily's upcoming visit to London. The clothes they would order, the people they would meet. Mama even grew romantic, detailing exactly what sort of gentleman Emily should marry, and Emily had blushed at the thought.

Then she handed her a necklace, a simple garnet cross on a gold chain, and all too soon their tea was over, and once again Emily had to share her mother with everyone else.

Less than a week later, her mother was dead. And nothing was ever the same again. The girl of sixteen was forced into a role not of her choosing.

Although they had Nanny and other servants, the task of overseeing the three younger girls fell to her. Their father became distant, closing himself in the library for days. Emily grew up very quickly.

As she tried her best to provide what stability she could, Caroline and Fanny became exceptionally close. There seemed to be a delineation, an unspoken line that divided the two from Emily. She felt keenly a sense of being out of place. She was no longer just a sister. The days immediately after her mother's death had changed that. The moment Emily took charge and made sure that the doctor was paid and the christening for the baby arranged, she assumed a different role.

When life resumed its normal pace, there was no chance to return to those earlier days. It was like unringing a bell—what was done was done. Final. She was no longer the eldest daughter awaiting her launch into society. Instead, all thoughts of her going to London were forgotten. Quite simply, other than Emily herself, no one even remembered the planned trip. It slipped into the realm of the forgotten, or the forsaken, along with Mama enjoying her daughters' weddings or her first grandchild.

It was not to be.

The notion of Emily as a youth was remote indeed when it was Emily who had to tell Caroline to clean up her shell project, or it was Emily who asked Fanny to play the pianoforte more quietly so as not to wake the baby. She was an outsider in her own home.

Within a few years Caroline was introduced to society with all of the pomp and ceremony that had been expected for Emily, followed the next season by Fanny, and both found suitable husbands before the new crop of debutantes charged into the ballrooms.

It had been Emily who took control, who followed through on the plans her mother had outlined for her own coming out. Instead, she had given the honor to her two sisters.

By now it seemed ridiculous for Emily to emerge. And something else had changed in her. No longer was she the dreamy girl at tea with her mother, imagining all sorts of glorious things in her future. And when she did dream, the sketch of the wonderful gentleman her mother had drawn for her, the man with whom she was destined to forge such a delightful future, grew blurry. No such man existed. And if he did, her chances of meeting him were more remote than the location of Fairfax Castle.

Besides, there was the baby Letty to care for. And as the middle sisters grew up and left the home, a special bond grew between Emily and her youngest sister. Her first duty was to the baby, the child whose arrival had so disastrously and enduringly altered the fabric of the family. Whatever happened, Emily was determined to keep Letty from any misfortune or unhappiness.

Whatever fanciful notions remained were redirected to her plays. That was her unexpected pleasure, the sheer joy of creating worlds she could control, places where nothing was taken too seriously and only the deserving were rewarded.

All was in order, until the arrival of Mr. Lucius Ashford into her life. He changed everything.

Now she was feeling the stirrings of those emotions of which her sisters felt her incapable. Now she longed for something, although she was afraid to articulate even to herself exactly what that something was.

Afternoon was turning into evening, and as her sisters prattled in the parlor, Emily felt a strange sense of the waning day echoing her own life. Soon she would return to Fairfax Castle. Soon her weeks would resume their normal path, comfortable and predictable.

"Emily!" Caroline clapped her hands.

Emily blinked and looked at her sisters.

"My, you seemed to be about a million miles away just now," Caroline said.

"I was just thinking of long-ago days, when we were all children."

Fanny was standing up, smiling at Caroline. "Those are wonderful days to recall. I find myself doing just that, with more and more frequency." The smile faded. "I will take my leave," she announced. "Thank you." The formal tone had returned.

"I am so glad you came," Caroline said rising. "But please, can you not stay for supper? Or even for the whole night? We could send word to Robert, and he may sup with us if he wishes. But if you do stay, you could sleep in Emily's room, and—"

"No, no I must not. I must return at once. He will—" She stopped. "But thank you. Thank you both. And," she straightened, with just a dash of the old sparkle in her eyes, "Let me assure you on that one final point. Long sleeves made of lace are soon to be worn by everyone of consequence." Fanny pulled on her gloves.

"I have rarely seen lace sleeves in the prints from Paris. Velvet, silk and muslin, yes. Lace, rarely. And the lace sleeves I have seen were so poorly rendered, I am certain it was an error on the part of the printmaker."

Emily sighed and stood to take Fanny to the door. "Oh, Fan. May we call tomorrow? Letty so longs to see you and have a proper visit."

"Well, perhaps. Or perhaps I should again visit here. It must be more convenient for me to journey here than for the three of you to travel all the way to my house. But perhaps . . . maybe, if Robert . . ."

Suddenly the maid entered. "Lord Ogilvie is here to see Miss Fairfax and Mrs. Edgeworth."

Emily smiled. "Thank you, Mary."

Fanny turned to Emily, and her eyes softened. "Do come round tomorrow. It is my turn to play hostess." And unexpectedly, she kissed her on the cheek—a brief gesture that seemed to confuse and even embarrass her. She reached out her hand and touched Caroline's arm.

Fanny swept past just as Lord Ogilvie entered.

"Lord Ogilvie, may we present Mrs. Robert Aubridge—" But Fanny curtseyed and left the room before Ogilvie began his bow. Her countenance had returned to the blank, dull one they had seen earlier.

"Good Lord, who was that ray of sunshine?" he asked with a chuckle.

"That was our sister." Emily curtseyed and he bowed.

"That person is your sister? In that case, I fear the London air has not done Letty any good, although true she has grown remarkably tall."

Caroline was on her feet and beaming at Lord Ogilvie. "Sir, how delighted we are to see you! And that was not Letty," she explained carefully. "That was our other sister."

"Mrs. Edgeworth, I cannot tell you how relieved I am to hear that."

Ogilvie looked much the same as he had in Ireland, although on this day he was clearly free of the torments of the previous night's drink. Although he was well dressed, and his dark blue jacket and brown pantaloons were clearly the work of a fine tailor, he seemed yet disheveled. There were bits of stray thread on his shoulder. His cravat, white enough to indicate a good laundress, was ever so slightly crumpled. The top hat in his hands was well brushed, but his hair seemed to sweep to the left, as if a great wind had just passed through the walls.

But overall, there was such a spirit of good

nature and kindness, that it was hard to truly find any fault with the man.

"Miss Fairfax," he continued. "Congratulations, I hear, are due. You have conquered the ton, no easy task, that. Now, if you will only use your newfound influence and send them abroad, you will have done your country a greater service than Wellington."

"Why, thank you, sir. I shall take that under consideration. And where do you wish me to direct the well-heeled population?"

"Anywhere you like, as long as you don't send them as a whole. I believe that would be considered unsportsmanlike on your part—no other land could possibly survive such a sneak attack."

Caroline looked between the two of them, slight confusion evident on her face. "Would you two excuse me? I must see to the children."

"Please, do not neglect the offspring on my behalf," he bowed.

"Good afternoon, sir," she nodded. "Emily, I shall have more tea and cakes sent up at once."

"Again, not on my behalf," Ogilvie said. "I predict that during your arduous visits, you have consumed enough tea and cakes to satisfy the most ardent lover of tea and cakes."

"You forgot to mention the watercress and cucumber sandwiches, sir," Emily admitted.

"Very well," Caroline said, and with the charming smile of an emerging hostess, she left the room.

"Please sit down," Emily gestured to the chairs, and he nodded and settled into the wing chair Caroline had just vacated. Emily sat again on the couch. "So tell me, where have you been in the long days since we arrived in London?"

"Up north, at my family home. There were some of my own matters to settle, as well as those of a friend."

"I do hope it went well."

"Tolerably." Then he grinned. "It is good to see you, Miss Fairfax. How is your father?"

"Very well. And I would imagine quite pleased with the sublime silence our absence had brought to the house."

"And how does Miss Letty find London? I hear that London has already discovered her, and wonder if the admiration is mutual."

"She's having a wonderful time. She adores the sights and sounds, the bustle of the carriages. But I believe if we stay here much longer, she will actually turn into marzipan from Poole's and berry ice from Gunter's."

"I have heard of London doing far worse to a person," he laughed. Then he grew more serious. "And how are you?"

"Fine," Emily answered breezily. "I am enjoying myself very much."

"I lunched at White's and heard the Prince Regent paid a call along with Brummell."

"Such news must travel fast. But yes, they did, briefly. I think he wants one of Letty's hats."

"Dear God, which one? Brummell or the Prince?"

"The Prince. And do not worry—it is for his daughter, not himself."

"That is a relief. I would not wish to face next season in a bonnet."

An easy silence descended upon them and Ogilvie tapped the rim of his hat. "I have tickets for the new Edgar St. John production at the Olympic."

"Good God." Emily straightened. "With everything else, I had all but forgotten." How relieved she was that her new version was in place!

"My dear Miss Fairfax, it is to open next week. Mr. Ashford informed me."

"That soon?" How clever the players must be to adapt to such an altered script so quickly.

Then he leaned forward slightly. "You have seen Ashford once or twice since being in town, have you not?"

"Yes, I have." She kept her voice as light as possible.

"This may be a peculiar question. Indeed, I know it is. But tell me, does your play in any way involve or refer to our mutual friend Ashford?"

She swallowed. "It does, sir. Well, it did. But they have a revised copy to perform. There is no longer any humor at Mr. Ashford's expense, thank goodness."

"Good. Jolly good, I am relieved to hear it. Tell me, Miss Fairfax, have you not heard about the bill he is proposing to Parliament?"

"I have heard him mention business, but that is all. I confess I haven't been following the politics here, as George reads those gazettes at the club, and Caroline favors the society columns above all else. Other than fashion plates, of course. But is some sort of trouble expected?"

"More than that. His proposal is nothing short of revolutionary in some circles."

"Is it?"

"Indeed. He wishes to regulate hours and wages for workers, and to limit the amount of time a child under the age of fourteen may labor. And further, to assist some of the poorer women who are forced to, well, to make ends meet as best they can, under the harshest and most demeaning of circumstances."

"That sounds worthy," Emily said. "It seems very rare to me that someone of his standing would wish to help those people. I have seen a glimpse of poverty on this trip, sir. From behind the glass of my brother-in-law's carriage, fleeting glimpses of such sadness and hopelessness. How remarkable that he is willing to do more than observe indigence from a distance and dismiss it as a sad but inevitable aspect of the human condition. How wonderful," she murmured.

"Perhaps. And one cannot help but applaud his tenacity and commitment to his cause. But he is making enemies, Miss Fairfax. Powerful enemies."

Their eyes met and he continued. "Much of the newly found wealth in this nation is built on the long hours and meager wages of such labor, including the labor of children. And with the advent of new machinery, the reliance on a cheap and pliant workforce will become even more important. Same for the workingwomen."

"I can understand the controversy of his ideas, but danger? Surely you mean political danger."

"Unfortunately not. There have been threats on his life, Miss Fairfax. Threats he claims not to take seriously. Yet he has kept to himself more than his usual custom."

"I'm sorry, I don't follow," she stammered, befuddled and more than a little alarmed by Ogilvie's words as well as his somber demeanor.

"I believe that he has seen you only twice since your arrival because he does not wish to place you or your family in any danger, physical or otherwise."

Emily weighed the information, wondering if Ogilvie was being an alarmist. But something told her no, that was not the case. For all of his good-natured temperament, he was not a fool. And above all, he was not the sort to raise concern for no reason.

"Why have you told me this?" she asked at last.

"For two reasons. One, I am deeply troubled by some of the talk I have been hearing. And if certain parties have no compunction about speaking so freely with me, his close friend, present, I can only venture to imagine what they say when they are alone, with like-minded cronies. I believe you can help him."

"What good can I possibly do?" Her hands were clenched in her lap, the skirt of her gown crumpled in her fists.

"If possible, could you speak to him? I have tried. He is now avoiding me because he finds my warnings tiresome and irritating, and I must admit I find myself annoying as well. But I venture to say that the same words of caution issued by you will have more of an impact on him. Voice your concern. His is indeed a noble cause, but if there is to be any chance of his proposal getting a fair hearing, it must be from Lucius alone. He has the force, the personality to make a difference. His martyrdom will make for impassioned eulogies, but will do no good for those he wants to help."

"Martyrdom?" A brief wave of queasiness came over her. She took a deep breath. "You don't think it is that serious, do you?" But even as she spoke she knew the answer. Of course he thought it was that serious. Why else would he be there in Caroline's drawing room. "Of course I will speak to him. But how shall I . . ."

Ogilvie reached into his jacket pocket and produced a folded slip of paper. "Here is the address of his apartment on Bond Street. It's a curious little place. Could use a woman's touch. But if you send him a note asking to see him, I know he will come at the appointed hour. Actually, he would come at the appointed minute. Please do convey all the urgency the matter requires."

"Of course I will do my best. Thank you," she

said, looking at the address. She did not see Ogilvie smile warmly. Then she looked up. "Oh, and what was the second reason?"

"Pardon me?"

"You said there were two reasons why you revealed this information about Mr. Ashford. You have only told me the first one, sir. What is the second?"

He stood up, the warm smile still on his face. "Madam, do you not know?"

There was a thundering noise on the steps, and Emily immediately realized that Letty was on her way down. Even the boys could not manage such a thud.

"Know what?" She wanted to hear the answer prior to Letty's inevitable burst through the door.

"I have been his close friend for most of our lives, and I know him as well as a brother. Indeed, we are very like brothers. I have seen him grow from a boy to a man, and on occasion I realize what is good for him before he himself becomes aware of the fact. This is just such an occasion, for I spent many hours in his company since he met you. And, my dear, Ashford is in love with you. Problem is, he may not know it himself."

Emily's mouth opened, but no words came out. Never before had she been so entirely astonished. Never.

Before she could regain the powers of speech, the heavy door flew open.

"Lord Ogilvie!" Letty exclaimed.

"Miss Letty!" he replied in the exact same tone.

Then Letty looked at her sister. "Have I missed something? Oh, please, if it was good, tell me!"

With that he patted Letty's head, winked at the still speechless Emily, and left the home of George Edgeworth with more hope for his good friend Ashford than he had felt for a long, long time.

Chapter Nine

Robert Aubridge was desperate.

He needed to find men as equally desperate as he was, which would be no easy task. And only a desperate, depraved man would consent to murder, especially for the relatively paltry sum he could afford to pay. To ensure success, he had decided to hire at least two such men, preferably three, for his prey—Lucius Ashford—was in devilishly fit condition.

With the information gained from his reluctant wife (and shouldn't a man's wife be a helpmate without question?), he would be able to find Ashford without any problem. Or he could send his emissaries to find him.

So he sought the dubious comfort of the Nail's Head tavern, one of the meanest places in town, an establishment so rough and dangerous that even adventurous young bucks seeking a thrill avoided it, no matter how intoxicated they became. That was precisely what Aubridge was counting on, for it would never do to be recognized by members of society. The same society he had been so briefly a part of, before his life became a living hell.

It was all her fault, he thought, clenching a fist. His wife, the harpy of misfortune.

In a darkened corner of the public house near Covent Garden he slowly examined his hands. As he suspected, the trembling wouldn't cease. There were marks and scratches on his hands, and he knew they had been scratched by his wife, the way she would cower like a dog and hold up a hand to deflect his blows. She deserved each one, and then some, yet he was the injured one. Another wave of anger began to rise, but he squelched it, knowing he needed a clear head and steady wits to solicit the help he required.

Even in the dim, flickering light, with the stench of stale drink and acrid, unclean patrons elbowing each other for a prime place at the bar, he could see the fraying linen of his cuffs. A single thread was hanging, and against his better judgment he tugged it once. Nothing happened. The second time he yanked harder, and succeeded in ripping a three inch length of cloth from his sleeve.

Although his threadbare clothing was simply a disguise to help him blend in with the other customers, he was all too aware that the attire could prove prophetic. If he was unable to enlist the help he needed, he could very well become a regular at just such an establishment. He, who had rubbed elbows with the elite nobility, with statesmen and even princes, was brought to this reduced level by his wife. It was she who had kept him from greatness, whose constant doubting of his business skills had forced this situation.

If only she had kept her mouth closed, he would be at White's this very moment.

The barmaid, a woman with conspicuously rouged cheeks and, he could easily tell, a matching rouged bosom, leaned over him.

"What's your pleasure, lovie?" Her breath was hot and thick and vaguely corrupt. One of her front teeth was missing, and the other was a leopard-spotted brown. Yet he found her perversely alluring.

"Ale," Aubridge said, avoiding all eye contact. His usual drink was fine wine or an aged brandy, not coarse ale. Even if this place could furnish a more refined beverage, no one would buy it.

The barmaid lingered, running a dirty finger up his arm. It wasn't that he wouldn't have been interested in a fast, furious romp with the wench. She would prove a welcome change from his wife, who had become a skinny hag. But it would keep him from his real business. And that was something he could ill afford.

She waited for his response, and when he again stared at his hands, a huffing noise came from her. She walked away, swinging her heavy hips just as he pulled his jacket sleeve down as far as it would go, to cover the offending cuff.

The jacket wasn't much better. It had served several years earlier as a best jacket purchased on credit. But of course he needed a new one soon after, and then another one. He simply needed to keep up appearances, which was something his wife never seemed to acknowledge.

"It takes money to make money," he had told her. And when she made an infuriating whimper about living more cheaply, with more economy than flash, he had been forced to silence her with the back of his hand.

She deserved it. Fanny, the rich heiress from Ireland. How soon he went through her dowry, and then her annual income. Indeed, her annual income for the next several years was already promised to some moneylenders. He knew it was gambling that led to this place, but he was always certain that just one more hand at faro, one more roll of the dice, and his fortune would be made.

Aubridge hunched over the ale when it arrived, wanting to avoid all contact with the other customers. The trembling in his hands would lessen. It had to. It must.

For he knew if he failed to accomplish his mission of hiring someone to silence Lucius Ashford, he would be ruined. And the ruination, unlike his previous temporary setbacks, would last forever.

Three men slipped onto the next bench, tilting the end of the table.

He took a large swig of ale. The trembling of his hands was beginning to subside. That was good, he thought. Very good.

The three men looked vaguely familiar, and he realized he had seen them before, perhaps at this very tavern. Then he turned his full attention to eavesdropping on their conversation.

"What I wouldn't give for five guineas," one of them moaned.

"What are ye, daft! How could you ever come up with that much money?" snapped another man. The third, with a shaggy hat atop an even shaggier mop of hair, pushed his companion's shoulder.

Their voices were lowered, occasionally one would shout "Go on with ye!" The sounds in the pub were rising, the laughter and clanking mugs and the continuous clamor of raucous conversation. Aubridge struggled to listen. Whatever they were talking about, he wanted to hear it.

Five guineas. Three men at five guineas each. That was within his price range. But were they capable of the job required? After all, murder was no simple matter.

Very casually, he inched toward them, remaining in his hunched position as he moved. They were speaking in low tones now. With a large swallow of the ale, he turned toward the men and nodded.

All three eyed him with suspicion, and one who had a large, disfiguring scar over his lip sneered. At least Aubridge thought it was a sneer. With the pull of the scar, it was difficult to tell.

Aubridge cleared his throat. This was it—time to make his move.

"Would you gentlemen be interested in making five guineas in the next day or so?"

"Five guineas each, or five guineas split between the three of us?" The Sneer asked.

Aubridge hesitated for an instant. Could he possibly succeed for a mere five guineas total?

The shaggy-haired man in the shaggy hat set his jaw in a most unpleasant manner, and Aubridge decided to be more generous. "Five apiece," he said with a tone that he hoped passed for authority.

"What sort of business will this entail?" The third man, who was missing most of his left ear, leaned toward Aubridge. Instinctively, he leaned back.

"I'll not mince words," he said. "You would be killing a man. But in all truth he is a most troublesome sort, with no wife or children to mourn him."

"Why do you want him dead?" The Sneer asked reasonably.

Aubridge debated whether or not to tell them the truth, that he was hundreds of thousands of pounds in debt, that he owed moneylenders who were now threatening to send him to debtors' prison, that his wife was a hag and that if he could only borrow a little more money, he knew he could rise in both social position and fortune. But he decided not to reveal all.

"Many, many people want him dead, for he is an inconvenient man," was his nonanswer.

"Murder is a hanging crime," said One Ear. "Seems five guineas a man is not much considering the risks. Should be more like fifteen a man."

Aubridge swallowed. Where would he ever get such a sum? "Ten," he said, his mouth dry.

The three men glanced at each other; Shaggy

Man wiped his mouth with the back of his sleeve. "Will ten do, men?"

They nodded grudgingly.

"When do we get paid?" One ear growled.

"Half up front, the rest upon completion of the deed," Aubridge said.

"I don't know. This sounds dangerous." Shaggy Man was having doubts.

"Not for us." The Sneer tilted his glass. "But for the bloke they want dead it's right dangerous. But for us, three against one. Can't get much better odds."

One of the men laughed uncomfortably.

"A lot of money," One Ear said reverently. "Who is that unfortunate gentleman?"

"I'll give you the particulars once you agree to the task." He drained the rest of his tumbler in a single gulp.

"Very well," Shaggy Man concluded.

Aubridge slipped them the coins he had, outlined what Ashford looked like, and where he was likely to be found. As soon as he possibly could, he left the pub, hoping they would just kill the damn man and get it over with. Should they not be able to find him, he would give them further information on Ashford's whereabouts from his hag of a wife.

He couldn't wait to leave the place, the men, the thought of what he had just commissioned.

Back at the pub, The Sneer announced, "Gentlemen, in a very short time we'll be ten guineas richer, with a bit of sport into the bargain."

And with that they toasted themselves, good fortune, the soon-to-be deceased Ash-something, and lastly—with great feeling—Bess the barmaid.

Lucius Ashford settled back into the chair and reread the note for the third time.

Dear Mr. Ashford,

I have information of great importance to share with you. Could you please call at my brother-in-law's home tonight at eight this evening? The matter is urgent, otherwise I would not press.

Yours most sincerely, Emily Fairfax

He closed his eyes for a moment, wondering what she could possibly have to tell him. Was it that the Prince Regent called upon her this afternoon?

No. She would not bother with such nonsense. He had seen her face as she met the Prince, and she seemed far more amused than impressed.

Could it be that she met Brummell? Or that Letty had fashioned a new design, this one for men?

No and no. Although she excelled at light conversation, she was not the sort of woman to send a note without good reason.

Perhaps it was at last about the letter he had sent her, the pages of confessional she had yet to respond to in any way.

Maybe. Just maybe that was it.

Opening his eyes, he looked around his room. It was decent enough, in a bachelor sort of way. But now he observed it as if for the first time, critically and unemotionally.

It was comfortable. It was practical. There was even a bit of art—a painting that had reminded him of his dog Pepper, the one who ran away when he was eleven. It wasn't a particularly good painting, but then again, Pepper hadn't been a particularly good dog. The beast's main appeal was that he had a large spotted tongue, could put both front paws over his eyes on command, and above all, Pepper was his.

What would Emily think of such a room? Dozens of them could easily slide into Fairfax Castle. Even her brother-in-law's comparatively modest town house could accommodate his home several times over.

She would probably observe every detail of his abode somberly, make a gracious comment or two about whatever she could, such as the generous size of the windows or the useful shape of the chair cushions. And that would be it. Nothing more, nothing less.

He smiled. Then, in a gesture that somehow embarrassed him even as he performed it, he held the envelope under his nose. Of course there was no scent there. And if there was, by chance, a sprinkle of rare cologne on the buff colored paper, it belonged to George Edgeworth's footman who delivered the note, not to Miss Emily Fairfax.

Of course he would see her at eight.

Then the smile faded from his face. He knew what she wanted to tell him, the important information.

She was getting married.

What else could it be?

Opening the note for the fourth time, he reread the words, hoping for a clue. But there was no clue there.

Hadn't she said she would never marry? Never. He recalled that distinctly. Their conversation at Fairfax Castle had left no room for doubt. Emily Fairfax was determined never to marry.

But perhaps someone clever enough could change her mind. Perhaps some damned fortune hunter, unscrupulous knave, had worked on her, had flattered or written poetry in the heavy-handed style of those new romantic aesthetes. Useless, long-haired men.

He hated poetry.

Taking a deep breath, he relaxed, running a hand over his jawline. He needed a shave. That is what he would do, shave. Perhaps put on a fresh shirt. He would have done that anyway, even if he hadn't been going to visit Miss Fairfax. Probably. And a neckcloth. After shaving, a new neckcloth was always required.

In fifteen minutes he would walk over to Grosvenor Street. The walk would do him good. There he would see her, talk to her, allow her to share whatever information she had to share. And whatever that information was, he vowed to be happy for her. Very happy indeed.

It was Ashford himself who would be miserable.

* * *

Emily knew Caroline would be delighted to have Ashford come for a visit. And she was.

"How wonderful! Such a gentleman! Oh, Emily," her large blue eyes filled with heavy tears. "How very happy I am for you."

And of course Emily knew that Caroline would be sure to leave her alone with Ashford. Then she could explain to him what she had heard from Ogilvie, and maybe even touch on why he never responded to her letter. Of course the main purpose was to warn him, to let him know just what danger he was in.

Was it possible that Ogilvie was right about Ashford's feelings for her? It mattered not, she told herself. There were more important issues to discuss that evening.

She had chosen eight o'clock for his arrival, for that was when dinner was served, and the rest of the family would be busy with the meal.

Emily paced for a few minutes, then decided to make herself comfortable. With a keen sense of anticipation and a little worry—how would he react to her?—she sat on the steps and waited.

Ashford was glad he had decided to shave. The brisk evening air felt crisp, bracing. It was still quite dark, not all of the lamps had been lighted yet. But he knew the route so well, he could walk it blindfolded.

Pausing to look up at the sky—the stars were brilliant—he heard the unmistakable sound of footsteps behind him. They shuffled to a halt when he stopped. Very slowly, he began to walk again. And the footsteps also began again.

He was aware, of course, that he was not the Tory favorite at the moment. He wasn't even the Whig favorite. There were too many rumors and misconceptions concerning his upcoming proposal to make either side comfortable.

In truth his notion was not radical or politically wild. It was a beginning, a gentle beginning to some genuine reform. Once those in power—meaning the landowners, the emerging manufacturers, and the chronically wealthy—became aware of the general good a few simple changes would initiate, they would no longer fear those changes. Change, after all, was what the aristocracy and the newly rich feared most.

He picked up the pace, then stopped. The footsteps mimicked the same pattern.

Perhaps he should have been more forthcoming about the changes he intended to propose. But the heated discussions his supposed ideas had ignited were helpful. By keeping the interest high, and even fanning some of the fears, he was ensuring that his proposal of the bill would be well attended, if only by the curious and those who were already burning the late night oil drafting rebuttals.

If the footsteps continued, he would not see Emily. He would simply circle back to his own rooms. The last thing he wanted to do was endanger her in any way.

Instead he wanted to protect her.

Only a few more blocks, a handful of steps. No one else seemed to be out. He was in a fashionable area, and all of the fashionable people were inside their fashionable homes dining at this hour.

And then, all at once, they were upon him.

It happened so suddenly, the first blow to his midsection stunned him. Another hit smashed into his arm. All he could see was a trio of scruffy-looking men who, from the smell of them, had spent the better part of the afternoon and evening in a pub, and the better part of their lives avoiding soap and water.

Yet they did not make any attempt to retrieve money, or his watch. At once he realized they were not intent on mere thievery. They wished to do him serious harm.

And then he reacted instinctively, employing the techniques he had honed at Gentleman Jackson's boxing rooms. There was no time to think. With one left hook, the largest of the men—taken off guard—went reeling into a tree. He heard a thud and a moan, then nothing but silence from that one.

For a moment the other two just looked at each other. Ashford was still in his boxing pose, fists raised, feet planted firmly apart. Then they both rushed him at the same time, and with a swift left-right they, too, were silenced.

His left shoulder was a bit painful, and he rotated it to ease the stiffness. And his new jacket was torn.

Perhaps he should have quizzed them as to who

had hired their services, for he doubted these men held a political or social grudge. But someone else clearly did.

Yet he could still see Emily, for there was no danger of them following him. All three remained motionless. He continued on his way to George Edgeworth's town house, moving his shoulders to ease the pain he still felt from the scuffle.

And just before he lifted the oversized brass knocker, he realized that this may not be the last such attempt on him. He looked over his shoulder, just in case there were yet more marauding criminals in his trail. But the coast was clear, and consulting his watch, he realized he was three minutes late.

With his left shoulder still throbbing from the punch, he rotated it once more and was about to knock again when the door opened. And there she was, bathed in the yellow candlelight. Even in her simple dress of some flimsy fabric—he couldn't very well examine it at the moment—she took his breath away.

"Miss Fairfax." He removed his top hat.

"Good God!" Her hand flew to her mouth. "Please come in." With that she took his elbow and led him into the hallway.

"Yes, I am a bit late, but according to my watch it is only by three minutes—"

"No. The blood, sir."

"Blood?" He patted his face. "Perhaps while I was shaving—"

"Were you attempting to shave off your left arm?"

"Pardon me?"

Very gently she led him upstairs to the parlor and closed the door. "Really, Miss Fairfax. This is quite—"

"Please sit." She pushed his right shoulder, but he resisted.

"After you," he gestured to the chair next to the one she had pointed out, and he stopped. "Oh, I have that same artificial ancient Greek urn. I use mine as an umbrella stand."

"Please sit down, Mr. Ashford. I fear you are wounded more seriously than you think."

"They were nothing but harmless footpads."

"Foodpads?"

"Well, perhaps footpads with a strong desire to interfere with my political career."

"Exactly my point, sir. Please sit down and allow me to attend to your wound," she said. This time he did not resist her efforts to ease him into the chair.

As he settled into a comfortable position, he glanced down at his shoulder. Now, in the lighted room, he could see why Emily had been so concerned. "Good Lord," he prodded it cautiously with a finger. "The jacket is ruined."

Not only was his jacket torn, it was covered with blood. And since the stain was still spreading, he could only conclude that the blood was his own.

"I'll be right back," she said softly. Before she left the room, she again placed her hand briefly on his right shoulder.

It was a very pleasant sensation. Quite worth the pain in his other arm.

The realization that several men had tried very hard to harm, if not actually murder him was a peculiar sensation. That they did not accomplish their goal was almost beside the point. Three men had just made an attempt on his life. And no doubt they, or someone else, would most certainly try again. And try harder.

Someone had tried to kill him, he who had attempted to stop duels and negotiate disagreements with words rather than fists.

And that thought made him furious.

Within a very few minutes she returned with a basin of warm water, clean white cloths, soap and a needle and thread.

"Oh, you needn't bother, Miss Fairfax. I am certain my tailor, Mr. Weston, can stitch up the jacket." How dare they visit their base sentiments on him!

"This isn't for the jacket. It's for you." Very gingerly she removed the jacket, which was entirely soaked in blood on the left side.

"I had no idea," he mumbled. "I would not have come. It was dark, and—"

"And some men attacked you," she concluded, wincing as she pulled his shirt away from the wound. "There is a rather nasty scratch along your cheek," she added, examining it to see if it was as bad as it appeared.

Unexpectedly, he grinned. "That one was self-inflicted." Then he looked up at her, their eyes only inches apart.

How could they be so very brown, she marveled.

How could they be so very bluish green, he wondered to himself.

Abruptly, she returned to the wound on his shoulder. "Did you see what kind of knife he had?" she asked, her voice rather weak.

"No. I hate to admit this, but I didn't even see the knife. I thought it was a lucky punch. Lucky on his part, that is."

"Did he follow you here?"

"No, not at all. I left the three of them insensible by the park. And I would never have led them here, to you."

"There were three of them?"

"Yes. But I do some boxing and indeed it came in rather handy tonight and . . . Miss Fairfax? Are you unwell?"

"I think I need to sit down," she breathed.

"Forgive me," he rose halfway out of his chair and helped her into the one beside it.

She had grown very pale, her lips almost white.

"Miss Fairfax—"

"Do you know what could have happened just now?" Her voice was a bare whisper.

"The thought did cross my mind. But it didn't happen."

"Did they attempt to take money or your watch?"

"No."

"Oh, Mr. Ashford. I fear they were trying to kill you."

"I know that as well."

"And this is the important information I had to impart to you."

"That someone is trying to kill me?"

She nodded. "Lord Ogilvie told me, hoping I could urge you to have more care. He fears you are not heeding his warnings, and those of your other friends. And in the very act of attempting to save your life, I just came very close to helping them end it."

"Now you're being overly dramatic."

"Overly dramatic? Sir, please look down. No. Slightly to the left."

"Yes?"

"Tell me, what color is your shirt?"

"White. Sort of."

"No. You are color-blind, sir. Look again."

"Well, there is a dash or two of red."

"It is fully soaked in scarlet, sir."

"Well . . ." He touched it, and had to admit it was beginning to hurt like the blazes. It was larger than he realized, and deeper. "Perhaps I am just an empathetic supporter of our army, our brave men in red."

Finally Emily stood and walked briskly to the basin. "Please remove your neckcloth and shirt."

"Are you going to try to get the stain out?" he asked hopefully.

"No. I am going to attend to your wound."

"Yes, I see. But . . ."

"But what?"

"Well, it's just that the stain will set."

Emily stopped for a moment with a wet cloth in her hand. "Sir, your shirt and jacket have absorbed perhaps a pint of blood. Both the jacket and shirt have also suffered major gashes, as have, incidentally, you. I fear that even if we race the shirt and jacket—and neckcloth. . . . Look." With a pointing finger she directed his attention to the torn fabric. "Even if we rush them both to Mr. Weston and pull him from dinner, the clothes are goners."

"Yes. I'm afraid you are right," he admitted, sitting bare-chested on the striped chair.

Dabbing at the wound with a corner of the cloth, she was unable to keep herself from staring at his almost naked body.

Never before had she seen a man without his shirt on. And even if she had, she suspected he would look nothing like this.

Lucius Ashford was quite simply the most splendid thing, man or beast, she had ever beheld.

His arms were large. Massive. They looked as if each one had been honed from the trunk of an enormous tree. Each muscle was so well defined, she could almost cut herself on the edges.

But his skin was soft, so soft, and bronzed by the sun.

Where did he go naked in the sun to acquire such color?

"Are you unwell?" he asked. His breath ruffled her hair as he spoke. "Perhaps overheated?"

"No. Um, not at all. Why do you ask?"

"Because your cheeks are flushed."

"Are they?" She cleared her throat. "Um, I don't believe you will require a single stitch."

"A single stitch of what?"

"Clothing. I mean, thread. For your wound. I will just clean it and wrap it in fresh cloth. That is what I mean."

"Oh. Thank you."

He took a deep breath and she watched his chest expand. The muscles there were sharp as well, and covered with crisp dark hair that seemed to go all the way down to . . .

She could not stop herself. Before she realized it, she was touching his chest. She had to. There was no way she could stop herself and . . .

"Miss Fairfax? What are you doing?" There was a smile in his voice.

"Oh, well. Cleaning your wound, of course. That is the medically sound, um, thing for me to do."

"But you are rubbing my chest. The gash is on my left shoulder."

"Sir, I am cleaning the blood from your skin, and preventing further damage to your entire body." She bit her lip.

"But madam. You have dropped the cloth."

With horror she realized she had been rubbing his chest with her bare hand.

Hands.

When had she begun to use both of them?

And when did she abandon the cloth?

Suddenly he placed his hands over her wrists. "Emily."

She remained very still. Slowly he eased her forward, then he lowered her onto his lap.

"Sir," she tried to say. But the only noise she made was a slow murmuring moan, like a deeply contented teakettle.

His right arm went around her, and before she was conscious of what she was doing—an occurrence remarkably similar to what had happened just before with the washcloth—she bent her head down to meet his lips.

It was soft, gentle. She felt dizzy, as if she were the one who had just lost so much blood, and he held her on his lap.

Was this happening?

There was a tumble of emotions coursing through her, heightened by the purely physical luxury of touching him, of being touched by him. She was breathless, heady, unable to distinguish where her body ended and his began. It was an entirely new experience, as if her senses had been suddenly awakened to something magnificent, something profound.

"Emily," he repeated.

"Mr. Ashford," she mumbled.

"Emily, I have to go."

"No, please."

"Yes. Please." There was a strain in his voice, and she pulled back.

"Are you unwell?"

"Not now. But I will be very unwell presently if I do not leave."

She had a vague notion of what he was implying, and wasn't certain if she should be flattered or offended.

She was flattered.

"I do not wish you to leave," she heard herself say.

And it was the truth. She wanted him to remain with her for as long as possible, no longer caring about propriety, or what should be left unspoken, even unthought.

"And I do not wish to leave," he responded softly. "I must. But," he touched a coil of hair by her neck, "I hope to return. Very soon." Then he held the strand of hair to his lips, and she thought she would melt.

He prodded her with a light nudge, and gently she stood up. "Shall I borrow some clothes from George?" Her mind was still in a haze, her thoughts still unclear.

He shook his head. "No. They would be far too large for you."

"I mean for you, sir," she smiled.

"I know. But it's dark enough that no one will see me. And if they do, I will claim it's the latest rage in Paris, and by next week all men will be wearing torn jackets and red shirts."

"What about the men who attacked you?"

"I will take another route. In any case, I do not believe they have yet awakened."

"You hit them that hard?" she asked in awe.

"No. They were that drunk. Here, can you help me with the waistcoat?" As she eased the vest on, she lingered over his back, savoring the feel of his muscles, the warmth of his skin. "Thank you." His voice was husky.

"We should go there at once, then, and apprehend them!"

"Miss Fairfax . . . Emily," he slipped on the torn, bloody jacket. "This is not one of your plays."

"But do you not wish to bring them to justice? To see them pay for their heinous crime?"

"Firstly, I doubt the crime was their idea . . ."

"Then we should force them to tell us who put them up to this! If we go immediately, we should—"

"Secondly, they have paid. I suspect none of them will feel remotely healthy for the next few days."

In a few moments he was dressed. If he didn't look quite presentable, then he looked something very close.

They stood, and with a smile he leaned down and kissed her softly. "I will see you in a very few days."

"You will?"

"The play. Your play. I have been invited to share your box."

"Have you?" The play. With any luck, the new version would please him. She hoped it would be so.

"Thank you."

She blinked. "For what?"

"For trying to warn me. Did anyone besides Ogilvie tell you of this?"

"No. Just Ogilvie."

"I reckoned as much. But thank you."

"Even though it almost got you killed?"

"Think of it as a very pointed demonstration. Always an effective teaching tool. I will be more careful, for the next ones may be more effective."

They stood in awkward silence, and then he spoke.

"I must go. Good night."

"Well?" Caroline said from the next room, craning her neck through the door. "Are you betrothed?"

"No, Caroline." Emily stepped quickly to the basin and linens, and hid it with her skirts. "I'm afraid not."

"Oh. Shame." Caro's face fell. "But there is time, dearest. Do not give up yet." And then she was gone, leaving Emily alone and feeling that Lucius Ashford was more of an enigma than ever.

Chapter Ten

"I really must hurry breakfast, for I do have so much work to get done today," Letty announced with bland importance as she reached for a muffin.

"Your work?" Emily smiled as she checked the tea. "Tea is almost steeped. Would you like tea or cocoa?"

"Tea, please." Letty examined the muffin. "Cocoa leaves me much fatigued."

Emily resisted the urge to burst out laughing. Why did she feel so giddy? But of course she knew exactly why, even without looking at her lap, where a white napkin lay folded.

Just like the white cloth she had used the night before, mere hours before, on Mr. Ashford.

On Lucius.

Or rather, the white cloth she had used until abandoning it to the floor and applying her greedy bare hands to his entire torso with unladylike vigor.

And how she had enjoyed every blessed second of it! The feel of his skin beneath her fingers. The warmth, the muscles . . .

"Em, are you unwell? Your cheeks are all splotchy."

"I am fine, thank you, Letty. Very fine indeed."

Then there was the kiss. The kisses. How could such a large man—for he had to be well over six feet tall, perhaps six and two—be so very gentle?

Up close he smelled of soap. Up very close.

"I cannot tell if these are currant muffins or if there are bugs in the flour again." Letty crinkled her nose and sniffed. Then she pulled off a piece and handed it to her sister. "Can you taste this and tell me?"

Emily felt like kicking up her heels and dancing. She wanted the world to feel just a fraction of the sheer joy she was experiencing.

Instead she remained seated as she offered Letty milk and sugar. "Since I cannot recall ever willingly eating bugs, I can be of no help to you, dear. I wouldn't know how they taste."

Squinting, Letty looked more closely at the muffin, and then she sniffed it.

"Oh no! No! Heavens!" Caroline shrieked from below.

"Best not eat that," Emily advised. "From those screams, I'll venture there are bugs in the flour again."

"And maybe mice. Or rats!" Letty added with relish.

"One can only hope."

The distinctive sound of Caroline marching up the steps seemed to shake the house.

"I see where the boys inherited their stair technique," Emily whispered, and the two were giggling when the door flew open, clattering against the brass doorstop.

"I have the most dreadful news," Caroline said. "Em, did you bring any black gowns with you? I hardly know how to tell you."

"Why would we need black gowns? Is it Papa?" Emily said quietly, fearfully.

"Letty, dearest, you had better go upstairs. You should not hear this. I need to speak to Emily alone."

"I will not leave!"

"Letty, perhaps—" Emily began.

"I never get to hear the interesting things. You always send me away just before the subjects get good."

"Caroline, could you please just tell us who this concerns?" Emily asked as calmly as possible. A knot was beginning to grow in her stomach.

"It is someone you both know," Caroline said gently.

"Please, who is it?" Emily demanded apprehensively.

"Mr. Ashford, dear. I'm afraid he has been murdered. . . . Emily?"

She clutched the edge of the table. "No. There has been a mistake." She almost laughed. Of course it was a mistake.

How rumors do spread in this town! "No, it is just a nasty story. It is not true."

"But it is, dearest," Caroline said gently. "I am so very sorry, Em. So very sorry indeed."

Letty dropped the muffin and said nothing, but her chin began to quiver.

"Impossible," Emily managed to say. Suddenly she was unable to breathe. "It is all impossible. Just a mistake. Tell me, what did you hear?" Then she felt her throat catch. "What did you hear?"

"Not in front of Letty," Caroline said. "I'll fetch the smelling salts—"

"How!" Emily shouted.

"It is most unsavory. I heard it from the servants—one of them saw Mr. Ashford's man early this morning, and he related the dreadful news."

"Damn it, Caro!" Emily snapped. "Just tell us what the bloody hell happened!"

"He was set upon last evening not far from here. Must have been right after the short visit he made to see you," she stammered, stunned by her sister's language as well as the event itself. "Stabbed right through the heart. Thieves, they say. I have ordered new locks on all of the doors, so you needn't worry. We are snug here, all safe."

"It's a mistake," Emily concluded. "It has to be a mistake."

Tears were streaming down Letty's face, and she was unable to respond.

"Poor, poor thing," Caroline shook her head and placed a protective arm around her youngest sister.

"It is a mistake," Emily repeated. "He was indeed set upon, but the wound was not serious. I tended it myself, and he left here on his own."

But as she spoke she wondered what had happened after he had left.

What if the three men had set upon him once

again? He had been rather unsteady when he left, as she herself had been. But she had not just suffered a significant injury and lost so much blood.

Perhaps his judgment had been impaired.

Another terrible thought crossed her mind: what if the puncture had been much worse than she had thought? Her mind had been distracted. She had not paid proper attention to his condition.

What if he had left her side, walked all the way back to his rooms, and then perished?

He would have died alone, then. All by himself.

Was it possible?

It was her fault. She had beckoned him, had penned the very note that drew him from the safety of his home. Because of her he was in the streets at that time.

And then, later, had she examined the wound more carefully, she would have seen how deep it was. But she had not done that. Instead she had allowed him to kiss her, then leave on his own, by himself, to walk home. To die alone.

She had murdered the man she loved. Not once, but twice.

And with that thought, the breakfast room began to tilt. Tightening her grip on the table, she heard a distant clatter of silver. Someone called from downstairs. Letty rushed from the room in a pink-and-white blur. Caroline shouted something, but it seemed to come from the other end of a long tunnel. Then—as if in a strange dream—the world went entirely, mercifully black.

* * *

Emily awoke slowly.

At first she thought she was in her bed, but then a fierce pounding wracked her head, and she frowned, recalling a hideous nightmare she had dreamed during the night. It had been so realistic, so terrible. Even the thought of it made her feel ill.

That Lucius was dead.

A dawning of awareness began to creep into her mind, but she kept her eyes closed. Turning her head to the side, she realized she was on a carpet.

And she remembered. It hadn't been a dream.

"No," she cried softly.

Her entire body was numb. And all she could hope was that she, too, would die rather than face the pain of coming awake. Part of her willed herself to die, to just cease living.

"She looks positively ashen," she heard Caroline's voice coming from someplace above her. "I will have Dr. Ward sent over at once. He can bleed her."

Emily wanted to tell her not to bother, but she couldn't speak. Good, she thought. It was working. She was already dying. And luckily, Caro had her mourning gown prepared.

"Is she smiling?" The voice of her sister seemed to yell from beyond the tunnel. "That is a most unattractive smile."

"No, it is not. It is a beautiful smile," spoke a soothing voice close to her.

It was the voice of a ghost.

It was Lucius!

Then she was almost there, on the path to Heaven. This was it, the moment of her death. And he was greeting her halfway. It was just as the poetry books had said it would be, a dreamy, lovely feeling. All of the worldly woes had dropped from her, and she was a pure spiritual being.

"Emily, can you hear me?"

Of course she could hear him!

And then, miraculously, she felt his hand over hers. It was warm and large and she felt safe, so safe. Now she could let go.

"Oh dear, is she drooling?"

"No," the ghost voice replied. And then she felt a gentle thumb by the corner of her mouth. "Well, perhaps a little."

Then she stiffened.

This was wrong, all wrong. Elegant ladies were not supposed to meet their loved ones drooling. Impending death was no excuse for bad manners.

Unhurriedly, she opened her eyes. And the first face she saw was that of Lucius Ashford.

"Are you dead?" she asked.

He did seem rather pale. But as she spoke a grin spread over his face, and his eyes creased into the most welcoming of glimmers. "I was just about to ask you the same question."

"What happened?" She tried to sit up, but his firm hold kept her down.

"Don't get up just yet. Lie there for a while. This

is the last chance you may ever get to see your sister's breakfast room from this prospect."

"Do you want the brandy now, Mr. Ashford?" Caroline asked.

"Yes, please."

Emily could see Letty eating her muffin at the table, her legs swinging from the chair.

Caroline handed him a crystal cordial glass filled with brandy. With extraordinary care, he raised her head just slightly and held the brandy under her nose. The sharp odor snapped her to her senses, and she lifted her head farther to take a sip.

"No you don't," he said. Then he raised the glass to his own lips and in a single swallow finished it off. He handed the empty glass back to Caroline. "Thank you. That did the trick nicely."

"Would you like another one, Mr. Ashford?"

"No. One is quite enough." He looked back down at Emily.

"What happened?"

"There seems to be a rumor floating about that I was murdered last evening."

"Yes. I do believe I heard something to that effect," she said weakly.

Caroline busied herself with tea, keeping a watch on Ashford and Emily.

"I gave the jacket and shirt to my man Addleston to bring round to the tailor. I was hoping it could be salvaged."

"But how did the rumors circulate?"

"Well, Addleston is a delightful gentleman in

most ways, but he is rather fond of telling a tale. Usually that fondness works to my advantage, for I have learned the surest way to circulate information is to give it to Addleston in strictest confidence. Within hours it has passed throughout the entire city, within a matter of days it has gone abroad."

She was finally beginning to relax, listening to him speak, watching his changing expressions.

"So, as you can imagine, he was most delighted to be handed a torn and bloodied jacket this morning. There is nothing I could have done or said to have made him happier. He happened upon several of his acquaintances in service, one of whom is the butler here, and thus my tale of a ruined suit of clothes became a dastardly act of murder."

"You realize that it is only sheer luck that you are not dead."

"Sheer luck? What of my boxing skills?"

"You said they were drunk."

"Tipsy is a better word."

"And they stabbed you without your knowledge."

"That is how it is usually done. On the sly."

"Still, when I think of what could have happened . . ."

"What *could* have happened, you say? The jacket is completely ruined. As are, of course, the shirt—a particularly fine one—and the neckcloth. The waistcoat came through tolerably well, but only just."

"What are you going to do about what happened?"

Leaning his right elbow against his knee, he thought for a minute. "There is nothing to do but shoot them."

"The men who did this?"

"No. The clothes. There is no way to save the jacket, best to take it round back and shoot it cleanly through. The linens, too, I fear."

"I am serious," she began to get up, and this time he helped her into a sitting position, his hand resting on the small of her back. Although she was fully awake, she still felt light-headed, a little unsteady. But that, she realized, was because he was there, safe and well and very much alive. Now they were both seated on the breakfast room floor, with Letty and Caroline enjoying their meal at the table. "Lucius, I'm worried that . . ."

Then she paused, observing an annoyingly handsome smirk on his face. "Why are you smiling?"

"I just enjoyed the way you said it."

"That someone tried to murder you last night? That I suspect they won't stop until they succeed?"

"No. My Christian name. Could you please say it again?"

"Mr. Ashford."

"I faced the jaws of death last evening. My best jacket is ruined and my left shoulder is stiff. Not to mention most of London believes I am stiff as well. The least you could do is grant my humble request."

"Lucius," she whispered.

"Thank you," he whispered back, and very

slowly he began to lean toward her. Very slowly, she began to lean toward him.

"Emily!" Caroline chirped, and they both jumped apart. Caroline did not even look up from her eggs. "I believe we should cancel the theater for tonight."

"Why?" Letty cried.

"Because, dearest, your sister has just been through a terrible fright . . ."

"Is uttering my name that much of a trauma?" he said so softly, only Emily could hear. She began to laugh at the absurdity of the entire scene, and he, too, started laughing, a low, rich chuckle.

"See, Letty? She is quite hysterical. You should take to your bed, Emily. Take to bed at once. It would be fashionable for you to remain there for at least a week, perhaps two," Caroline admonished. "And you, too, Mr. Ashford."

Their eyes met briefly, and again they laughed. Letty smiled as she watched them. Caroline continued to eat, pinching grains of salt over her plate as she observed their progress, satisfied.

At last Ashford stood up and offered his hand to Emily. After only a slight hesitation she accepted, and he drew her smoothly to her feet.

"Mrs. Edgeworth, I do believe what Miss Fairfax needs is an evening at the theater."

"Is it tonight? Is this Wednesday?"

"Yes, of course. The new St. John play—"

"No, no! It is next week, is it not? Next Wednesday, not tonight," Emily cried.

"It's tonight," Ashford confirmed. "What do you think, Miss Letty? Do you think your sister should go to the theater tonight, or spend a fashionable week abed?"

"I agree with you, sir. The theater is the thing," she replied, delighted to be included in such an important decision. Her eyes sparkled as she looked at Ashford, so strong and so very alive in the breakfast room.

"And what think you, Miss Fairfax?"

What did she think? That she was nervous and excited. That she hoped he would find pleasure in her play. And maybe all would be well.

"Perhaps an evening at the theater is just the thing," she agreed with hesitation. "As long as it is a decent play."

"It is the new one by Edgar St. John," Caroline said. "I have seen one or two of his works, and they are quite amusing. Not as brilliant as Shakespeare, of course."

"Of course," Ashford nodded in agreement.

"But decent enough in a small way."

"How small?" Emily asked.

"Quite small. Now I must see to the children," Caroline concluded. "Mr. Ashford, we are delighted that you are in such good health, sir."

"Thank you. And I do hope to see you this evening at the Olympic."

"Perhaps," she smiled, and with a gracious nod she stepped away from the table. "Good morning," she curtseyed.

He bowed, "Good morning."

Then it was just the three of them.

"I must go." He plucked his hat from the table. "Business and all."

"Mr. Ashford?" Letty asked. "How on earth did you discover that rumor about you being dead so early this morning?"

He took his gaze from Emily, then stepped over to Letty and placed his top hat upon her head.

"Does it suit me?"

"Perfectly," he answered, tilting it so that it didn't cover her eyes. "I learned of the rumor quite early indeed, when an undertaker called to apply for the job."

"How gruesome!" Letty declared with approval.

"Yes, it was." He then removed his hat from Emily's head. "Good God, I do believe I should go round and let Ogilvie know it was a rumor. His coachman is a good friend of Addleston's."

"Run, then," Emily said with unmistakable affection.

"I shall. Until tonight," he bowed. She watched as he tapped Letty on the top of her head and left.

"I like him," Letty said. "I'm ever so glad he's alive."

"So am I, Letty. So am I."

Letty waited until everyone in the house was occupied with their own activities. Uncle George left for his office, wherever that was. Caroline went out to do some marketing with one of her maids.

The boys and the baby were upstairs making a racket, and Emily, well, she just seemed out of sorts and confused.

This was the perfect time, then, to sneak out and see Fanny. After all, no one bothered to tell her Fanny had come over for a visit the day before. Furthermore, they hadn't given her any news at all about Fanny and Robert. So it was up to Letty herself to check on her.

There was an element of excitement to the adventure. It wasn't too far to Fanny's house, but it was London. Anything could happen, she thought with glee. How shocking to think of a twelve-year-old girl out alone in town! How Caroline would cry, and Emily become furious!

That alone made it all worthwhile.

It was almost too easy to slip out of the front door. "Really," she mumbled as she descended the steps to the street, pausing by the cast-iron boot scraper to remove imaginary clumps of mud from her shoes. "They should take much better care of me. This is nothing short of irresponsible."

And then she was on her way. The freedom was glorious! She saw all sorts of sights, people of all colors in every manner of dress imaginable. There was a vendor selling fruit tarts, and she made a mental note to pass that way upon her return.

The shops were marvelous, all of them seemed to be filled with splendid window decorations that gave little indication of what was sold within. A draper's shop had a large crystal bowl filled with glass orbs of all sorts of colors for no reason, she supposed, other than it was pretty. An apothecary had dozens of fascinating-looking vials, with a sign that leeches were available within. Letty thought it capital to be able to walk into a shop and buy as many leeches as one could want.

No one seemed to think it unusual to see a young girl out on her own. And then, all too soon—for she was having a wonderful time—Letty was at Fanny's house.

The same sense of gloom came over her as before at the sight of the somber, sad-looking town house. All of the shades were drawn, as usual. But she squared her shoulders and marched straight to the front door.

She was just about to knock, when a loud noise from within stopped her. It sounded as if someone had broken some pottery, or dropped a stack of plates.

"No, I won't!" It was Fanny's voice, Letty was sure.

Then she heard a male voice. Robert, no doubt. Letty glanced behind her to make sure no one was watching, then pressed her ear to the door.

"Yes, you will, hag. I need more information. It will be a small thing for you to tell me of his visits to your sisters and brother-in-law." Robert's voice was so strange-sounding, harsh and ragged.

"You had something to do with the assault on him, did you not?" Letty was surprised by the strength in Fanny's tone. "And it did not succeed, so you will try again. Your vile associates want Mr. Ashford silenced, so again you will do their bidding. So now you will have blood on your hands."

"That is not your business."

"Yes it is! Robert, please. Save yourself, save us. There is no shame in admitting financial failure. No moral disgrace. I'm sure my family can help us."

"Do you think I want that pompous Edgeworth to know anything about us?"

"I'm sure he knows more than you imagine. I'm certain everyone knows."

"Be quiet!"

"Very well, then. But I will warn them of you, of what you have become. I will tell Mr. Ashford that—" Then her words were cut off by what sounded like a slap.

Suddenly Letty felt as if she would become ill. All thoughts of a pleasant visit or shop windows or fruit tarts left her. Now she just wanted to get back to Caroline's home. She wanted to tell them all about Fanny. They could get her out of there, away from that monster.

Already in her mind he was no longer Uncle Robert. He was a beast.

Suddenly she was feeling far from safe herself. Without further thought, she ran as fast as she could, her bonnet flying off without her caring, the soles of her slippers wearing thin. Nothing mattered but to get away from that horrible place.

Chapter Eleven

❧

Emily did indeed sleep for most of the afternoon, an exhausted, dreamless slumber for which she was thankful. It wasn't until she awoke from the sleep that she realized how very fatigued the previous day and a half had left her, how her spirits rose and fell with such great frequency, and to such great depths and heights, that she was amazed she was able to wake up at all.

But wake she did. And with a nervousness she had never known, she began to dress for the theater.

There was a faint knock on her door while she was deciding on gloves. "Yes, come in," she said.

It was Letty. "Em? Can I tell you something?"

"Oh, Letty, you are nowhere near dressed! Your hair is a fright."

"Yes. Em, can I tell you something serious?"

"Of course, but may we talk later? Tell me, which gloves do you think will go with—Letty?"

She had turned to leave the room.

"Letty? Pray, do come back. We can have our talk now if you wish."

"No. I guess it can wait." She smiled.

"We'll have more time later," Emily began. "Letty, would you like to wear one of my necklaces?"

"No thank you. I'll get ready now." And then she stepped out of the room.

Puzzled, Emily stared at the closed door. It was probably something about a hat, or perhaps one of the boys had said something nasty, as boys tended to do. They would sort it out later, after tonight.

How odd it was to be dressing for her own play!

It was her work, *The Reluctant Rogue,* and yet the only people in the world who knew her identity were Letty, Ogilvie and, of course, Lucius Ashford.

Given a choice, those were the three people she would have selected for such an honor. That is, if knowing the playwright could ever be considered an honor. From what she had heard of playwrights, they were a thoroughly disreputable lot, given to drink and debauchery.

At least all of the very best ones were.

She had heard amusing anecdotes concerning Mr. Richard Brinsley Sheridan, a fellow Irishman, former MP and onetime owner of the Drury Lane, who wrote plays such as *The School for Scandal* and *The Rivals.* Several years earlier, his theater, the splendid Drury Lane, burned to the ground. Everyone in town, especially Sheridan himself, knew it meant his certain financial ruin.

He watched the flames from the safety of a window in a nearby Covent Garden coffeehouse. When someone suggested that witnessing leaping flames engulf his life's passion, watching his very future turn to ashes in the inferno, might not be a prudent idea, he replied, "May not a man be allowed to drink a glass of wine by his own fireside?"

Emily thought of him as she dressed, wondering if he might even be in the audience that evening. If so, perhaps he would applaud her words. Maybe even wish to seek out the author.

Vain, silly thought. One she was certain all playwrights experience, the same thoughts she used to have when her plays were only for the amusement of her sisters and on occasion—if the gazettes were late—her father.

Would the play be any good? She tried to keep the amusing scenes in, removing the character of Sir Luscious Ash-Heap altogether. Perhaps it may not be quite as comical, but she was rather pleased how her hurridly written replacement had turned out.

Indeed, she recalled laughing out loud as she scratched the words on the paper, dipping the ink from bottle to bottle as she raced through the writing.

And now there was nothing she could do but sit in the audience and judge the play, just as everyone else would be doing.

How odd it would be to watch one of her works, ideas from her own mind, performed by professionals, by seasoned actors who knew precisely what they were doing.

How odd, and thrilling.

Her only hope was that the minor play would live up to the expert production Mr. Elliston of the Olympic was certain to provide. Her only hope was not to be embarrassed before Letty, Lord Ogilvie and, most especially, Lucius Ashford.

Henry Hughes was beyond terrified.

Terror was what he felt when he first arrived at the Olympic that afternoon and discovered that Julian Nichols, the play's solid second lead, had come down with an inflammation of his throat. Throughout the rehearsals he had seemed invincible, a real trouper, as the others said. An actor who had not missed a performance or a line in over thirty years.

But now his voice was gone, vanished. Nichols had been his foil from the very start. But on this night, when he needed him the most, he was below sipping a hot whiskey and lemon and allowing the new actress from Perth to rub his feet.

Elliston himself would play the part, which meant that Hughes would actually be sharing a stage with his most severe critic.

That was terror.

In the ensuing hours, he discovered that nerves had caused him to pass wind. This had never happened before, although he had laughed along with everyone else when some new young actor would suffer that peculiar symptom of stage fright. Unfortunately, the acoustics at the Olympic Theatre were excellent. The audience would be regaled with his nerves as far back as the last seat in the last row of the top balcony.

That was terror.

But as he applied his stage paint, he heard that Edmund Kean was to be in the audience. Kean himself.

Hughes stared at his reflection as he drew his brows darker and lined the rim of his frightened-looking eyes with black.

Kean had been a success but a few months, after years of struggle as a strolling player, just like himself. Hughes had grandly announced that the name Henry Hughes would soon be on everybody's lips.

Unfortunately, that was likely to be the case when the audience stormed the box office to demand a return of the ticket price.

Now Kean would be there to watch him, to judge and appraise him, as he had done when Kean played Shylock. How amazing it had been, Kean as Shylock! An absolute revelation. He shouted lines that were usually uttered softly, he mumbled words usually shouted. It was topsy-turvy and passionate, bringing new life to a role etched out hundreds of years earlier. His was not a classical performance, a clear reading of a speech the way the greats of the last century had performed. Instead the story seemed to be unfolding as he watched, as if the audience were interlopers witnessing the events from behind an invisible wall. There was no posturing, no posing like a Greek statue.

In a matter of minutes, it would be Henry

Hughes on the stage, with Kean in the audience.

He imagined catching a glimpse of Kean's glowing eyes. And then his imagination took him further, to what would happen next. His mind would become free of every word and action in the play. The prompter offstage would shout his lines. Other actors would be forced to take over his part to see the play through.

Henry Hughes had left the realm of terror long ago. For the rampaging, bowel-loosening, vomit-inducing panic he was experiencing at the moment, there was, as far as he knew, no name.

Emily came down the stairs slowly, careful not to trip on the delicate lace hem of her new gown or slip on the smooth soles of her fragile slippers.

Caroline and George were already in their outer cloaks; Letty, in her cape of peach, was uncharacteristically quiet.

This was the first time Emily had worn the gown, and she was well pleased with how it had turned out. She hadn't been sure. When Madame Tellier had first shown her the fabric and sketched out a pattern, she had been dubious at best.

But Madame Tellier, known as Bridget Murphy when she was growing up in Cork, had a keen eye and had known Emily for years, ever since she had been her mother's own seamstress. The pairing of a gauzy yellow with a pale blue satin overdress was absolutely stunning, and very unusual. It was puckered above the waist, and both the neck and back were scooped low, to display Emily's lovely throat and back. Small ruffles of off-white lace rimmed the neckline and the length of the overdress. Her hair, piled high with loose ringlets framing her face, was fastened with small satin flowers of the same blue satin fabric and a few curling ribbons.

"Great Lord," George exclaimed. "You are a treasure!"

"Are those lace sleeves?" Caroline scrutinized her arms. "You may very well regret it if those are lace sleeves. Sleeves at all are something of a concern. Lace sleeves are an absolute controversy."

"You are quite right, my dear," George agreed. "I believe that very issue is to be taken up in Parliament next session."

"If it is any consolation, the sleeves are of a very sheer muslin. I do not believe that anyone in their right mind would dare to call them lace." Emily allowed her sisters to touch the fabric.

"If I even hear the word 'lace' used in reference to those sleeves, I vow to call the liar out," George said with a flourish. "Besides, as you ladies know, no one looks at the women anymore in society. All that matters is what the gentlemen are wearing. Did you know that Beau Brummell will only polish his boots with the froth of champagne? A waste of champagne, I say."

Caroline did not seem to hear her husband. "Well, your gown is quite beautiful, whatever it is," she admitted, closing her own roomy cape more tightly about her. "Will you wear a pelisse?"

"Just a wrap Bridget made from the same blue satin," she replied, feeling very self-conscious, and wondering if Lucius would approve of the way she looked.

"Oh dear," Caroline sighed. "Well, perhaps you had best take the corner seat, the one by the column. Perhaps slightly behind it."

"Thank you, Caro. That will set my mind at ease."

She could not help but smile. Caroline was trying out her society manners, and they did not become her.

"Will Fanny be at the play? Or her husband?" Letty whispered when they settled into the carriage.

"What was that? Could you please speak up?" George asked.

"Letty was wondering if Fanny and Robert will be in attendence tonight," Emily repeated.

"We did send a note round to their house," Caroline answered. "I forgot to mention it to her the other day. But I never did receive a response."

"Oh," Letty looked out of the window.

And with a jolt and a bump, they were off.

There were so many carriages already wedged and packed into the small amount of space in front of the Olympic, the Edgeworth vehicle was forced to park quite a distance away. And the carriages were beyond lavish! They were painted in every color imaginable, and a few beyond that. There were britskas and curricles, high phaetons and glorious tilburys.

"Dear me," muttered Caroline. "My shoes will simply not tolerate this mud or the loose cobbles."

"Uncle George should carry you," Letty suggested.

"Uncle George would not stand upright for a week," he said to no one in particular.

"George! How very ungallant of you!" Caroline cried.

"It was not a comment about you, I am sure," Emily interjected. "I believe it was an all-too-honest declaration on George's lack of physical . . . well, you know what I mean."

George laughed. "Go ahead, dear sister. Say it."

"What do you wish me to say, sir?"

"That you have seen better physical specimens hanging in the window of the butcher shop."

"Better preserved, at any rate," she nudged him.

"Well said," he agreed. "But speaking of physical specimens, I heard something of interest at the club today."

"The club, the club. Always the club," Caroline moaned. "Oh dear. It seems a very large and healthy horse recently passed by here. Mind your shoes, Letty."

"At any rate," he continued. "It seems the rumor circulating about Ashford this morning was not far off the mark."

"What mean you?" Caroline asked.

"He was indeed set upon by three men. And they did stab him on the left shoulder, quite deeply, I understand. His arm may even be in a sling tonight, although he refused one this afternoon when it was giving him some pain."

"Heavens! Did Ashford himself say this? He seemed perfectly fine when he appeared this very morning. But now that I reflect on it, he did seem to favor the left hand." His wife stepped over another puddle.

"Of course he would favor that hand. But in any case, Ashford would say nothing of the event. No, the three men themselves admitted it. They were found quite insensible this morning, baking in the sun by the park. He took all three on, and broke one of the men's jaw."

"To whom did they admit this?" Emily asked.

"This is the curious part—to none other than dear Fanny's husband."

"Robert? How very odd." Emily grabbed Letty before she stepped in front of a horse.

Letty stared down at the stones. "What did he say?"

"He happened upon the unfortunate trio, and had them sent to Newgate. They were saying all sorts of ridiculous things, as criminals do when they wish to save their own skin."

"But I have a question. Did—" Letty began, only to be cut off by Caroline.

"Here we are! Now remember, we take the other door. We are not in general seating, for we have a box."

The crowd was uncomfortably close as they took their place outside and slowly filed into the theater.

A lone young man with a frantic expression was directing the patrons. "Pit or gallery? Box or pit?" he called as they passed.

The single door open for the pit audience was jammed, and the doors for the box holders was only slightly less packed. Hems were torn as feet trod unintentionally on gowns; feathers and ribbons were jostled from hats and hair. Yet there was no sense of distress or irritation. Everyone was in an amiable mood.

Emily took in every sight and sound, the stray bits of conversation, the brilliantly colored posters declaring *The Reluctant Rogue*. Then, in smaller letters, "A New Play by Master Edgar St. John."

Emily bit her lip. No one had ever called her a master before.

The interior was filled with gaudy but, upon closer examination, rather cheaply made decorations. Gold-painted wood was applied to resemble expensive molding, at least from a respectable distance. The floors, from what briefly viewed patches could be seen through the fleeting crowd, were etched and drawn to mimic inlay. On several walls were lavish, swooping drapes of rich red velvet. It was absurdly exravagant, ridiculously lavish, and, in fact, utterly fake. The yards and yards of cloth were simply cleverly painted flat plaster walls.

The entire building was made to resemble a grand country house, which it was not, inhabited by wealthy nobles, which it most definitely was not. The theater was layer upon layer of joyful deception, as everyone there knew. And that, of course, was a good part of the amusement. Everything beyond the threshold was false. Reality was left behind for the duration of the evening.

They had no difficulty locating their box, which was the first box in the first row to the left of the stage, first tier. There were no obstructions to their view, no shadows or blind spots. Only the one column Caroline instructed Emily to sit behind.

As they settled into their chairs, with the three sisters in the front and seats for the men directly behind them, Caroline turned to George with excitement.

"Dear, could you please fetch us some refreshments?"

He obliged, taking orders like the most accomplished of waiters. Although it was but a little after six, Caroline asked for champagne and cakes and perhaps a savory or two.

"You must try the lemon ice. It gets quite warm during the play." Caroline looked around with satisfaction as her husband left. Theirs was certainly one of the best boxes in the theater. "You may yet regret those sleeves, Em."

"Well, it's a bit too late now." The pit was already filled with the less exalted classes, some dining on entire joints of meat, others enjoying rather bawdy dalliances with other members of the pit audience. Also in the pit were the dandies, the young bucks dressed to the hilt and anticipating the most merry of entertainments, regardless of the play. They were having a marvelous time, some faced away from the stage, their backs turned solidly away from the juggler who just appeared. Others were shouting or singing or pouring wines and ales from great skin jugs.

Part of Emily wanted very much to be down below, and she laughed along with everyone else when a woman in a rather flimsy and very low-cut frock poured a full measure of wine atop the head of an overly ardent admirer.

The audience in the boxes was of a vastly different breed from those below, almost a different species, in all ways imaginable. Even in the late afternoon light, the sparkle and blinding flash of jewels seemed to dance across the whole theater, blinding some patrons, fascinating some of the rather unsavory creatures in the pit. The women were elegant; the men—some of them in knee-britches, as if going to court—were well pleased with themselves.

Emily allowed her shawl to slip against the back of the cushioned chair. Now she could better observe the people in the other boxes, many faces familiar from Lady Duff's levee, and many faces familiar from the calls. She saw Lady Jersey, a woman not much liked but certainly feared, and the lovely Lady Conyngham, declared by the French to be the most handsome woman in Europe. In the center box, first row, was Lady Caroline Lamb, her dark hair cut short as a boy's, her slender, elfin figure covered in an exquisite gown of silk. But her celebrated beauty seemed off, her behavior frantic rather than lively. She was speaking with great animation to the gentleman beside her, a well-dressed young man who was certainly neither her husband nor her famous ex-lover, Lord Byron.

Beau Brummell arrived at a box three down, and she watched in fascination as he flipped open a small box and indulged in a pinch of snuff, using only his right hand. The left remained immobile, in languid, elegant repose.

How long had he practiced that particular motion, Emily wondered.

The boxes were almost full, the ladies and gentlemen nodding and smiling, some with quizzing glasses peering blatantly, without shame, at everyone other than the performer—now a lady singer—on the stage. They gave the distinct impression of having someplace else to be, of bestowing their presence out of their own kindness rather than their own amusement.

"Is it always this crowded?" Emily asked Caroline.

But another voice answered. "It is because of the playwright," Ashford explained, slipping her shawl back about her shoulders. "Edgar St. John is quite popular. Directly opposite us is Edmund Kean. He's here because the Drury Lane is closed until autumn, so he observes his competition with his usual contempt."

"Which one is he?" Letty stood up to get a better view.

"I'm afraid he is that rather shifty-looking fellow in bad need of a shave. He's taking a swallow from a bottle now. And dribbling most of it down his chin."

"That's Edmund Kean?" Emily said with disappointment.

"I assure you, he is much more impressive on the stage than he is in the audience."

"He has strange eyes," Emily concluded. "Dark and conniving."

"Yes," he agreed. "I would gladly pay to see him again in Shakespeare, but I wouldn't want him within thirty paces of my pocket or the second-best silver."

"Mr. Ashford!" Caroline held out her hand. "Delightful to see you! My, I have heard such exciting things about you and about your unfortunate adventure last night. You held out on us, sir, this morning. Why, it was far more thrilling than you led us to believe!"

"Was it?" He looked directly at Emily, and she shook her head very slightly.

"Everyone is talking about it. My husband, of course, heard it all at the club."

"It must have been an extraordinarily slow day at the club." Ashford sat in his own seat just behind Emily.

"Thank goodness you survived," Caroline continued. "Three men! You conquered three men! And look, not even a sling. Why, when you came round this morning we had no idea of what an ordeal you had endured."

"They were rather small men, sickly as well. I'm sure Miss Letty could have performed the same deed. Look—on the stage. The play is about to begin."

Emily turned to Ashford, and he smiled. "Good evening, Miss Fairfax. You are looking remarkably well tonight. Very pretty dress."

"Good evening, Mr. Ashford. Thank you. You, too, are looking well. No slashes on the jacket. Neckcloth white. Very well-thought-out attire."

"I thought I would try something different," he said dryly.

Just then Lord Ogilvie stepped into the box to whisper good luck to Emily, and to exchange a few pleasantries with everyone else in the box.

"Now I must attend to Miss Lloyd," he said miserably.

"I thought you swore you would rather dine on arsenic than pass another evening in Miss Lloyd's company?" Ashford asked.

"There was no arsenic to be had at such short notice," Ogilvie admitted. "Believe me, it was not for want of trying."

"Who is Miss Lloyd?" Emily asked.

"The question is more accurately phrased as 'What is Miss Lloyd?'" Ogilvie then pointed to a box on the second row. "Do you see the woman with the beautiful eyes? The dark glossy hair with two ostrich feathers? Tight gown? Figure beyond compare?"

"I do! Good gracious, sir, Miss Lloyd is lovely!"

"That is not Miss Lloyd. Miss Lloyd is the large woman next to her with the overly large ears and the strangely pin-sized head. She's waving at me. Can you see the size of her hands? Enormous. She can tear the head off a rampaging tiger with those things. I am now waving back. I fear those hands."

"Oh," Emily stammered. "Miss Lloyd seems very nice. Very nice indeed."

"Yes, well," Ogilvie bowed as he left. "She is quite handy to have about when one throws a carriage wheel. Or needs large furniture shifted. Good evening, ladies, Ashford," and then again, to Emily, "good luck!"

George arrived with the refreshments, which delighted Letty and Caroline.

And then the play began.

Emily took a deep breath as the curtain rose.

On the stage was the solitary figure of a young man in the ridiculous, exaggerated costume of a modern dandy.

"My name is Sir Luscious Ash-Heap," he proclaimed as he minced about the stage in a small circle. There was a slight pause, then the entire audience swiveled to see the box where Ashford sat.

No! This was all wrong! There was no Ash-Heap in the play! She had taken that out, along with all of the other elements that could harm Ashford.

Behind her she heard nothing, only silence.

The actor continued, his face illuminated with an eerie greenish cast because of the new gas lamps in the wings.

His voice grew stronger. "And it is my solemn, God-given duty to prevent every duel in England, Ireland, Scotland, Wales, the Americas, the Continent . . ."

He paused, and there was an enormously loud, crude bodily sound.

The audience in the pits roared their approval, the boxes were laughing delightedly.

Then he continued, as if pleased with his own words, relishing his own self, oblivious to the audience's response.

". . . . Africa, Australia and the Poles. North and South, not Warsaw and Krakow . . ."

Emily stared at the stage without blinking, stunned by what she was seeing.

The monologue continued, but she was no longer concentrating on the play. Her entire being was focused on Lucius, inches away from her, so close she could feel his breath on the back of her neck.

The action seemed to fall into a jumble of farce and comedy. The actor in the Ash-Heap role grew larger by the moment, enveloping the entire theater with the absurd, fully-formed character. Just when it seemed Ash-Heap would dissolve into the realm of unbelievability, the actor would give him a human gesture, a shrug or a brief look of sadness, even those terrible body sounds gave the character an almost touching humanity.

It seemed very real, this silly play. There was an element of truth that drew the audience to its feet again and again.

She was afraid to turn around to Ashford, but she looked over at Ogilvie several times. Miss Mary Lloyd was laughing heartily, her large hands clapping over the rail of the box. Lord Ogilvie was very still, and once their eyes met, and Emily looked away, ashamed.

The breath on the back of her neck seemed to blow hotter, and with more frequency. At one point a line was said, Emily no longer cared, and everyone in the audience, almost everyone, turned to their box and laughed. The hilarity was so thick, so constant, it felt as if the entire building would float to the sky.

There was no break in the play. No pause between acts, and even through her misery she realized that the manager did not want to interrupt the momentum. Never before had she heard of this done; the play ran straight through.

As an audience member, she thought the ploy brilliant. As the playwright who had much to apologize for, she thought every moment excruciating.

And still he sat, saying nothing.

Then came the most dreadful moment of all.

Ash-Heap was seducing a fair maiden. It was dandyism at its very worst, most flagrant, and offensive. Ash-Heap had been accidentally wounded by stopping a duel, and the fair maiden was attempting to bind his minor wounds. And somehow, the entire scene played like an obscene parody of what had transpired between them the night before.

Emily no longer cared what was happening on the stage. All she cared about was Ashford. She could feel him behind her as the scene progressed, hear a slight sound as he shifted in the chair. When the applause grew loud and furious after the scene ended, she slowly turned to speak to him, to say something, anything.

The chair was empty. Ashford was gone.

But the play had two more scenes to go. By the end the audience was cheering. The actors came for their call, and when the actor who played Ash-Heap appeared, he was pelted by the people in the pit.

Pelted with flowers.

The actor started to make a speech when another actor with thick lips pulled him off. Still, the roars continued. Across the theater, Ogilvie's box was empty.

George, Caroline and Letty were strangely silent as they made their way through the lobby to their carriage. Everyone else was laughing, repeating their favorite lines. Some were even hoping for the ticket box to open, so they could secure more tickets.

Once or twice Letty looked up at Emily, confusion in her eyes. "I thought you liked him," she said once, when George and Caroline were walking ahead. "I thought you said you replaced the nasty play with a nice one."

"I did! And I do like him. Very much." She barely recognized her own voice. It was broken, rough.

"Oh, Em," Letty all but cried. "How could you?"

She wanted to accuse her youngest sister, who had sent the play without her permission. She longed to blame Ashford himself for prompting her to write such a play. Elliston who had not used the revised play.

She wanted to blame everyone, anyone.

But there was no defense. For she alone had written it. It was indeed her fault for putting pen to paper and not burning it at once, back in Ireland.

Letty was right. How could she?

When they reached the carriage, Caroline finally spoke. "I confess, I did not enjoy it at all. It was mean-spirited, cruel. Poor Mr. Ashford. I did espy his face before he left, and he seemed most upset."

"Angry?" George asked.

"No. That was the curious part. He seemed wounded, hurt. As if he had been betrayed."

The carriage began to roll forward, and Emily allowed her forehead to rest against the side of the window. The wind dried her tears as they rolled down her face.

"Who is this Mr. St. John? And why does he dislike Mr. Ashford so?" Caroline was indignant.

"I know not," replied George, without his usual good humor. "But I vow, if I were Ashford, I would call him out by dawn."

"George! You would never!"

"I would, if I were Ashford. As it is, I have half a mind to do it myself. Ladies, you were all witness to something terrible tonight."

"What was that?" Letty asked softly.

"You just saw an attack more vicious than the one he suffered last night."

Emily heard him. And with great despair, she realized he was absolutely right.

Fate would have been kinder had he indeed been killed the previous night.

Henry Hughes could not feel the ground beneath him.

This was one of those rare moments when the actual event surpassed the years of dreaming, of hoping and praying such a moment as this would happen.

From the second he stepped onstage, it had been a miracle. It was dazzling, perfect. The mistakes were perfect. Even when his stomach betrayed him during the first few lines, the effect was so tremendous that when he relaxed and the sounds no longer came, Elliston hurriedly retrieved the body noisemaker device he had created months before.

The only unfortunate moment occurred when Elliston prevented him from making a speech. But he could do that another time, another performance, another role.

He was backstage, surrounded by the cast and crew and the high-ranking audience members. Was that Lady Caroline Lamb, lisping sweetly into his ear? Brummell suggesting they lunch the next day?

Women were fawning over him—not barmaid sluts but women of quality. Next to him was a stunningly beautiful creature with two feathers in her hair and a radiant smile. Could he dine with her soon?

"Of course," he bowed.

Then someone was shaking his hand with too much vigor. It hurt. He turned to pull away, and there he was. Edmund Kean. He was saying something about comedy being so difficult. About the true worth of an actor being found not in the lines of a play, but in the lines of his face. About humanity filtering through, of touching emotional truth and that, sir, defines comedy.

Hughes just nodded.

Elliston handed him a silk pouch filled with coin. He accepted it, stunned, delirious.

So on a whim, he did the most logical thing he could think of. He invited everyone to his favorite pub for drinks. Jingling his coins, he added the first round was on him.

More cheers, more praise. Several ladies told him they thought he was the most handsome man in London. The most handsome man anywhere.

This was far better than any dream. For this, he knew, was his destiny.

Chapter Twelve

Lucius Ashford dismissed his man Addleston the moment he reached his rooms. He did not simply want to be alone. He wanted to be the only human being on the entire planet.

"Are you sure you require no brandy, sir? You look rather off, begging your pardon."

"No, Addleston. I fear there is no brandy strong enough for what I really need." He untied his stock and tossed it to the floor.

Addleston frowned and picked it up, smoothing it against his forearm. Then Ashford began to remove his jacket. When Addleston reached over to help, Ashford pushed him away.

With his good arm he shrugged off the sleeve, but with the left arm it stuck, and the jacket fell away with the lining pulled out from the cuff.

Ashford kicked it across the room.

"Sir!" Addleston exclaimed. "That is super-fine!"

"Then let it be damned."

Addleston blanched. It was one thing to curse the French, a racehorse, a bad shipment of Bordeaux or a badly misplayed hand of cards. It was another thing altogether to curse an expertly tailored superfine wool jacket.

Making himself as inconspicuous as possible, Addleston walked stiffly to the abused garment and cradled it in his arms.

"You may leave now," Ashford ordered.

Hadn't he already dismissed him?

The man remained in place, silent and unyielding.

"I said you may leave now," Ashford repeated tersely.

Again, Addleston stood with military stiffness, as if no words had been spoken.

Ashford glared, then began to unbutton his shirt, only using his right hand. The left shoulder had started to throb again.

The buttons were stuck.

After spending what seemed to be hours on the first button, Addleston stepped forward.

"Get away," growled Ashford.

The man did not reply.

It took another unreasonably long span of time to undo the second button, and with one ferocious pull he ripped the linen from his body.

"Savage!" panted Addleston.

"You may wish to avert your eyes," Ashford warned. "I am particularly furious at the trousers."

"Sir, please see reason," he pleaded.

"Haven't I dismissed you?"

"I did not hear you, sir."

With a malicious twist, Ashford began to turn

the top button on his pantaloons. Harder and harder, his teeth gritted into an unpleasant smirk.

"Please, please," Addleston begged to no avail. Desperation had caused his voice to rise to a high-pitched shrill. "You will ruin the line! They will never again fall right, never. They will pucker and bunch. You are stretching the fabric, sir!"

Ashford continued twisting the button.

Then the manservant tried a different tack. With a false air of calm, he began conversationally, "Have I ever told you about my friend who runs the opium den near Haymarket?"

The button popped off.

"Very well," Addleston said. "I refuse to be a party to this any longer. I am leaving. But sir, I warn you—I am taking with me your three best jackets and four pantaloons. They will be returned unharmed when I am confident they will be safe."

"Good night, Addleston." Ashford closed his eyes and slumped into a chair.

"Sir?"

"Yes, Addleston."

"It is none of my business . . ."

"It never is."

"But the play will not succeed."

His eyes opened. "What did you say?"

"The play will pass. It is no good, sir. *The Reluctant Rogue* will not last."

"How did you hear about it?"

"A friend of mine has a brother who works in the public house where Mr. Elliston, the manager, frequently drinks. He is quite mad. Furthermore, the actor who plays the lead is just about as mad. The two of them together will ruin it. Mark my words."

"Well, thank you, Addleston."

"Good night, sir."

The servant left the room silently. From the next room came a thumping, then a clicking. The sound of a lid slamming shut.

"What are you doing?" Ashford asked.

"Sir, I am taking your better clothes, as I stated previously. I am having some trouble with your trunk."

"Do you need a hand?"

"No, sir. I have it now. Good night."

He heard the sound of Addleston dragging the heavy trunk down the hallway and bumping up the short flight of stairs to his own room.

Then he was alone.

"Work," he said aloud. That is what he needed to concentrate on. Work. His speech. Helping people who so richly deserved to be helped.

Not rich people who deserved nothing.

Perhaps a glass of brandy would help.

He walked over to the sideboard and poured himself a snifter. Then, tilting the lead crystal decanter, he added another hefty splash.

Usually he avoided too much brandy, for it tended to make him numb. Now that was what he most wished for, numbness. To end the pain. Not of his shoulder, but of his heart.

How could he have been such a damned idiot?

He should have known the moment he saw her galloping over the field in Ireland, blinking at him with those blasted eyes, smiling with that ridiculously crooked smile of hers.

Only slightly crooked, he amended. Not askew enough to mar her beauty, to blemish her in any way. Indeed, the trifling curve was devilishly attractive. And her lips were so soft, so warm—

"Enough!" He hadn't meant to shout. But it felt good. Damned good.

"Sir?" Addleston cried from the other side of the closed door.

"Go away," Ashford mumbled.

"I am away, sir," Addleston mumbled back.

"Then go farther away." Taking another sip of brandy, he again fell heavily into his favorite chair. It was an old battered thing that most people with any pride would have abandoned long ago, but Ashford loved it. It was his. It was honest and true and could never be accused of betrayal on any level.

The brandy burned as it traced down his throat, and he could feel it in his stomach, spreading out like warm fingers.

Then he remembered he hadn't eaten. He had planned to sup with Emily after the play.

He took another swallow.

Maybe this was all for the best, for he had an inkling that he would have asked her to be his wife tonight. He would have gone down on one blasted bended knee and asked her to spend the rest of her damned life with him. The rest of his Goddamned bloody life.

Of course he would have phrased it differently.

Another sip.

And then, next season, he would see a humorous rendition of their wedding night performed with sound effects. Pure comedy, with tragic undertones only Ashford himself would find remotely tragic. The audience and the playwright would be howling with laughter. It would be yet another great play by Edgar St. John. Master Edgar St. John.

Master indeed.

Master of misery. Master of deception and betrayal.

"Ogilvie should have shot her when he had the chance," he said into the snifter.

Then he poured himself another.

After he left the theater, Ogilvie caught up with him, muttering some nonsense about the play being a mistake, a grave error. That Emily had not meant it for the public, that she had written it for her own amusement (how he could imagine her laughing at her own cursed wit!), that Letty sent it to London without her permission.

But it mattered not.

The material point was that Emily had, indeed, written the words, lampooned him in such a manner as to make him ridiculous.

So this had been her real response to his confessional letter.

So now he knew, without a doubt, her genuine sentiments.

When was the last time he felt like this? Certainly not when the affair with Cecily Trevor ended. That was a painless conclusion to an almost painless liaison. There had been a few bad moments, of course. When it turned out her husband was still alive, that was a bit of a bump. And then when he learned her other lover was his good friend from school. That, too, had been awkward, but in the end they all laughed about it and Cecily's husband finally did pop off, and she married an elderly duke.

There had been other affairs, of course, other loves. At least experiences that he mistook for love, which in the moment can be much more agreeable than the real thing. And in the long run, was certainly much more enjoyable and much less painful.

That he had fallen in love with Miss Emily Fairfax was not even a question. He knew he had. He was aware of it from the very beginning, with the same sinking certainty one knows an arm is broken, or a rowboat has sprung a leak. That was the precise feeling. It had happened. Then, after accepting the event, he was forced to cope with all of the ramifications.

The vexing part was that it wasn't necessarily her most attractive traits that charmed him so. It was not her money, for he had enough of his own. He did not live as if he had money, but he did. A lot of it.

It was not her position in society that enticed

him. Although she was firmly placed amongst the aristocracy, she was Irish.

One had to deduct for that, in all fairness.

Yes, she was beautiful, but not brilliantly so. She did not walk into a room and leave the place agog, unless, of course, she was wearing one of her sister's hats.

Or unless one knew her.

Hers was a more subtle beauty, one that seemed to come from her very core. It wasn't based on even features or a trim figure, although her figure, he was forced to admit, was his notion of perfection. But there was something more to her, so much more than conventional beauty. Her very being seemed to sparkle. Even without seeing her face, one would take her for comely. More than comely.

But what had truly done him in were her peculiarities, the characteristics that would send most men running. Most wise men, at any rate.

She was very close to being a bluestocking. She read too much, caught on to what she didn't initially understand far too quickly, and picked up jokes like a man. No coy games were employed to imitate shock or confusion.

Indeed she refused to be shocked, and furthermore refused to pretend she didn't comprehend the very issues that shocked most women. It was an unfashionable trait, bordering on the reckless. Furthermore, she only fainted when there was no significant audience, when she had absolutely nothing to gain by insensibility.

Most undesirable.

And she was not a snob. She spoke to everyone as an equal, from the postman to the Prince. She would invite Lucifer himself for tea if he happened to look a little peaked. Her crooked smile was not reserved for a few, but given to everyone, without charge.

Then there was her profession. The fact that she had one at all was remarkable. When she first announced that she was Edgar St. John, well. The little part of him that had not been in love with her during the previous few seconds fell in love with her then.

There were other things as well, important things.

And there was Letty.

How she reminded him of his own little sister. Elizabeth was just about Letty's age when she died, but she had been ill for so long, she seemed much older in many ways. Before her illness, though, she'd had the same spark, the same joy that Letty had in such abundance.

Emily had it, too. Usually.

Then an image came to his mind. It was of the expression on Letty's face during the play. She turned to him, their eyes met, and she understood. Letty knew the betrayal he felt, even if she did not understand the exact details, the precise emotions he was experiencing. In her eyes he saw compassion and confusion and above all, genuine friendship.

But Emily did not even bother to turn around. She sat rapt in her own creation, motionless, fascinated, no doubt. He had watched the back of her slender neck, observed the fine hairs curled against her nape.

He could even smell her, a light scent of flowers, a bouquet sent his way to tantalize him even when she was unaware of his existence.

Never again would he fall in love. It was not worth the pain.

She had made him the laughingstock of London, but that was not what plagued him so.

He realized soon after the play began that this was the long-awaited response to his letter. Now he had his answer.

What was tearing at his very soul was that the play showed precisely what she thought of him. The words were uncompromising, clever. Witty. But she made her point.

Emily Fairfax saw him as a vain, pompous idiot. A buffoon. She had mocked him with her tenderness. He had been close to revealing himself, so close to telling her that he loved her, that he could not imagine living without her by his side.

"Enough!" he shouted. This self-torture could not continue.

Thank God for that play. Without it, he may never have known. He would not have known that she had played him for the fool, for her own amusement all along.

"Damn it all!" He threw the snifter at the wall,

where it shattered into a hundred sharp, glimmering splinters. The last of the brandy slid down the wall in long, slithering talons.

There was a knock on his door.

"Sir?" Addleston called from the other side.

"Yes."

"I have come to collect the boots."

"The boots?"

"Yes, sir. The good riding boots with the turned down top. I wish to take possession of them until the danger has passed."

With a deep sigh, Ashford finally relaxed. It was over. "Very well. Take them."

"Thank you, sir," Addleston said as he entered the room, grabbed the boots, and started to leave. Then he stopped and, noticing the smashed snifter, took the remaining three and left.

"Good night," Ashford said aloud.

The farewell had not been to his manservant.

It had been to his dreams.

Emily's first instinct was to go back to Ireland immediately. To flee. To put as much land and sea between her and London as possible. That would be the easiest thing, the one that would require the least explaining. The solution that would be no solution at all, for she would always have herself to face.

How would she ever explain the play to herself, much less justify it to anyone else?

That was not the way out. That was not going to

ease the intense pain that seemed to envelop her. It enveloped everyone, for that matter.

It was a long, silent carriage ride back to Caroline's house. Nobody was in the mood to chat. The play that had been written to amuse herself had instead dampened countless spirits.

While she was undressing, she could envision Ashford's face. She was well aware that he was beginning to treat her very differently from other women. Although she had never experienced it before, she knew she had fallen in love with him, and he was falling in love with her.

A mere few hours ago, the world had seemed the most welcoming, wonderful of places. She could not wait until the next morning, until the next day, the next week. The future, she knew, would be filled with love and joy and happiness.

Because in the back of her mind, unwilling to admit it even to herself, she knew the future would be Ashford.

Now that had changed. Now she did not know how she would survive the next minute, much less the rest of her life. It was as if a horrible illness had overtaken her, a physical hurt that touched her very soul. It was painful to even breathe, a clamp of metal agony was tightening about her chest.

Caroline and Fanny would be proved right. She would be alone, rattling about in an echoing Fairfax Castle. Alone.

Splashing cold water on her face, she then

rubbed it hard with a towel, so her cheeks were painfully red. It was a small distraction. It served a purpose.

There was a light knock on the door.

"Yes?"

"It is me," Letty said.

"Come in," Emily replied, although she really didn't want to face Letty.

She was far too ashamed.

Letty opened the door slowly and stood for a moment, as if deciding whether or not to come in. Her hair was twisted into rags, just the way their mother used to twist their hair every night to create curls. Finally she came in and closed the door behind her.

But she remained silent.

"I know you are angry at me," Emily began.

"No. I'm not angry." Her voice was strangely composed. "I just don't understand why you wrote the play."

"Didn't you read the whole thing before sending it to Mr. Giles?"

Letty shook her head. "I just read the beginning. I didn't know the rest. So I too share the blame. I know that. Really, I do."

"Oh, Letty. No. I am the one to blame, the only one. I'm always telling you not to write down anything that would do you shame, and that is precisely what I did. It matters not that I did not intend this play for public viewing. I wrote it."

Letty frowned, and she opened her mouth. Then

closed it, pursing her lips as if to prevent herself from speaking.

"Please, go on," Emily urged.

"I think maybe Fanny is unhappy with Robert," she said.

"Were they at the play? I did not see them. Indeed I saw little after the opening lines." Emily was slightly perplexed by the abrupt change of topic.

"No. It's just that, well. Today, while you were resting before the play, I . . ." Then her voice petered out. "I went for a visit . . . I . . ." She slumped forward, as if suddenly weary. "I thought you liked him, Mr. Ashford, I mean," she said softly.

"I did." Then she corrected herself, sitting on the edge of the bed with the balled up towel in her hands. "I do like him."

"I thought you could help him. Emily, people want to hurt him."

"I know, last night—"

"But other people. And Fanny."

"Fanny? Letty, I don't understand what you are saying."

"I thought you liked Mr. Ashford!" Letty blurted again.

"I do like him. Very much indeed."

"Then why did you hurt him so?"

"I . . . I tried to stop it. And I thought I had, really. But that matters not, for this is the play everyone saw. And in the end, all that matters is that I did, indeed, write the thing." It was painful for her to speak. "I didn't intend to hurt him. To hurt anyone."

"But you did."

"I know," she tried to say, but the words failed to come out.

"I saw his face just before he left."

"You did?"

Letty nodded.

"What did he . . . I mean, how did he . . ."

"Do you remember when old Mr. Palmer's wife died? Papa had him come home with us after the funeral. I will never forget that, for Papa turned round to reach for a book on the library shelf to give him. It was some poetry book about love and loss. There were no pictures or drawings. While Papa's back was turned, Mr. Palmer looked at me."

Letty folded her arms, her face more grave and serious than Emily had ever seen it.

"Did he say anything?" Emily asked.

"Mr. Palmer? No. He just looked at me for the briefest of seconds. But I will never forget his face. I don't know how to describe it. It was grief, pain. His eyes seemed blank, as if he no longer expected anything from God or the world now that Mrs. Palmer was gone. Hopeless. That was it. He was hopeless. Hollow. And the expression Mr. Ashford had this evening, right before he left, it was the same look."

Emily looked down at the towel.

"But it was worse," Letty continued. "It was far

worse to see such an expression on someone so young as Mr. Ashford. Someone as alive, as funny and nice. Mr. Palmer was an old man, he had already lived a good life. He already had stored memories to look back on, to keep him company. To reflect upon when he sits alone in his chair. Mr. Ashford just looked alone. Empty."

At last Emily looked up, tears rolling down her cheeks.

Letty took a deep breath. "Well, good night," she said.

"Aren't you going to say anything?" Emily sobbed. "Aren't you going to tell me how awful I am? How ashamed you are of me?"

Letty walked to the door and placed her hand on the knob. She began to turn it.

"Please, Letty. Say something. Anything."

She spoke without turning around. "I don't need to."

"Why not?" Emily's voice shuddered, as if broken.

"Because now you have it too, Em. You're wearing the exact same expression."

Miss Emily Fairfax was indisposed for the next several days. No callers were admitted, and she attended no soirees or levees or balls, nor did she take a turn in the park or even poke her head out of the window of the Edgeworths' elegant home.

The rumors about town spread quickly. One was

that the suddenly famous Miss Fairfax had found city life too hectic, and she had retired once again to the family estate in Ireland. Another story that gained immediate popularity was that she had replaced the Ladies Conyngham and Jersey as the Prince Regent's favorite mistress. That story garnered further credibility when the Princess Charlotte appeared at an official function with a hat of gigantic proportions featuring a kangaroo and large portions of fruit.

This was clearly a design inspired if not created by Miss Letty Fairfax. Another rumor was that Miss Letty was not, in fact, a child of twelve, but a dwarf of thirty-eight. Anyone who observed Princess Charlotte's millinery wear realized at once that this was the work of a twelve-year-old.

Finally, there was the ever popular rumor that Miss Emily Fairfax was dead. That particular rumor was always employed when no one had a better story. By most accounts, the King himself had been declared dead so often, that when that tragic event did eventually occur, it would be something of an anticlimax.

All anyone knew was that Miss Emily Fairfax was indisposed. And in spite of all of the celebrations in London, of all the fetes and parades and fireworks, the extraordinary visits by European royalty, the magnificent displays to welcome a momentary peace, the summer itself was feeling very dull indeed.

* * *

Henry Hughes saw no end in sight for his meteoric success.

How glorious life had become! And how wonderful it was to be the center of all that glory!

In the past week he had been admitted into the finest houses in London. Not just admitted. Invited. Begged to show up and drink vats of champagne and eat buckets of food, and then relieve himself over a balcony just the way he saw "Golden Ball" Hughes or Buck "Romeo" Denton do it.

And the women! The women were nothing short of spectacular. And the women of quality were every bit as lively as the barmaids were, sometimes even more so, for they were not going through the motions for a few shillings, but for the pure love of the sport. They would take him back to their elegant, lavishly furnished homes, usually when the husbands were still out gaming. They would drink more champagne, play more cards. They would even turn their back when he was near to the family silver, for he was trusted not to pinch a spoon (although he had taken one or two, just as souvenirs).

This was the life he was meant to lead all along.

And he had been busy at work as well. With some careful thought, and a little consulting with his new friends of elevated rank, he had altered his performance in the play. Instead of a lewd comedy, or even a comedy of manners, he would turn it into high tragedy. He would wring the drama of the human condition from every line, make the audience weep with his greatness.

That is what he was, he declared at every chance he could. A great tragedian.

The first night he performed the play his new way, the audience had seemed perplexed. Of course they had! They had been expecting a fool, and instead they were gifted with brilliance.

Elliston kicked him once, in the posterior, backstage. But everyone knew, especially Hughes, that Elliston was simply jealous. He had never been able to rise to such heights, and he did not want to see another man succeed where he had failed.

The next performance was even better!

Some members of the audience left, proving that his performance had so moved them, they were unable to rein in their emotions. They were forced to escape and give way to their weeping in private. Those who stayed did not laugh. They understood. This was his audience.

When Elliston threatened to replace him in the play, Henry Hughes knew he had proven his point. He needed a tragic role. Elliston replied that soon enough a tragic role would be his: The Unemployed Actor.

The final performance of the play was sparsely attended. Henry Hughes was at his finest, for he knew that the audience was his, almost as if he had selected them himself. He owned them. They were in the palm of his hand.

Let Elliston fire him. That was exactly what Henry Hughes wanted, what he had been hoping for. It was the only way he could leave his contract, be free to seek employment where he would be fully appreciated—at the Drury Lane. All he had to do was wait until the Drury Lane reopened in the autumn.

How excited they would be to see the great Henry Hughes on their threshold, offering his services in the role of Great Tragedian!

There, at last, he would be with the only man on earth worthy to share the stage, his stage.

He would at last be peer, friend, and professional companion of Edmund Kean.

Together, they would make theatrical history.

Chapter Thirteen

Emily had written the address of Mr. Edward Giles so many times, on so many letters and manuscripts to post from Fairfax Castle and in recent days, that she knew the address as well as her own.

But what she did not know was the part of town in which Lambeth Road was located. It was across the Thames from Mayfair, not far geographically. She consulted a map, and decided to slip out of the house and walk there, without using the carriage, which would have prompted too many questions, and without telling anyone, especially Caroline.

Besides, after her long days indoors, it would be good to experience a stimulating walk. To take some fresh air. To shake the cobwebs from her mind.

With her plain bonnet over her face, shielding her from the bright sun as well as impeding her peripheral vision, she felt the stares of others rather than seeing them herself. She kept her head down, and walked forward as if she knew precisely where she was going, glancing up only to consult the street names fastened to corner buildings.

She did not have serious doubts about her destination until she crossed the bridge. And then, the sights and sounds that assailed her caused her to doubt not only this one errand, but everything else about her life as well.

Ever since she was a small child, she had been aware that not all people lived as they did. Her parents had made a concerted effort to teach their children how very fortunate they were to have such material comforts, not to want for food or warmth, to always have nice clothes and shoes.

Although they had understood in a vague way what their parents were talking about, seldom did they leave their rarefied world. When they did, it was for short visits to tenants' homes, or passing through a nearby town in their well-appointed carriage, viewing the poor at a distance.

And they were never alone. There were butlers, footmen in livery, abigails and manservants. There was always an umbrella of protection in the Fairfax name alone, always a sense of safety. Even when they strayed away from the environs of County Mayo, their identity was established. They were always the Fairfax family, and thus shielded from the harsh realities that others faced every day.

But now she was alone, in a part of town that was populated with individuals who seemed to be coarse, harsh. She was no longer Miss Emily Fairfax. She was simply a woman venturing alone in unknown territory without an escort.

No one at her sister's home, including the servants, even knew she had left the town house.

Should she be accosted, should she have any sort of mishap, her whereabouts would be unknown to her family.

There were children on the streets as well. For some reason she hadn't thought of that, of children wandering about unattended, with no shoes and nothing but filthy rags for clothing. Wouldn't their feet suffer injuries? Where do they sleep, or eat, or wash? How do they grow up, become adults, without any comfort or security in childhood?

She imagined Letty stripped of all she knew, left to survive on her own in these streets, and she shuddered. No child should be forced to live this way. No adult should be forced to live this way either.

How sheltered she had been all her life. Ignorant and protected. She reminded herself that when life is such a daily struggle, one doesn't have time for the niceties to which she was accustomed. Manners. Civility. Basic order. All of those things must assume secondary importance when the primary concern is mere survival.

Just last week she had thought it the end of the world when she did not like her hat. Now she was even more ashamed of herself, at her flimsy values. At what her thoughtless actions had done. No matter what she had always believed about herself, the reality was that she had always been wealthy. And that had made her a rather selfish being.

She had no clue about real life, about the world in which the vast majority of humanity dwelled.

And then she thought of Ashford, that the bill he had proposed would have helped these people. Although she had not the faintest notion about their daily lives, her thoughtless actions had dealt them a severe blow. And none of them knew it, none of the people she passed on the street had any clue that this solitary, anonymous woman had prevented their lives from becoming so much better.

Any element of fear that had formed within her quickly disappeared when she thought of Lucius Ashford. He wouldn't be afraid walking these streets. He wouldn't hesitate to make eye contact with the other pedestrians.

Then again, he boxed regularly, which seemed to be excellent, not to mention prudent, practice for just such a situation.

Now she paused and looked around at her surroundings.

It was as if she had stepped into an entirely different city, in some foreign land forgotten by all those on the other side of the Thames. The buildings were old, but not well maintained. Some were ancient Tudor half-timber structures. Others were of more recent construction, but still they seemed to be crumbling, with bits and chunks missing. Everything, no matter what its age, was in the process of decay.

The very air was different in Lambeth, an atmosphere thick with conflicting scents, with open sewers running down the streets, the fragrance of bodies too warm that had been bathed too infrequently. A window across the street suddenly opened, and a pair of arms dumped a full slop bucket below—and onto the heads of two passersby. Their vociferous protests and fist-shaking caused others to laugh, and Emily to venture an uncertain smile at the scene.

She then passed a rough-faced man standing by a large sign. Teeth Pulled, it proclaimed. He wore a blood-spattered canvas apron, and by his side was an iron device that resembled a pinching claw. Both the man himself and his equipment were uncomfortably filthy. As she passed he grinned, exposing what seemed to be a mouth entirely free of teeth.

Carriages rattled by. A muffin man passed in his cart, shouting the day's offerings. A fight broke out in the doorway of a public house, and three gentlemen and a lady were tossed to the curb.

Clutching her reticule, she felt conspicuous, out of place. And in spite of her attempts to avoid drawing attention to herself, her mere presence alone in that area provoked comments and whistles.

"Missy! Come on over here, no need to walk . . ."

"I'll give yer a ride, I will . . ."

"Fancy a drink at Vauxhall, milady?"

And then she saw it, a small brass sign. "Mr. Edward Giles, Esq.—Theatrical and Literary Facilitator."

The door was painted green, with a large brass knob in the center in dire need of a polishing. Beneath her gloved hand the knob turned, and with a hard push the door opened, revealing a narrow, dark staircase within.

The interior smelled of last week's cabbage. Apparently Mr. Giles shared his office with others—people who were no doubt great admirers of cabbage—for there were several doors with various names and professions displayed. She located his office on the second floor, and knocked once on the partially opened door.

"Yes?" someone barked from the other side.

"Mr. Giles?" There was some sort of response and, assuming it was an invitation to enter, she opened the door. There sat a portly gentleman surrounded by stacks of books, both bound and unbound. There were papers of various sizes scattered about, some covered with handwriting in different styles and shades of ink.

There was no attempt at decoration, no potted plant or framed print or ornamental anything in sight. And if at one time there had been an effort in that direction, it had long been buried under books and papers.

Dust swirled everywhere, and beneath her feet was a carpet of indeterminate color and design. Perhaps it had once been a burgundy, or a blue. There might be a touch of green. It mattered not, for now it was a deep gray with only occasional patches of slightly less gray to hint at what it had once been.

"No, no, no," he said as he looked at her without standing up, without any other sort of greeting. He was quite bald, with tufts of white hair fringing the bottom quarter of his head. His eyes were set deeply into comfortable folds. He seemed to squint a great deal, and Emily had an immediate suspicion that he needed spectacles. She also suspected there were indeed spectacles within that very office, perhaps more than one pair, but that they had been lost under the mountain of paper.

"Mr. Giles?" Emily ventured.

"I said no. I am not in the market for a ladies' novel. Or poetry. Or, God forbid, your ode to the lake country."

"Well, sir, to be honest I—"

"Unless you have a cookbook. Do you have a cookbook? Everyone's always looking for a decent cookery book."

"No, I'm afraid I do not. You see, sir, I am involved in the writing of plays, and—"

"No!"

"Sir?"

"Forgive me, madam. I am sure you are a lovely woman, and quite the rage with the amateurs at your country house. Nothing like a rousing play, is there? And they are so very entertaining to perform, what with the costumes and the property and all of that. Especially when the shooting is off or the weather bad. But madam, I assure you, the professional theater is no place for a lady. Nor is it a place for society playwrights. End of discussion."

"Please, sir!"

"Would you be so kind as to close the door on your way out? Good day."

He returned to the stack of papers on his desk.

The morning sun reflected off the shiny flesh atop his head.

Emily looked about the office, wondering if her own manuscripts were somewhere in the stacks. All along the wall, even piled against the window, were rows of books and papers. How could he find anything in this mess?

In the corner, under a vast stack of papers, parchments, and books, she spied the forgotten legs and back of a chair. Just the top and bottom were evident. The chair and its contents were in peril of tilting over at any moment under the strain. The only thing keeping it upright were the stacks on either side of the chair bracing it like a vise.

Without asking his permission she removed the papers to the floor, dragged the chair across the office, and placed it directly before his desk.

Then she sat.

"I beg your pardon," she began.

He looked up, astonished to see her still there, and now sitting in a chair.

"Madam! How dare you! Please, replace those files at once."

"I am here to see you about a play."

"As I stated before, I am not—"

"It is about a play you already represent. *The Reluctant Rogue* by Edgar St. John."

"What about the play? It is, of course, the greatest success in the history of the Olympic Theatre."

"Yes. But I would like to request the play be withdrawn."

"Excuse me?"

"The play must be withdrawn. Immediately."

Giles looked at her in disbelief, and then he started to laugh. "You wish me to what?"

"I am acting as Edgar St. John's agent."

He stopped laughing. "Are you his wife?"

"No."

"Sister?"

"No."

"Blackmailer?"

"No, of course not. However, I am acting as his agent, and he requests the play be withdrawn."

"Madam," he said plainly. "*I* am Mr. St. John's agent."

"No, you are not. Although he appreciates what you have done with his previous plays, he requests this one be withdrawn immediately. He has written you another play, a better play, to replace this one, and sign over all of the proceeds to you."

"Pray let me guess. Has there been another flood? Has he been brought down by a plague of locusts?"

"No, no. Please, it is of the utmost importance that you listen."

"Who are you, madam?"

"As I stated before, I am acting as his agent."

"Do you, how shall I phrase this? Do you share a residence with Mr. St. John?"

"Why, yes. I suppose I do."

Giles leaned forward, fascinated. "So you know him well?"

"Very well, sir. Very well indeed."

"Why does he want this play withdrawn?"

"Because it is a poor effort. He believes it is a bad play, and no longer wishes it to be offered to the public."

"Why does he not come here himself?"

"Well," she began, looking about the room. There was an enormous spiderweb in the corner, with dozens of insects dangling down or caught deep within the netting. It must have been there for weeks, months. Perhaps a full year.

"Yes, madam?"

"He is not well."

"I see." Giles looked at her for a few moments, twirling his eyebrows in contemplation. "Madam. I do not believe you."

"You do not?"

"No. It makes absolutely no sense for a playwright to withdraw his greatest success at the beginning of its run. Especially if he is unwell. I know writers, madam. They do not wish to toil in poverty and obscurity, no matter what they claim. Those who profess to enjoy obscurity are either liars, or attempting to justify their own stupendous failure. No. I do not believe you. Not one bit."

"It is true."

"Then prove it to me, madam."

This was what she had been afraid of, for there was no absolute way she could prove she was acting in the author's behalf. "His manuscripts arrive from Ireland," she ventured.

"Yes. And so do a great many others. Try again."

"His penmanship is quite good."

"Many people write with a steady hand. That proves nothing."

"You sent two gentlemen to Ireland. He was called out by Lord Ogilvie and his second, Lucius Ashford."

That surprised Giles. "Now this is becoming more interesting! Whatever became of that argument? They tricked me into it, you know. Otherwise I would not send a pair of assassins to visit my most profitable playwright. "

"It was settled peaceably. But how could I know that unless I knew Edgar St. John?"

"Perhaps you have seen him in passing. Perhaps you've met him once or twice, and hear of his business. I once shook hands with Lord Nelson, but that doesn't make me qualified to speak on his behalf."

"Then why on earth would I be here?"

"Madam, I fear you suffer from boredom. Perhaps your husband ignores you. The children are a mess. You have played every hand of faro possible, and this is your new game. Go back home, my dear. Do something less destructive than attempting to interfere with a man's career. Take up knitting, or charity work. Train hounds. Join a band of gypsies. Indulge in too much sherry. Anything. I beg of you. Just leave me in peace."

Without waiting for a response, he then returned to his work, head bent, shine still bouncing off the top.

"I did not want to tell you this, but I have no choice."

Ignoring her, he turned a page and continued reading.

"Very well, then. You have forced my hand. I will tell you."

Again, he ignored her.

"I *am* Edgar St. John."

There. She had said it. Now she sat and waited for his response. For the startled look, the dumbfounded stammering.

Instead he calmly turned another page.

"Did you hear me, sir?"

"I heard you. And please close the door behind you as you leave. Good day."

"You do not believe me."

Finally he glanced up. "You are either a very ill woman, or an even sicker man. Whoever you are—whatever you are—you are not Edgar St. John."

"I will prove it to you! Please, hand me a piece of paper and a pen."

"Really, I do not have the time. I—"

"Please?"

For a moment he simply stared at her. Then, with a harumph, he passed her a sheet of paper, a pen, and pointed to the ink bottle. Very carefully she wrote the name Edgar St. John, then handed it back.

"There," she said in triumph.

"Very nice. Very nice indeed. But still, this proves nothing."

"How can you say that? Right before you is the proof that you need. That, sir, is Edgar St. John's signature."

"Right before me is proof that Mr. Edgar St. John has a secretary. I presume he dictates his plays to you, and you handle his correspondence as well."

"No, please! Listen to me. My name is Miss Emily Fairfax. I do live in Ireland, but at present I am visiting my sisters. I write these plays under the name of Edgar St. John. I never thought they would be produced, never had the smallest notion they would ever be performed. Be that as it may, I am indeed Edgar St. John. Please withdraw the play, Mr. Giles. I beg of you."

"Tell me, madam. Or miss. Presuming you are who you say you are, why on earth would you wish to end this play?"

"Because, sir, it is harming someone."

"Who is it harming? As far as I know it is harming no one, and giving happy employment to many, not to mention great pleasure to the theatergoers in this city. Who could possibly be harmed?"

"Mr. Lucius Ashford. He's an MP from—"

"I know who he is. I just assumed this was St. John's way of getting even with Ashford for his role in that duel business." Giles tilted his head. "Assuming you are Edgar St. John, why did you write this play if you did not intend to destroy his career?"

"I, well, I was foolish. I did try to retrieve it, but

it was too late. I underestimated the power of my words, the power to harm, in any case."

At last he pushed away his papers and stared at her for a long time, frowning, shifting in his chair. "What is your name again?"

"Miss Emily Fairfax."

"Didn't I read something about you being visited by the Prince Regent?"

"Yes. I did make his acquaintance."

"Tell me, Miss Fairfax, what manner of person is our future King?"

"Well, he is quite gentlemanly."

"What of his appearance? Is he elegance personified?"

"He seems to be a very kindly, learned sort of man. And quite elegant as well."

Giles tapped the desk for a few moments. "What of his hair? His whiskers? Are they indeed false?"

"I . . . well, sir. I don't know," she hesitated. Why did he want such strange information? There was something decidedly odd about his questions.

"Please, Miss Fairfax. Do not be missish with me. I am asking if his false whiskers and hair are convincing."

When Emily did not respond, he sighed heavily. "You may not have noticed, but I too am beginning to lose some of my hair." Involuntarily Emily glanced at his shining head. "Very well. I have lost my hair. And I was wondering if His Majesty's false hair is convincing."

Emily took a deep breath. "No, sir. I fear it is not.

And speaking as a loyal subject, I cannot pretend that anyone who sees his gracious self would be the least bit convinced."

Giles thought for a while longer. "And what sort of person is Mr. Brummell? That is all I hear of these days, Brummell and Napoleon. One would almost think the pair had set up a fashionable shop. Perhaps 'Brummell and Napoleon—Haberdashers,' although I suppose by rights Napoleon should have first billing. What think you of Brummell?"

"I do not know what to say," she confessed, again at a loss as to the turn the conversation had taken.

"Just tell me," Giles urged. "I hear that Mr. Brummell is quite the rage with the ladies. Think you there is a special lady in his life?"

"I haven't the faintest clue," she admitted. "But . . ." she began, then stopped. "Well . . ."

"Go on," he urged.

"I do not believe Mr. Brummell would display passion of any sort if there was the slightest chance it would crease his linen," she said in a rush.

"Fascinating," he mumbled. Then, for the first time, he revealed a surprisingly pleasant smile. Although his teeth were not particularly good, and his features flattened a bit at the stretch, there was something wonderfully welcoming about his appearance. His entire face was transformed by the new expression. "Perhaps I am mad, but I am beginning to believe you. Just beginning. Now you sound like Edgar St. John. Now you sound like the playwright."

Relief flooded through Emily. "Oh, sir! Thank you!"

"I had thought as much. About Brummell, I mean, although we have never met, and about the Prince." For a moment he seemed disturbed. "I mean, about his hair, although I have never met the man." He looked at her as if for the first time. "I believe you may very well be who you claim to be, madam."

"I'm so glad! And I—"

"In any case, I never imagined that St. John could be a woman, and of such high degree. Always imagined him as either a mad vicar or a fop. Never a woman, which is to your credit. I can always spot the words of a woman. Usually. And unless they are in a cookery book, I confess, I cannot stand the way women write. Begging your pardon, of course," he said, slightly flustered. With that he pulled a kerchief from his sleeve and mopped his brow. "This weather is unseasonably hot." He leaned forward. "Tell me, do you fancy this Lucius Ashford?"

"Why, sir! I know not how to answer that question." Emily looked down at her reticule and straightened her skirts. "It makes no difference. What I did was wrong. I must do whatever I can to rectify the situation."

"I must tell you, Miss Fairfax. I, too, grew uneasy when I read of Ashford." Now he leaned back. "Felt the pinch of blame myself. He seems a decent enough fellow."

"He is. Indeed, he is the best of men." She swallowed. "Thank you for helping. Thank you for believing me." She felt as if a weight had been lifted from her. "When will the play be withdrawn?"

"It will not be withdrawn."

"Sir?"

"My dear, I signed the full rights over to Elliston at the Olympic. Do you not recall the papers you signed?"

Emily realized Letty must have signed the papers through the post. She decided not to mention her twelve-year-old sister's part in the deception.

"Neither you nor I have any power over the situation," he continued. "Elliston owns the play for the next eighteen months."

"Eighteen months?"

Giles smiled. "Now I am sure you are Edgar St. John."

"Why is that?"

"No writer ever reads the contracts he signs." He stood up and walked around his desk to her.

Emily was amazed by how short he was, perhaps four or five inches less than her height. Then he extended his hand to her. "It is a pleasure and an honor to meet you, Mr. St. John."

"Oh, thank you." She shook his hand distractedly. "Is there anything we can do?"

"Two things come to mind."

"Yes?"

"I will have a talk with Elliston. Your record as a playwright is already proven. There is no doubt in my mind that your next play will be at least as successful," he said, rubbing a stubby set of fingers over his mouth. "Would you agree to promise your next play to him at a rate he determines?"

"Absolutely."

"And to provide me with a mutually acceptable fee? Perhaps something substantially higher than our previously agreed rate?"

"Yes. Anything."

"And you must complete the play swiftly. Perhaps within the next month or so."

"Yes! Of course."

"Very well, then. To tell you the truth, I believe the play may have run its course, in any event. Sales are down, attendance has slipped. Elliston has been asking about other plays, which is something he would not be doing if he happened to be convinced that *The Reluctant Rogue* would continue for any great length of time. No, I believe this was a one-day wonder. We might have a chance with this, Miss Fairfax."

"Thank you, Mr. Giles," she said.

"I will do what I can. Now tell me, Miss Fairfax, how did you get to this part of town?"

"I walked, sir."

"Good Lord, not from . . . let me guess . . . Mayfair?"

"Yes. How did you know?"

"You all but have 'Mayfair' stamped upon your

forehead. There's a livery stable round the corner. Come with me, and I will hire a coach to deliver you home safely."

"Thank you, Mr. Giles. Thank you so very much."

"You are welcome. Would you prefer to contact me, so as not to prompt questions with your family when the post arrives?"

"I hadn't thought of that. That would be fine. Oh, and what was the second thing you said we could do?"

"Well, Miss Fairfax. It's about Mr. Brummell. Well," for the first time, Giles seemed ill at ease. "Could you ask him, if you happen to see him, of course, and if the matter comes up easily, what a rather shortish man should do about trouser length? What I mean is," he lowered his voice. "should one extend the length to best take advantage of the leg? If there is not much leg to speak of. That is what concerns me. Or is it better to shorten the length of the pantaloons to above the ankle? And if so, what sort of hose must a man wear? You see," he looked directly into her eyes, forced to cast his glance upward. "I was fine with knee britches, you understand. Perfectly at ease with them, for I must admit to possessing a rather fine calf. And particularly good knees. But with the new long trousers, I am at a complete loss. And as a result I do not go out in company, and my business has suffered, I assure you. It is no small matter. With the wigs and the knee britches, I cut quite the figure! I could dance the reels, the country dances. How I wish you could have seen me then! Now, well," he cleared his throat. "If you happen to speak to Mr. Brummell, could you ask him about my dilemma?"

"Of course," Emily smiled. Then she stopped. "Thank you."

"You are welcome, Miss Fairfax. Now let me escort you to a safe carriage home."

And as he walked her outside, he paused for just the briefest of moments. "Miss Fairfax, I do believe had you seen me in knee britches and a wig, you may have forgotten Mr. Ashford altogether."

"Mr. Giles," she smiled, looking down at his rather pudgy face. "Perhaps you are right."

That thought pleased the crusty Mr. Giles vastly.

Robert Elliston was furious.

That rodent Henry Hughes had thrown away a golden opportunity not only for himself, the fool, but for Elliston as well. For all of the actors at the Olympic. Hughes had destroyed one of those rare theatrical opportunities that happen once every few years, every decade or so, simply because he was stupid.

One of the greatest traits an actor could possess was a complete understanding of his own failings. That was what kept Mrs. Siddons from playing Juliette when she was too long in the tooth and too thick in the waist to do so convincingly, what kept the tone-deaf leading man from bursting into song. The very best actors were also the very best casting directors, for they knew exactly what they could play, and more important, they knew what they could not play. Furthermore, they managed to employ their weaknesses to advantage when it best served a role.

Hughes was not so blessed with self-knowledge.

Elliston had realized, of course, that Hughes was not an intelligent young man. But sometimes less intelligence was a very desirable trait in a performer. There was nothing that made one cringe more than observing an actor who mistook playing a brilliant, emotionally complex character for actually being brilliant and emotionally complex himself. That was always the danger in allowing a juggler to take on Othello, or a fire-eater to play Hamlet.

Similarly, a stupid actor who does well in a comedic role may fear he is being laughed at rather than being laughed with, that he as a person is the focus of the audience laughter rather than the role.

That was the rub with Henry Hughes.

During his first few performances as Sir Luscious Ash-Heap, the audience hailed Hughes as a refreshing newcomer, a genuine talent with a sharp gift for comedy.

Then the word "genius" was thrown about, mainly by Hughes himself. Expectations grew higher, unreasonably so, just as Hughes decided it was time to become the new Kean.

Never mind that Kean himself had yet to be proved, and had only been in the public's eye for a few months. Never mind that Kean had already demonstrated his dramatic proficiency in several of Shakespeare's most demanding, and diverse, roles. Or that Kean had been in the spotlight before, as a child prodigy playing the great roles well before his voice had changed. Kean knew the business, knew the audience, and above all, knew his own limitations.

And never mind that Kean had told Hughes, on that very first glorious night, how much he admired his ability to play comedy. Hughes, being a simple fellow, would not be satisfied with reaching the top of the profession using his own specifc, rather narrow capabilities. He was unable to realize the scarcity of such plum roles, how most actors wait their entire careers in vain looking for just such a magical match.

He mistook his simple good fortune, being in the right place at the right time when the right role came about, for much more than that.

He confused enormous good luck for enormous grand talent.

Elliston couldn't help but feel slightly sorry for the lad. Very slightly. He did not have time to dwell on the image of Hughes knocking on the door at the Drury Lane, expecting to be welcomed as a hero, but instead being told to apply again when the stable boy retires.

The Olympic had its own very considerable worries, mainly that a much-touted play had just lost a leading man. That the play, being topical and centered on one main character, was losing its popularity.

The Drury Lane was rehearsing a new production, as was Covent Garden. He had to find another play, or put a new twist on *The Reluctant Rogue*.

As he counted the take from the previous night, down by more than half from the night before, he hoped for something miraculous to save the Olympic.

Chapter Fourteen

Emily felt much more comfortable returning to Grosvenor Street in the hired carriage instead of walking, although the interior smelled somewhat of fish. She leaned back and closed her eyes, wondering what she should do next.

Perhaps she should make peace with Letty, tell her of her visit with Mr. Giles. Let her know that soon, hopefully very soon, everyone would forget about the play. Perhaps she should contact Ogilvie to see how Ashford was faring.

The carriage was becoming rather too warm in the springtime heat. The sun beat down with unfiltered strength, and the only way to remain in the shade was to pull down a canvas screen, which would of course prevent all hope of fresh air from entering the cab.

Not only was it becoming too warm, she noted as she pulled off her gloves, but the fish scent that had been vague before was becoming more powerful by the moment. It wasn't simply a fish odor. She felt as if she herself would take on the characteristics of a rotten fish is she remained in the cab much longer.

Who had been the last to hire this vehicle? A family of rabid fishmongers?

She suddenly remembered the trout back home that had been in the sun for two days before. . . .

That was enough.

"Excuse me! Driver!" she called from below.

"Sorry, mum. Traffic is blocked."

"No, please. I will get out here. Thank you."

The driver hopped down from his perch above and opened the door, and Emily handed him a half dozen coins as she stepped to the sidewalk.

"Thank you, mum." The driver tipped his cap, and she smiled, grateful to be in the open once more.

Glancing around, she took her bearings. Bond Street. Good, she thought. Only a few short streets from Caroline's home. It was just past noon now, and she doubted that her absence would have been missed. And if so, she could simply claim to have taken a stroll in Hyde Park.

Bond Street.

Ashford lived on this very street. She straightened, wondering if she would pass him on the sidewalk. Other young men, all well dressed and handsome to varying degrees, jostled by. Some tipped their hats. Others did a double-take at the sight of an elegantly attired young woman walking unescorted down the street known for men's tailors and a boxing academy.

Casually, very casually, she noticed the numbers. She remembered his exact house number from the note she had sent to him.

Had it only been a mere few days? Less than a week, in fact. And in that time so very much had happened, so very much had changed.

And all of a sudden, somehow, she was there, right in front of the home of Mr. Lucius Ashford, MP.

He would not be in, not at that hour. Of that she was sure.

But perhaps she should leave a note.

It was a bold idea, very nearly scandalous. Fanny and Caroline would faint at the mere inkling of an unmarried woman calling at a bachelor's establishment. Should Letty ever find out, it would be the worst possible example to offer a girl of her age. To visit a man's rooms alone. Unescorted. Unannounced, no less.

But she had to. It was intolerable to think of the misery Ashford had endured because of her. If she could ease his mind just a bit, even at the expense of her own reputation, it would be well worth any disgrace that might come her way. Indeed, she would welcome it.

She deserved to be shamed. And there would be no real damage to her life, for she would simply return to Fairfax Castle and live there the rest of her days, just as she had before. Nothing would change, except for her memories.

Without further thought she walked directly to his door. It was painted a glossy black. Off to the side was an iron boot scraper, and the doorknob was of highly polished brass.

His apartments were on the third floor, above a well-known gentlemen's hatter. Why did they insist on having such large glass windows at such establishments these days? It seemed quite unnecessary. And it provided the customers an unobstructed view of her passing by. She ignored the stares of men in that store as she stepped through the front door to the residences above.

Everyone knew they were the homes of wealthy gentlemen. No one could mistake her for a misguided shopper looking for the florist, or a confused woman seeking a cup of tea.

Within his building it was warm in the hallway, with no windows to allow an early summer breeze. It was hot and still and painted vivid, blinding white, which only served to make the place seem even hotter. By the time she reached the third floor she was breathing heavily, a thin sheen of perspiration on her face and visible above the neckline of her light muslin frock.

She knocked once, wondering as she waited what she would write on the note. His manservant, she knew, would open the door and perhaps look down his nose at her request for pen and paper to compose a note for his master.

So be it. She would suffer the disapproval of his man. Worse fates had befallen others during the history of the world.

But there was no answer.

She knocked again, envisioning Mr. Ashford's expression as he opened her note, realizing she had come to his rooms and that it had not been delivered by post or a servant and . . .

The door opened. And there was Lucius Ashford, in nothing but a collarless linen shirt, open at the throat and untucked, and snug gray pantaloons.

"Mr. Ashford!" Emily cried.

"Miss Fairfax!" he exclaimed simultaneously.

They stood for a moment, each uncertain of what to do or say.

His dark hair was tousled, and he seemed to require a shave. He was clearly not expecting company.

"I had heard, Miss Fairfax, that you were dead."

"No," she began uncomfortably. "That must have been a rumor. I mean, I know it was a rumor. Otherwise I couldn't possibly be standing here and . . ." She took a deep breath. "I had no idea you would be in, sir."

Leaning against the door, he took his time in answering her.

"I see." He noted her appearance, her flushed face and obvious discomfort. A single damp curl pressed against her throat. "You came by because you thought I would not be in. In that case, why are you here?"

"To leave you a note."

"Is that not why they have the post? It's a marvelous invention. Prevents people from having to deliver messages in person."

"Yes, of course. But I had something to tell you. Something important. I thought I should give it to you in a note, and wished to deliver it as soon as possible. It is most vital."

"Why does this seem so oddly familiar? Miss Fairfax sending me an urgent note?" He did not seem angry. He did not seem wounded or hurt. If anything, he seemed bored.

"Forgive me." She felt utterly stupid. She was so hot, so tired. Covered with dust and dirt from head to toe. Covered with humiliation to her core. "Good day, sir." She turned to leave, her head down.

All she wanted to do was remove herself from his presence as soon as possible.

"No, please," he said hastily. For a moment he closed his eyes, and she watched him, his extraordinary features. Then his eyes opened, deep brown, and he seemed to look her over before he spoke, as if uncertain of what to say. It crossed her mind fleetingly that in the short, potent span of their acquaintance, she had never seen him at a loss for words. "I am exhausted and not in the best of spirits," he explained at last. "It is I who should beg your forgiveness. That was horribly rude. Please, do come in."

Part of her wanted to escape now. It would be the perfect chance to exit, for she could always satisfy herself with the notion that she had tried to make peace with this man.

But that would be the coward's way out. As uncomfortable as it was, she had to speak to him, to explain, perhaps a little, of what had happened. And if possible, why.

"Please," he said again. "Do forgive me, Miss Fairfax."

Looking up, she simply nodded. How ironic, that this man whose life she had all but ruined was asking her to forgive him for a trifling breach of etiquette.

He took her by the elbow and guided her into his main room. There were wooden crates scattered about, stacked in the corner, some in the middle of the floor. Many were open, and she could see books and objects wrapped in cloth inside.

"Are you embarking on a journey?"

"In a sense. I am quitting London."

"You are? For how long a duration, sir?"

He cleared a place for her on the sofa, and gestured for her to sit. When she was settled, he looked about for a place for himself. Seeing no other space, he swept several more boxes off the sofa and sat.

"Miss Fairfax, I am quitting London permanently."

"But you can't! You are an MP! How can you possibly quit?"

Ashford watched her with no expression on his face, no emotion. When she finished he spoke. "I must. Due to recent events, I have been rendered less than effective. Any cause I have championed, or was to have championed, would be harmed by my presence. This is not simply my own notion. It has been told to me by others. In private, of course, for they would not wish to have their names sullied by association with me. For that I cannot blame them. Thus my seat will remain vacant, and will be filled by someone else at the next election."

"But what will you do? Where will you go?"

"Up north. Ogilvie has been kind enough to offer use of one of his estates. I will sort through my future then, my options, at leisure, secure in the knowledge that I am doing no one active harm."

"Oh." She was most dreadfully warm. It was becoming difficult to catch her breath. And he was sitting so close, she could feel heat radiating from his body.

For relief she pulled off her gloves, allowing air to reach her hands.

"I am busy, Miss Fairfax." There was a bite of irritation in his tone. "Forgive me for hurrying you, but what is the vital information you feel compelled to impart?"

"Nothing," she shook her head. "It's not important anymore."

"It was important enough five minutes ago when you rapped on my door. A rather bold move, would you say? Tell me, Miss Fairfax." Gone was the humor that used to lurk behind each word, the joy she used to see flashing in his eyes.

She had drained that from him.

"I must be leaving." She began to stand up.

But he grabbed her wrist, and for the first time she saw a genuine flash of anger. "Tell me. I believe

I deserve that small courtesy, Miss Fairfax. Thus far you have shown me precious little."

She felt ill, and wished she had never come. It had been a foolish gesture, stupid. So stupid.

Now what she had to relate to him seemed such a small concession, a drop of water to allay a drought. It seemed almost useless to speak any further. There was indeed nothing else to say.

But she sat down again.

He did not release her wrist. "Tell me."

"I have just seen Mr. Giles, the gentleman who—"

"I know who Mr. Giles is. We had quite a correspondence at one time, if you recall. Go on."

"The play will end soon."

Ashford said nothing. It was as if she hadn't even spoken, he simply stared at her.

"Do you understand? *The Reluctant Rogue* will no longer be performed. And I have every belief that it will be within the next week. Perhaps a fortnight at most. So there is no need for you to leave London. None at all."

There was still no response.

"And Mr. Ashford, it may further relieve you to know that I myself am leaving London next week. So you see, everything will be just as it was. As if I had never been here."

Finally he looked away, his expression shielded from her view. He dropped her wrist as if it were the most distasteful article imaginable, and leapt to his feet. Taking several long steps, placing as much distance as possible between them, he spun and faced her. "Do you really believe that all will be just as it was? Are you so naïve, so foolish as to—"

"But Mr. Giles will try, Mr. Ashford. He may not be able to accomplish it right away, but he will try."

"You do not understand, Miss Fairfax." He spoke through clenched teeth, his lips barely moving. "Had the play been withdrawn after the first night, it would not have made any difference. Had it been stopped in the middle of the first act the damage would have been done."

"But sir, you must not give up. You must rally. You must—"

"May I ask you a question, Miss Fairfax? One very simple question?"

"Yes, of course." She pressed herself toward the back of the couch as he stepped toward her. Gone was the bland expression he had worn earlier. Now his features were animated, his eyes gleaming.

"Why." It was not spoken as a question, but as a statement.

"Why what, sir?"

"Why did you write that play. Why did you make the lead character an absolute fool, and base so many of the particulars on me. I thought we were friends, Miss Fairfax. In Ireland. Perchance even more than friends, something deeper. Something—" He stopped and cleared his throat. "Perhaps I was mistaken, but I did think we were friends."

"But we were friends. We *are* friends."

"Madam, we most certainly are not."

"I honestly did not realize that—"

"You have destroyed the chances of this bill passing. You have ruined my political career, at least temporarily. I will make every effort to rebuild it, but the material thing is that the moment is gone, the moment of this bill. By God, Emily." He seemed to vibrate with emotion. "Why?"

Nothing he could have said, nothing in the world, could cause her as much pain, as much agony as those simple words.

"I did not mean to," her words were weak. Meaningless.

"Perhaps I have been the fool," he began, slumping back against the sofa. "I came here to London as an idealistic young man, inexperienced. Having been abused by the justice system, I thought I could help remedy some of the ills. That is why I sought to prevent duels. Not a very fashionable thing, I know. Duels do add spice to the gazettes, give one something to talk about round a fire. But that was what I wished to do above all else. And I felt that if men thought there was a way out of a duel, some way to save face and yet resolve an issue, well, perhaps duels would go out of fashion. A small thing, but a beginning."

Ashford stopped speaking for a while, and looked off, his memory someplace distant, his mind elsewhere.

"But why, sir, were you so interested? Were you ever involved in one yourself?"

"I told you all this."

"No, no, sir. You never did."

"Of course I did! In the letter I sent you!" For just an instant she wondered if he would strike her.

Emily shook her head in confusion. "But all you did was thank us for breakfast."

"Not that letter," he snapped. "The second one, the long one."

"But I never . . . there was only the one letter. That was all I received."

"How very convenient for you, madam. Your celebrated Irish postal system failed you this one time. Missing in the post." His voice was raspy with fury.

"But it is true! It is I who have been hurt, ashamed, for the second letter I sent to you."

"Ah yes. The water nymph."

Mortified, she began to rise.

"Yes. Leave, Miss Fairfax. It is what you do best."

"Excuse me?"

"Remove yourself from any unpleasant situation. Escape. Run. Then you are not responsible, you need not dwell on the offensive details."

She sat back down, breathing hard with emotion. "What did your letter say?" Her voice was an unsuccessful attempt at composure. "What of duels. Please, I did not—"

"My father died in one."

Shocked, she was about to reach out to touch him, but stopped. He glared at her hand with contempt.

"I am so sorry," she said softly instead, twirling her glove on her lap. "Now it makes sense. Your father lost a duel, and—"

"My father did not lose. He won."

"But you just said that—"

"He killed the other man, a neighbor of ours, another country gentleman, as was my father. They had been close friends all of their lives, as I was close to his son. But some argument over a fence sparked a quarrel, escalated beyond all reasonable dimensions. And then these two gentlemen of learning—good friends, best of friends—met at dawn one morning. My father shot him cleanly through the forehead. He shot my father in the thigh. The wound became infected, and within three weeks my father was dead as well. He was dead, but only after having suffered the unspeakable agony of knowing he had killed a good man for no purpose."

She said nothing. Words were fumbling, inadequate, idiotic.

"My mother died not long after that, then my sister, Lizzy. She was but nine then. Of different ailments, separate maladies. But both died from my father's duel."

"How old were you?"

"Twelve. My aunt and uncle took me in, saw to it that I received the finest of educations. Then I came to London. And now I leave. There is a symmetry to it. A circle of sorts."

"Perhaps while you are away," she ventured,

"you will discover something else, something about yourself. And no one will try to harm you there, the way those three men did last week."

"Those three men did nothing, Miss Fairfax. It is you who has inflicted the damage."

"They tried to kill you," she whispered.

He laughed, a short, staccato, unpleasant sound. "No one will bother now. I am already politically dead. It would be like putting Oliver Cromwell on trial—already over."

"Please," she said, closing her eyes.

"Please what, Miss Fairfax? What do you wish me to say, to do? Shall I pretend that all is well, that nothing is amiss?"

"No," she said, beginning to feel dizzy. She should not have come. He didn't want her, she was accomplishing nothing other than to make him more furious by the second. She was inflicting yet more abuse on this man who had attempted to accomplish such good. "I must leave. Forgive me for—"

And then his hand was on her throat.

For an instant she wondered if he would harm her in any way, but that was just a brief, confused thought. Instead of hurting her, he removed a curl that had been resting against her neck.

"There," he patted it into place, and began to move away.

Then he stopped. His eyes were close to hers, and she watched as he searched her face, as if answers he could not find elsewhere would be there.

Slowly his hand returned to her throat, and then his knuckles brushed along her jaw. With a flick of his thumb he untied her bonnet, which tumbled off her shoulder and then to the ground.

Still she didn't move, she just watched him, waiting . . . hoping.

"Emily. Oh God, Emily," he exhaled, his breath against her cheek. She leaned back against the couch, he moved forward resting his head against her breast.

She did not move at first. And then one blinding thought came to her.

This was Lucius.

A chaos of emotions rioted within her, but no single thought made sense. Nothing made sense in the world except for one single thing.

This was Lucius.

She felt as if she had tumbled off a cliff into a realm of uncertainty. All of the perceptions of her life were suddenly worthless, erroneous, for this one moment was the reality, the truth she had been seeking. She was falling, yes. But he was there, waiting to catch her.

At least for the moment.

Her hand gradually rose to the nape of his neck, where she stroked the lush, thick hair and touched the strong cords of his neck. And then, unexpectedly, she kissed his forehead.

He lay so still, she thought he had fallen asleep, and she, too, remained motionless. If he was asleep it was because he needed it so.

But he was not asleep.

Turning his head slightly, he kissed her throat, his lips warm and impossibly soft upon hers. Then he moved up to her ears with aching gentleness, flowering kisses along the delicate path, to her temple, finally, with a staggering hunger, her lips.

The sensation for both was shattering, and for a brief instant life itself seemed to cease within them.

And then it returned with an overwhelming urgency, as the single kiss deepened, and became something all-consuming, enveloping.

He pulled away, and for a moment they simply stared at each other, panting, startled by what was happening. Confusion was mirrored in both of their eyes, and then he saw something else in hers, something he had not expected.

Trust.

Her arms slipped around him, a sweet, artless gesture, as if she had done it always, as if he had been there always. In spite of his size and weight, she did not feel conquered in any way. Instead she felt a sense of comfort, of being safe. She could feel his every breath, every beat of his heart. His very life force was next to her, and she felt almost a part of him, he a part of her. It was such a new sensation of intimacy, such a marvel, she thought she would weep.

Clutching at his back, she longed to be even closer, to make the moment last forever.

Even as he held her and kissed her, his hand

drew up her skirts. She held on as he touched her, stroked her, coaxing a silken trail. It was as if she had been waiting for this her entire life, waiting without knowing what, but somehow knowing with whom.

She felt him shift, his trousers slip off, and then, after one brief stab of sharp, wondrous pain, they were united.

They lay together on the couch for a long time, holding each other, not speaking. The enormity of what had transpired, what they had shared, kept them silent, kept them from wishing to move.

At last he spoke. "Forgive me. I know not what overcame me."

She shook her head. "There is nothing to forgive, Lucius." She yearned for the moment to extend forever, to last as long as possible.

But unwelcome reality filtered through her consciousness. She must leave now, or stay forever.

And no matter what, she knew that could never be. Not after what she had done. This enchanted spell was broken. But this interlude had shown them what might have been, a glimpse of a paradise they could never again regain.

And it was all because of her.

She had to leave, or the pain of the rest of her life would be unbearable.

Reluctantly, she began to sit up, to adjust her gown, smooth her hair. He, too, pulled on his clothes, watching her as she moved. "I must go now," she said as she picked up her bonnet. But she could only find one glove.

"I will find it, and return it to you," he vowed.

"Thank you." He would return it by post, she realized. This was to be their last time together.

Then she walked to the door.

"Shall I—" he began.

"No. I'll be fine." Then she looked up at him, and his eyes were different now. Warm, caring. She knew that she would never see him again. And she drank in every detail of his face, of the crinkles by his eyes, the small cleft in his chin, even the whiskers that had scratched her. For she would live on this moment for the rest of her life.

These were her memories. This was her treasure. She took a deep breath, her emotions in check, barely so. "Oh, how I wish—"

"So do I, Emily." He cut her off. "So do I."

With that she walked the few blocks—the thousands of miles—back to her sister's house.

Lucius stood by the door and listened to her footsteps fade.

What had he just done?

What had *they* just done?

He returned to the sofa, his knees buckling beneath him.

Then he saw it. Her glove, the one she left behind. Picking it up, he held it to his face, inhaling her scent. Wishing with his entire being that things could be different, that this did not have to be the end.

But of course, it did have to be the end.

The glove held her scent. And it wasn't until later, much later, when he examined the glove, that he found it was damp.

The dampness had been caused by his tears.

Letty hid behind the corner of the boot maker's shop as her sister emerged from Ashford's apartments.

Emily, who was always so polished and elegant and beautifully dressed, was nothing short of disheveled.

At first Letty had an urge to giggle.

"She looks like an unmade bed," she whispered to herself. Then she stopped smiling.

There was something unsettling about Emily's expression, her appearance. It reminded her of something, of someone. What was it?

Emily tucked a strand of hair beneath her bonnet. Even from across the street, and from between carriages and horses and pedestrians and a young man wobbling about on a hobby horse, she could see that her sister was flushed and distracted.

Then it came to her. Where she had seen just such an expression, just such a demeanor. It was at home, at Fairfax Castle, when she accidentally intruded on the undergardener and the new maid, Mary. They were behind the stable, and she watched them together, then watched Mary leave, smiling, flushed.

Her sister and Ashford?

But it was impossible! How could he . . . after she . . . and then . . .

Letty cried out, clamping her hand over her mouth.

She was all alone. Now she had no one to turn to. No one at all.

Chapter Fifteen

It was clear to everyone who passed by the elegant town house of Mr. and Mrs. George Edgeworth on Grosvenor Street, Mayfair, that a major social event was in the making.

The first evidence of the event's magnitude was the complete and total absence of their three children, who had been sent, along with their nanny, to their country estate. Letty, it was presumed, would be allowed because she had become something of society's pet, a child not yet out, but still desirable at parties. As the year 1814 reached its halfway mark, Miss Letty Fairfax was considered an asset. One could not possibly grow *blasé* with her there, *pas du tout*. Along with her charming sister Emily, she had become quite *on dit*.

There were deliverymen carrying boxes filled with new china and the specially ordered silverware, with a massive silver tureen for the *potage aux tortue*. Caroline had hired three new maids, all from France—or at least from the French district of outer London—to assist with the final touches, to ensure that everything was *comme il faut*.

A day before the grand event, with Caroline

working herself into a fever pitch, the menu was finally set. From the *noix de veau à la jardinière* to *l'epigramme de poulardes au gratin* and *la charlotte à l'Américain* (in honor of the Princess, who was expected to arrive fashionably late, and an American diplomat, who was expected to arrive unfashionably early), everything was falling into place.

While everyone *chez Edgeworth* rejoiced in the preparations for the upcoming party, two members of the household were noticeably subdued.

Emily was more reserved than usual. Of course she smiled when it was required, helped Caroline make decisions on where to place various *objets d'art* and with the seating arrangement, flowers and candles and all of those touches that would make her soiree so magnificent. But those who knew Emily could not help but notice a lack of sparkle in her eyes, a faraway expression that would cross her face when she was unaware of being watched.

George thought she was homesick for Ireland. Caroline thought it was due to Mr. Ashford, his terrible disgrace and his own sudden removal to the country.

There was a distinct change in Letty as well. She, too, did not smile as much, and although she would laugh and enjoy herself on some occasions, as if forgetting herself, she spent more time alone in her room than before.

No one seemed to note the distance between

Letty and Emily except, of course, for Letty and Emily.

It was not that Emily did not try. Her efforts were nothing short of valiant, from attempting to assist Letty with her hats (she told Emily if those ladies had wanted a hat designed by Emily, they would have asked for a hat designed by Emily) to buying a set of slingshots to use in the park. Nothing worked.

Letty was not ready to forgive Emily, and was still confused by her own emotions. And there was no possible way for Emily to rush her.

And then, twenty hours before the party, a note came from Lady Duff.

She was sorry, but was unable to attend the party of Mr. and Mrs. George Edgeworth.

Caroline was slightly surprised, a little upset, but allowed it to pass over her. Lady Duff was an unfortunate guest to lose, yet there were plenty of others. It had been quite the coup to have her agree to come in the first place, that was the material point. Having her not attend was actually a blessing, really it was, for no one would be comparing the two women as hostesses.

By that evening, seven other regrets had arrived. And by nine, there were thirty-five.

"What is happening?" Caroline asked frantically. She paced, she tore at her hair, although not too much, as the French hairdresser told her it was bad for the curl.

"I see no pattern, Caro," Emily said. "It could

very well be that business has called many out of town, that an alarming number of relatives have taken ill, or that country estates have indeed been flooded."

"Nonsense," Caroline replied.

"Here's a different one," Emily offered. "One lady has to go out of town because her daughter is having a baby."

Caroline barely blinked at the news. "Really? Who is that?"

"Let's see. It's a Mrs. Dinwiddy."

"Mrs. Dinwiddy? But her daughter had the baby two months ago! We were at the christening, and gave her an absolutely charming silver cup."

"Yes. But could it be another daughter?"

"The Dinwiddys do not have another daughter."

"Oh."

It occurred to Emily that the Dinwiddys were attempting to make a point with their ridiculous excuse. That could be the only reason for such a blatant lie.

Just then they heard George arrive below. He was not himself, not in the usual mirthful mood. This night he was somber. He did not even bother to joke with the servants, to call up to Caroline that he was home at last—a habit she detested as hopelessly middle class.

Instead he came in quietly. "Good evening, ladies," he said, giving a particular smile to his wife.

His seriousness was not lost on Caroline. "Lord, George. Is there bad news? Tell us. Is it Papa?"

"No, no. Not at all. Nothing like that. I just, well . . ."

Emily had never seen George so very uncomfortable, so ill at ease.

"This concerns all of you, but I fear Emily and Letty may be the most affected."

Ashford, Emily thought. Something has happened to him.

"I fear, my dear ones, there is some gossip going about town."

Emily let out a sigh. "Thank God, George! For a moment you had me frightened!"

"It is of a most serious nature."

"What?" Caroline snapped. "Let us have it, George. Do not sugarcoat it."

"There is no way to sugarcoat this. To begin with, the Olympic Theatre is running announcements revealing the true identity of Edgar St. John."

Letty and Emily exchanged quick glances.

George noticed. "Is it true, then?"

"Is what true!" Caroline shrieked.

Emily remained calm. "Yes, it is. I am sorry, George. That is why I took such pains to write under an assumed name."

"Do you mean," Caroline began. "Emily? You are Edgar St. John?"

She nodded. "I am."

Caroline needed more explanation, after which she seemed quite pleased. "There is nothing to worry about, George. Her plays are quite the rage. Imagine our sister is the famous playwright!"

"That is not all, I fear," he continued gravely. "There are to be items in tomorrow's gazettes."

"About me being Edgar St. John?"

"Some will be. Others will be of a more scurrilous kind. Indeed, the word is already out. And dear Caroline, I'm afraid you will soon have a platter full of regrets from your invited guests."

"What are the rumors? What is the gossip?" Emily asked.

"Letty," George said kindly. "Why don't you go upstairs to bed?"

"No, Uncle George," she stated. "Some of it concerns me, does it not?"

He nodded.

"Then may I please stay? I do have a right to know what is being said."

George looked at Emily, and she nodded. "Very well. Most of the rumors concern Emily, however."

"Go on, please."

"They say that you are something of a courtesan, a mistress to many, many men. To be frank, they are calling you a leader of the demimonde, a fashionable, impure—"

"I understand your general drift, George," Emily said. "They say that about me?"

"That's ridiculous," laughed Caroline. "Why, Em is, well, quite pure. Is that not so? It is almost silly."

Emily looked down, her face flaming, and Letty bit her lip.

The smile faded from Caroline's face. "Emily, look up."

George continued. "They say that you were forced to flee Ireland after making too many conquests. That you were driven out, in fact. And since coming here you frequent Bond Street in search of new prey. That you visit gentlemen's apartments during the day, for pleasure."

Letty made a gasping sound.

"Of course it isn't true, Letty," George soothed. "But sometimes, with gossip, it takes quite a while to get straightened out."

"What is the part about me?" asked Letty.

"This is the most absurd of all. They say, Letty, that Emily is not your real sister. That she is, in fact, your mother."

"That's not true," Letty said. "Is it?"

"Of course not!" Emily said.

"The best part is who your father is supposed to be, Letty," George said with a wink. "You might enjoy this bit."

"Who is that?"

"The Prince of Wales."

"Never!"

"This is not to be believed!"

Caroline was furious. "Slander! Libel! We will sue for defamation!"

"Well, that is almost impossible," George explained. "The papers are very careful with how they phrase their information. They start with a small grain of truth, in this case, the rather sensational news that Miss Emily Fairfax is the noted playwright Edgar St. John. And then that the

Prince Regent is quite taken with her, which was clear to everyone at the Duffs', further compounded when he called here. Then they build carefully, always citing unnamed sources, always using vague terms. It is next to impossible to sue, Emily. I consulted with a solicitor this evening, just to make sure. That is why I am late."

"George," Emily reached out, and he took her hand. "Thank you. No brother could be better."

"So what shall we do?" Caroline asked. The reality of the situation was beginning to sink in. There was to be no party because there were to be no guests. "Whatever shall we do, George?"

"I suggest we all pack it in and head to the country. The children are already there, and we all know that the most difficult part is getting them there. It will be a jolly lot of fun, all of us together. Emily and Letty can try out their new slingshots."

"Thank you, George, but I believe it would be best if Letty and I return home," Emily said.

"That is not necessary," he began.

"But it is. We will return. And you, of course, will come to Ireland for a holiday when you are able. But just now, perhaps it would be best if we leave as soon as possible."

"Dear Emily, I really don't think that—"

"But I don't want to go," Letty said. "I can stay, and Emily can leave."

Emily shot a glance at Letty, who raised her chin.

"Not this time, dear," Caroline patted her. "In a

few months you may come back, perhaps for Christmas. Wouldn't that be most amusing?"

"I don't want to go," she muttered. "I don't see why I have to, just because everyone is saying nasty things about Emily."

They all remained silent, each lost in their own thoughts. The clock on the mantel ticked, the room—festive, decorated for a party that was not to be—seemed artificially bright.

"Well, I am going to bed," Emily said. "But first, I do want to apologize to everyone. I am so very sorry, George, Caroline, and you, Letty. Most especially to you."

"There is no need," George started to say.

Emily looked at them all, her family, the people whom she loved so very much, whom she had managed to hurt so very deeply. And they all looked down, except for George, who gave her a sympathetic smile.

"Good night," she said once again.

There was little sleep to be had for Emily that night.

The fact she was fodder for the gazettes was bad enough, but not tragic. The announcement that she was Edgar St. John was not earth-shattering. It was bound to happen sometime, she reasoned. The more plays she wrote, the more likely it was to be revealed, especially when she was in London.

No, what was tormenting her was the grain of

truth that George had spoken of. For she *had* been on Bond Street, visiting a gentleman.

She had been seen by someone on the street, perhaps someone who knew her from Lady Duff's, or from the night at the theater.

While she suspected her unmasking as Edgar St. John may have come from Mr. Giles, or perhaps someone from the Olympic, what truly bothered her was the second part.

Bond Street.

Would Ashford have taken revenge by offering those details to the papers?

Never, she thought.

Impossible.

After what happened, after that last sublime afternoon together, could he have turned around and betrayed her?

Just as she had betrayed him.

She turned over and punched her pillow in a vain attempt at getting comfortable.

As much as she hated to dwell upon it, the truth was she was no longer pure, as Caroline had assumed. She had tried to keep the negative aspects of that afternoon at bay, for there was nothing to be gained by them. But she had allowed him to take her, not only without a struggle but with her full and absolute consent. Of that she had no doubt.

Perhaps she had even forced him. It was possible. He had not taken her, *she* had taken *him*. Everything was vague, hazy when it came the actual who did what to whom part. They did it to each other.

And she had found it heavenly.

Punching the pillow again, she curled onto her side.

She had thought it meant a great deal to him, but perhaps it had not.

Perhaps that had been his ultimate revenge.

Sleep. She would try to sleep. The next day they would return home, back to Ireland and Papa and all that was familiar.

Her life would stretch before her, one long yawn. She had tried something different, to come alive, to be a part of the world beyond Fairfax Castle, and it had been nothing short of disastrous.

But she did have memories, at least she had those now. Just like old Mr. Palmer whose wife had died, just like Papa when he thought of Mama. Now she would have her own memories. Perhaps there were not many of them, maybe in time they would fade, just as the newsprint on the gazettes would fade, the paper itself flake and dissolve into nothing.

That would eventually happen to her, to her sweet, secret memories. But until then, they were hers.

And she would treasure them, keep them fresh and alive, like a flower pressed into a book, for as long as possible. For in spite of all the wretched events, of all the wounds and harms and misunderstandings, this had been the most glorious time of her life.

* * *

"Please, please, I beg of you! Give me another chance!" Robert Aubridge held his hand up to deflect another blow.

"We gave you a chance," the Major growled. "You miserable, good for nothing—"

"But he is ruined! Ashford is the laughingstock of London!" Aubridge pleaded. "His bill is dead."

"That was not of your doing. You are the one who hired the three imbeciles. Did you know they are out of jail? And they will cause us more trouble, mark my words."

"But I—"

"Shut up. Now you have no way to pay your considerable debt to us, do you?"

"I will! I promise I will!"

"How? You have nothing. You are nothing."

"My wife's family is wealthy. They will give me the money."

"You wife despises you."

"No, you are wrong," he sniveled. "And I have an idea."

"It is too late for your ideas, Aubridge."

"Please! I will make it worth your while, I promise!" And frantically, as if his life depended upon it—which it did—he outlined a rough plan, one he had been mulling over but had never dared to enact. He had never been this desperate.

Until now.

The Major and his men listened. And to Aubridge's relief, they agreed to give him another chance to repay them. One final chance.

* * *

Emily rose early the next morning.

She was in no hurry to dress. She was leaving, but she knew there would not be a boat until later in the afternoon. She took her time packing, folding her clothing neatly and stacking it into her trunk.

Then she heard shouts, calls. Thumping on the steps, even though the boys were in the country and not there to do the thumping.

And soon enough she learned the cause of the distress.

Letty was missing.

Chapter Sixteen

Three days later, there was still no sign of Letty Fairfax.

It was as if she had dropped from the face of the earth, or vanished like the morning dew.

Naturally, all plans had been called off immediately upon discovering Letty's empty bed. She had taken a few clothes, a very few, from what Emily could tell. The small comfort derived from that knowledge was the feeling that meant she had not been taken with force, against her will. There were no signs of struggle, and any invader would have been most hard-pressed to take an unwilling Letty anywhere. It was difficult enough to wash her hair. A kidnapper stood little chance, especially from the third floor.

There was also her recent interest in a novel, published under the name *A Lady,* concerning an ill-treated heiress who abandons her home and her cruel father, who forces her to eat a great deal of mutton and wishes her to marry an ancient but wealthy duke or baronet or some such person. She disguises herself as a footman, and eventually falls in love with another poetic footman who happens to be the heir of a nearby estate.

This, everyone knew, was just Letty's style.

And one of the footmen believed a jacket and trousers were missing from the wardrobe, although he wasn't certain. It was either taken from the wardrobe, or borrowed by one of the servants who had gone to the country house with Nanny and the children. He could not recall which.

There was no note, which again relieved their immediate fears that she had been kidnapped, or that she would be held for ransom by some evildoer. George, after consulting some so-called experts in the field (some of the men at the club who had experienced wayward daughters), decided it was best to keep her disappearance a secret.

"They say that in cases such as this, an individual happening upon the missing person could do harm. And there is nothing to prevent a blackmailer from claiming to have her, when in fact they do not. No," George concluded. "I quite agree. Best to keep it amongst ourselves."

That first morning, when it became apparent that Letty was gone, Emily was forced to tell them everything, from the duel in Ireland, to the reason Letty was so furious with her for the play. It was another painful admission.

"So you see, again this is my fault," Emily explained. "She decided to run away rather than to return to Ireland with me. That was her dilemma, and she made her choice."

"If that is the case," Caroline had suggested, not

meaning to be cruel but simply being pragmatic, "perhaps it would be best if you did return to Ireland. Then Letty might come back here, where she is safe. Or feels safe."

But Emily remained in London anyway, helping where she could, riding about London in carriages to see if a glimpse of Letty could be had, doing whatever she could to help find her sister.

They reassured themselves that Letty had done this before. The previous spring she had made a valiant attempt at joining a family of sheepherders from Ireland's far west, getting as far as a distant hill before her shoes gave out, the shepherds asked her to leave, and she grew weary of the constant baying of the animals. Another time she had tried to get herself adopted by one of their tenant families, who informed their father. He allowed her to live with them for two days, which she enjoyed a great deal until she heard Emily was to take a trip to Dublin for some new kitchenware. She left her new family then, although she still ate the occasional meal with them, just to remember her humble past.

Emily blamed herself for allowing Letty such free rein. The others disagreed, but allowed that perhaps Letty, when she returned, should be taught reason.

That was little comfort to Emily, who tortured herself with images of Letty in peril, wandering the streets of Lambeth or worse. She feared the rougher elements of the city, people who would abuse Letty, or hurt her, or worse.

Her own misery, the discomfort of the gossip or

the events with Mr. Ashford, were pushed far to the back of her mind. Those issues were nothing compared to the life of her sister.

On that third day, George returned from an errand.

"I have with me two men who know England backward and forward," he said as the gentlemen entered.

It was Lord Ogilvie and Lucius Ashford.

Emily was only momentarily taken aback. Then she spoke. "I thought you were to be in the country, sir," Emily asked of Ashford. There was no awkwardness, no hesitation on either side. The situation was far too serious for such behavior. And she was far too numb, and terrified, as each hour without Letty passed.

"I was, but then George contacted me about Letty. Ogilvie came down at once. Tell me," Ashford said briskly. "Is there any further news?"

"None."

Ashford's manner was businesslike. "Have you notified your father yet?"

"No, not yet. We were hoping it would not be necessary, that the situation would be resolved by now. But as you see, sir, it is not."

"Miss Fairfax . . . Emily. Please. We will find her, and soon she will be back home, with you."

Emily, who had been at a breaking point for three days, felt herself unravel. "I . . . I can only . . ." Then she did something none of the sisters could ever recall seeing before.

Emily Fairfax cried.

"Here," Ashford said, settling her into a chair.

"Water, please?" he asked of Caroline, who quickly brought over a pitcher and a glass.

After a sip of water, he urged her to tell him all. Speaking softly, swiftly, Emily told Ashford everything, including Letty's fury with her and all of the gossip from the gazettes.

Of course he knew of the gazettes, but was rather surprised to hear of the situation between Letty and Emily. But Emily felt she must inform him of all she knew, for something in that information might lead to finding Letty. In the process of confessing the awful facts, she stopped crying. It was a relief to share the story, to unburden herself freely and completely.

"Please tell me, in all honesty. You do not think that I had anything to do with the gazettes? That I would do such a thing as to inform them of your identity as some sort of revenge?" Ashford asked, his voice so low only Emily could hear.

She looked into his face, and saw nothing but openness there. "I did have some fears on that account. After all, I deserved it. The revenge would have been perfect," she acknowledged. "But then I thought it wasn't possible. Now I know it wasn't possible."

"Thank you," he said with a brief smile. Then back to business. "Ogilvie has a map, and we can go over it and see if we can come up with likely places for Letty to be. Ogilvie and myself have searched some spots we thought promising, such as puppet shows and a hot-air balloon over by the river. No luck. We have also alerted the coach lines and taverns and inns on the major roads, so if she tries to leave London, we would know."

"I do not know what to say," she began.

"Then say nothing. We do not have the luxury of time. Ogilvie?"

Lord Ogilvie looked up from the map. "What of your other sister?"

"Fanny?" Emily asked.

"Yes. Does she know what is happening?"

"Of course," George stated. "I went directly to their house in case Letty was there. But Fanny was shocked to hear the news and promised to let us know if Letty came to her."

"What of her husband? What is his name?" Ogilvie asked.

"Robert? He's away on business, I suppose," Caroline said.

Ogilvie and Ashford exchanged glances. "Good God," George slowly stood from the map. "You do not suppose that Aubridge had anything to do with this, do you?"

"I'm afraid it's a possibility," Ashford admitted. "We've been asking round town, and it seems he has enormous debts. He has resorted to some less than savory characters to relieve his predicament, and you can well imagine the rest."

George looked over at Emily and Caroline. "I will go to see Fan at once, and bring her here."

"Oh no," Emily whispered. "But there has been no ransom note, no request for money?"

"Perhaps that will come," Ogilvie replied, adding, "I hope."

Caroline shook her head. "What do you mean, sir, that you hope . . . that you," then she stopped and clamped her hand over her mouth. "No. He wouldn't harm her. He couldn't."

"We are ahead of ourselves," Ashford said briskly. "George, you go to the Aubridge home."

"I will. And I will not leave until Fanny is with me."

There was a knock on the door and one of the servants entered. "A letter for Miss Fairfax," he bowed. "I thought it might be of importance."

"Thank you." George removed the letter from the silver tray and handed it to Emily.

"The ransom note?" Caroline cried.

But the moment Emily held it, she knew precisely what it was. Thick, clearly a letter of many pages. Misdirected several times in Ireland from the scrawls by the address, finally sent to her father who had forwarded it directly to London. The letter was not stamped but franked, one of the advantages of being a Member of Parliament.

"Well?" Caroline asked. "Are you going to open it?"

Emily looked at Ashford, who ran a hand through his hair. "It seems, Mrs. Edgeworth, that the postal service in Ireland is not as marvelous as some of us thought."

"Pardon me?"

"No, Caro. It's not a ransom note." Emily ran her finger across Ashford's name on the return address.

"Well, then. We should spread out now while we still have the daylight," Ogilvie announced.

"Yes, yes. Of course. Would you like the best carriage?" George offered.

"Depends on where we are going. I may just go on horseback," Ashford said to Ogilvie. "One of us should go on foot. You decide."

"Your speed." Ogilvie nodded.

"Right. That will do."

"Map?"

"You should. I know the way."

Emily watched the exchange with fascination. It was a brief diversion for the very serious nature of the situation, watching these two such dissimilar men working so closely together that they only spoke in clipped, partial sentences. When the two men had finished, she asked him a question she had been meaning to ask since she met the two unlikely friends.

"How did you and Ogilvie become such fast friends?"

For the first time since entering the house, Ashford gave a brief smile. Then he called to his friend. "Ogilvie, Miss Fairfax wishes to know how we became friends."

"Do you?" As he answered, Ogilvie was writing directives to George concerning places they had yet to cover. "We have been friends since boyhood.

Don't remember not knowing him, in fact. He was just always there. But what really cemented our friendship was when our fathers killed each other. Don't you think so, Ashford?"

"Yes, I believe that made us uncommonly good friends."

The others stared in shock, but Emily understood. Now it made sense.

"Duels do forge some peculiar friendships," she agreed.

Then they continued the search for Letty.

"Please, Uncle Robert. May I just go home now?" Letty begged, exhausted and hungry.

"I am not your uncle," he said, pacing back and forth.

"Where are we?"

"Shut up. I need to think."

It was his wife's fault again. It was such a slight thing he had asked of her, just to write a note to Letty begging her to come at once to their house, that she needed Letty's help. That was all. And she had done it happily, the idiot, thinking he was honestly inviting the little rat for a visit. And Letty had arrived within an hour.

He'd had no time to prepare.

Once Fanny realized what he had planned, to hide the girl in the cellar until money came from Ireland or the Edgeworths, she had almost ruined it all. Disaster had been averted only when he slapped her the last time, and she hit her head.

There had been nothing for him to do but tie her up in case she awoke (which didn't seem likely— there was a lot of blood). Then he had to get the little rat out of the house without seeing what had happened to Fanny.

Now they were stuck in some cheap inn, and his limited funds had gone to getting a room and keeping the little rat fed.

Nothing was going right.

Last time he saw Letty, she was just a small child, pliable. Easily led. She sat quietly and played with dolls. It was only a few years earlier. But she had changed.

"Uncle Robert?"

"Shut up!" Not so many questions last time he saw her. He thought he could hold her, collect the money, and with Fanny's help, the little rat would say she had been with her sister and no one would believe her because who listens to children? Everyone knows they make up stories.

Now what would he do?

He had probably killed his wife. It had been a mistake to tie her up, he realized too late. It would have looked like an accident had he simply left her there.

And then he knew what he had to do. He had to get rid of the little rat and make sure that looked like an accident, too. Then he could leave England, go someplace on the Continent. Italy, perhaps. He had always fancied the idea of Italy.

He could start over. That's precisely what he

could do! One could live cheaply in Italy, he had heard. They practically paid you to live there.

There was a knock on the door.

"Damnation," he muttered. He'd been forced to pay for a room at the inn so there would be a place to send the money. But he hadn't even had a chance to compose the ransom note. The little rat had kept on asking what he was doing, asking if she could help him write because everyone knew that girls had better handwriting than boys.

Another knock.

"Come in," the little rat chirped.

Why hadn't he tied her up, gagged her?

Because he had tried, he admitted to himself. She was far to fast. Hadn't had the chance yet.

The door opened and a young man with unnaturally bright eyes entered. "I'm to ask if you'll be having supper sent up," he said.

"No," Aubridge spat. "We're—"

"I know you!" Letty shouted.

"Miss?"

"What are you doing here?" Letty continued. "You were the lead in *The Reluctant Rogue,* were you not?"

Henry Hughes preened. "Yes, I was. Did you see it?"

"Oh, you were wonderful! What are you doing here?"

"Shut up, the both of you. And no, we are not eating here."

"But Uncle Robert, I—"

"Leave," Aubridge ordered. Henry Hughes wavered and looked at Letty. "I said leave."

"Yes, sir," he bowed and retreated.

Whatever he did, Aubridge decided, he would have to do it right away.

On the other side of the door, Henry Hughes was disturbed. Of course, he had been disturbed since taking the lowly position at the tavern after he had been let go at the Olympic. Another actor had sent him to the place, a grimy inn run by the actor's stepfather. For now he would accept the position. That is, until he found another part to play, and another theater.

He had heard that Scotland was quite the place now. When he saved his money, he would go to Scotland.

But the man and the little girl had seemed odd from the start. Acting had taught him a few things about human nature, about the way people behaved around each other, about dramatic tension and miscast characters. And if anyone was miscast, it was the pair in that room.

She had called him "Uncle Robert." But still, something wasn't right there.

And so with a shrug, he went in search of the innkeeper.

Something just wasn't right.

The doctor came down the stairs, his leather case in hand.

George Edgeworth rose to his feet, as did Caroline and Emily. "Dr. Jenner," he began.

The doctor, his white hair blown over on one side, shook his head slightly. "Mrs. Aubridge should recover fully."

"Thank God," Caroline sighed. Emily reached over and held her sister's hand.

"I don't know what would have happened to her if you hadn't found her, Mr. Edgeworth. She had been there two days, and—" Then he looked at the women and stopped. "In any case, I have something to help her sleep."

"Thank you, Doctor. We cannot thank you enough." George patted the man's shoulder.

"She said something about Robert having Letty. Does that make sense?"

"Yes." George walked over to the brandy. "We suspected that, but now we know. Would you like a drink, sir?"

"No, thank you. I've other patients to see, but I'll return tomorrow. And again, she'll be fine. All she needs is rest and wholesome food, and she will be right as rain."

Emily willed herself to remain silent as the men conversed. For no matter what happened, no matter how much wholesome food and rest they all got, she wondered if they would ever again be right as rain.

Chapter Seventeen

They all realized there was a very real possibility they would never see Letty again.

Emily was afraid to utter those words, or even form them fully in her mind, fearful that once they were articulated, they might actually become a reality. And the most tormenting aspect of the situation was that she was fully convinced it was her fault.

But there was no need to fan the fears that already gripped them all. They had one sister upstairs and safe. Now they would hope for Letty.

"We will find her," George reassured them the moment the doctor left. "Ashford and Ogilvie already know it was Robert. I have a feeling the two of them know very much what they are doing."

"I know we will find her." Emily tried to smile.

"I feel so horribly responsible," Caroline confessed softly. "Letty was here, under our protection and in our house. How could we have let this happen, George?"

"Oh, Caro," Emily began.

"Here I was, so concerned with the blasted party," she continued. "With my social position, all the airs and fripperies. What I wouldn't give to have Letty back!"

"Now, dear." George stepped to his wife and placed an arm around her.

"And what of Fanny?" Caroline sniffed. "For so long she's been suffering horribly, and I was nearby yet did nothing. Absolutely nothing. I thought she was jealous. I thought she was just of a sour disposition."

"But Caro, you have your own children to watch. Fanny hid it from you, from me, from everyone," Emily said. "Perhaps even from herself. There is no use in blaming yourself. And if anyone is to blame it is I, for—"

Just then the front door crashed open, followed quickly by thundering footsteps.

"Caro? Em?" came the shout.

"Letty!" And into the parlor flew Letty—her hair a mess, her face dirty—followed closely by Ashford and, huffing behind the two, Ogilvie.

The next few moments were a swirling tumble of noise and shrieks, of handshaking and back-patting and hugging and rushed explanations of what had happened.

"Fanny?" Letty shouted above the din. "Is she . . ."

"Upstairs," Caroline laughed. "George found her, and she'll be fine."

Emily found her way to Ashford's side. "What happened?" It was the first time she had been able to form a coherent phrase since Letty's entrance.

Ashford, his handsome face beaming, leaned closer to her so she could hear his words. "I followed a hunch and visited some taverns and inns on the outskirts of town. And in one particularly seedy establishment I saw a young man who looked familiar. It took me a moment to place him, and then I realized it was the actor who played Ash-Heap in your play."

"No!"

"Indeed, he's been out of a job of late, and working at the inn. I went directly to him, inquired if he had seen a little girl traveling with a man, and the fellow, this Henry Hughes, immediately took me to the room where Letty and Aubridge were ensconced."

"What happened then?"

Letty jumped between the two of them. "Oh, Em, it was wonderful, just wonderful! Mr. Ashford punched him right in the nose, and he fell over like, well, like a big dead tree! Henry Hughes thinks he broke his nose, but I think it was smashed. And on the way here Mr. Ashford bought me all sorts of sweets and things I'm not supposed to eat."

"Forgive me, Miss Fairfax," Lucius said.

"How's your hand?" Emily asked.

"Fine. But I fear I used a little more force than necessary." Then he grew more serious. "And your sister Fanny fares well?"

"Yes, yes. Thank you."

"Emily, you should write Henry Hughes a play!

A wonderful play!" Caroline suggested, tears streaming down her face.

"Excellent notion," Ogilvie agreed.

"I just might do that."

Suddenly Letty paused. "Emily?"

Emily simply smiled down at her youngest sister.

"I am so sorry. It's just that, well, I was so mad at you for hurting Mr. Ashford's feelings so."

"Not half as mad as I was at myself," Emily admitted.

"Not nearly as mad as I was at her as well," added Ashford, and they laughed. Then he bent over to be on her level. "But Letty. I have forgiven Emily. With all of my heart."

Emily stood motionless, unable to fathom what he was saying, unwilling to let the moment end.

"If I can forgive her, if I can love her still, do you not think you could as well? For my sake? For all of our sakes?"

With that Letty, whose eyes had filled with tears, threw herself into Emily's arms.

It seemed impossible that so much happiness could be contained in one room. But it was. Even Ogilvie wiped away a tear, muttering something about the London dust.

Emily reached out and Ashford took her hand automatically, without a glance. "Where is he now?"

He knew precisely who she meant. "I believe he may be with the magistrate, unless . . ."

"Unless?"

"Henry Hughes suspected that three gentlemen of my earlier acquaintance may have wished a word or two with your brother-in-law."

"You mean the men who attacked you?"

"The very same. And you know, they are not half bad, once you get to know them."

Then Emily felt a tug on her gown, and Letty looked up and smiled. "Oh, Em. Wasn't this a grand adventure? And aren't you glad you took me to London?"

And later that evening, after the toasts and talks and a festive meal made from all of the elegant food Caroline had prepared for her grand party that never was, they all agreed that it had, indeed, been a great adventure.

It was an early evening for most of the household. The servants had been dismissed, the family was abed. Ogilvie had long ago returned to his own home.

Emily closed her eyes for a moment, listening to the tick of the mantel clock. "It has been a long day."

"It has indeed," Lucius agreed as he stretched his booted legs out. They were but inches apart on the settee. The fire crackled, taking the late night chill from the parlor. "It has been a long few months."

Emily smiled. "Interesting. Now how long have we been aquainted?"

"A long few months."

"Rascal," she laughed.

"Emily." Something in his voice made her open her eyes and look at him. In the evening light, long shadows playing against his face, he had never been more handsome. More compelling. "Emily, I love you."

Her breath caught in her throat. "I love you, too, Lucius."

"Then the rest is simple." He took her hand and planted a light kiss on her palm. "Emily, my dear Emily. Will you marry me?"

He was right. So simple. "Yes. Of course."

For a moment they just looked at each other. Then he grinned, and pulled her onto his lap. "Promise not to write any more nasty plays about me?"

"Perhaps," she began, tracing a finger down the front of his waistcoat. "Oh, Lucius! I've never felt this way. You inspire me so. Perhaps I should write about—"

But no one would ever know what that play would have been, for her words—indeed, every thought in her mind—were silenced by one single long, blissfully magnificent kiss.

Epilogue

"I am still not quite certain why you have dragged me here," complained Jeremy Fairfax. "I do not like London. I do not like the theater. And this box is most inconvenient. Why, we are practically on the stage."

"These are considered the best seats, Papa," Emily smiled. "And this is the famous Drury Lane. You have heard of it, Papa. I know that."

"Perhaps I have. But . . . Gad! What is that sound?" He placed a hand beside his white curled wig.

"That is a champagne cork, Mr. Fairfax," said Lucius Ashford. "Your daughter Fanny and her future husband have brought champagne to celebrate."

"Good God, I thought we were being shot at," Mr. Fairfax mumbled. "There is not enough light to read in here, Emily. Not nearly enough. What they require is a good fireplace to cast more light. Then I could read. I believe it is growing even darker."

"That is because the play is about to begin. The play I wrote."

"Well, I always like to read when I am sitting. I do not like to sit without reading."

Letty finished her ice and looked over the railing, waving at familiar faces. The recipients of her greeting responded in various degrees, some smiling hesitantly, glancing about in search of subtle clues from others before committing to any action. Others returned the wave with enthusiasm. Only a few pretended not to notice the elaborately gowned girl in the first box.

After all, it had been a mere eighteen months since the entire Fairfax family was thoroughly dragged through the muck of scandal. There had been ruined reputations, shocking revelations, presumed alliances of a most unsavory sort, concluding with the mysterious disappearance of one of the sisters' husbands. Some said he was shanghaied to the South Seas by a trio of rogue sailors. Others claimed to have seen him in Italy, of all places. Most concluded he had met an unfortunate, but richly deserved end.

Then, in a matter of days, an even more remarkable story emerged, all the more remarkable because it was the truth. Instead of a family devoid of all proper morals, closer examination—and endless hours of discussion in clubs, parlors and country homes—concluded just the opposite was true. For once, society viewed a family of four high-born sisters as just a family. Perhaps the early death of their mother tugged at gold-plated heartstrings, although a mother's early death was hardly rare. Maybe it was the simple fact that they were raised in Ireland, which elicited sympathy from the more fashion-minded matrons.

The Fairfax sisters suddenly became a most fascinating topic in that festive summer of 1814. Indeed, everyone found something close to their own experiences in the four sisters. What family didn't have at least one member who married rashly and unwell? And what a relief it would be to have that unfortunate husband removed so neatly and without remorse!

Most families could boast at least one high-spirited tomboy. Then there was the one steady, least interesting sister who married a solid gentleman and had three perfectly respectable children. Her very existence proved there must be some deeply ingrained goodness in the family.

And when it came to Emily. Well. Who had not done something foolish for love, only to have the gesture backfire disastrously? Furthermore, most people took great comfort in the knowledge their foolish-for-love actions had been far more private affairs than that of Miss Fairfax.

Their redemption had been swift, and had included one wedding, an engagement and a political rebirth so complete, the formerly disgraced Lucius Ashford was now reckoned to be amongst the most influential voices of his party. He had given up his seat in Parliament, but there were high hopes he would return one day very soon.

Furthermore, once it had been revealed that Miss Emily Fairfax was the well-known playwright Edgar St. John, and had written *The Reluctant*

Rogue as a private diary about her conflicting feelings about Mr. Ashford, the romantics of society embraced them both. Those more cynical members of the ton enjoyed the irony of the situation, and its near-ruinous results. And everyone relished the emerging tale of the thwarted duel that brought them together in the first place.

Then, just as all attention was focused on the sisters, another scandal rocked the leading families to the core.

Lady Duff, the premier hostess of London that season, ran off with one of the animal trainers hired to locate a missing kangaroo. At last Lady Duff had found the true passion that had so eluded her with all the endless hostessing. Lord Duff took the abandonment in cheerful stride, but others admitted her parties would be sorely missed for their humor value alone.

The Prince Regent stepped into his box across from the sisters, and when he saw Letty he bowed deeply at the waist. After that, her waves were lavishly returned, and some competition emerged over whom the valuable greetings had been intended in the first place.

The curtains of the Fairfax box opened, and Mr. Edward Giles entered, resplendent in knee britches and a lavish wig. "I do so appreciate the advice from Mr. Brummell," he whispered to Emily.

"Mr. Giles, how magnificent you are!" Emily replied.

"I thank you." He stood straighter to allow other

patrons to view his impressive self more fully. "Although Mr. Brummell just said my knees are not all one would hope, I do trust the rest compensates for that deficit." After a final pose, his profile this time, he left for his own box.

"What a remarkably well-dressed gentleman," proclaimed Mr. Fairfax. "Although his ankles are rather unfortunate."

Lord Ogilvie began to pass flutes of champagne, handing Letty a very small glass. "Take little sips, my dear. We do not want a tipsy thirteen-year-old."

"William?" Fan took a rather large gulp as she nudged her fiancé. She alone addressed him by his Christian name. Everyone else just called him Ogilvie.

Fanny looked positively radiant, her eyes outshining the massive diamond necklace her husband-to-be had bestowed upon his bride. "Who is that woman waving at you? The one with the large hands and tiny head?"

"That would be Miss Mary Lloyd."

"Is there something wrong with her, my dear?" Fan asked.

"Why do you ask?"

"Her hands, William. They frighten me. I wish she would stop waving them about so."

John Philip Kemble, the great actor turned manager of the Drury Lane, stepped into the box. "Gentlemen, ladies. I welcome you to the new production of Mr. Edgar St. John." He chatted briefly and amiably with the family, shaking hands with all before returning backstage.

"Who was that man?" Mr. Fairfax demanded.

Letty explained it to her father, allowing him to switch places with her, since she was closer to the gaslights and he could read more easily.

Caroline and George were not at the play that night. Their party was the very next day. Since Lady Duff had run off, Lord Duff had insisted they borrow her staff, and thus were unable to leave their home. Too many servants to train, Caroline had sighed. So much to do.

And, Emily suspected, they couldn't be happier about it.

She looked at Lucius, positively breathtaking in his new jacket. His man, Addleston, who had gone with them on their bridal trip, had indeed taken beautiful care of his clothing. And now, Emily's wardrobe was in his capable hands as well.

The play was about to begin.

The excitement mounted.

This was her first play since *The Reluctant Rogue,* and was pure comedy with absolutely no basis in reality. Henry Hughes was the lead, and Mr. Elliston—who had been at the Olympic—had a prime character role.

The other lead was Edmund Kean, who delighted in the notion of playing a comedic role created just for him.

Lucius slid his arm around the back of her chair. "Say it."

"Say what?"

"My name, your name."

"Lucius and Emily. Exactly how much champagne did you and William have at the club?"

He ignored her, his fingers resting lightly on her shoulders.

He never knew such happiness was possible. And such fulfillment. His proposed bill had been taken up by some of the most powerful MPs, and was being voted on during the next session. The chances were excellent that it would pass, especially now that it had been embraced by the Prime Minister, and even endorsed by the Prince Regent.

In a few days they would return to Ireland. There he would start a new phase of his work, to bring about reform in the English-owned factories. They had taken a town house in Dublin's Merrion Square, just off Clare Street. There Emily would write her next play. And there, soon, they hoped, their family would grow.

He had not heard of a single duel in the past several months.

He looked at Emily as the lights darkened. How foolish he had been to think he could live without her!

Ogilvie laughed at something Fanny said, and Lucius looked at his friend with warmth. He wanted to embrace the world, to shout his exultation to the blue skies!

It was probably the champagne.

No, on second thought, it was the pure delight he felt being there, with his family.

Letty turned and smiled, and he returned the smile. She would live with them in Dublin, it had been decided, much to Jeremy Fairfax's relief and Emily and Letty's joy.

"Say it," he said again to Emily. Someone in the audience told him to hush.

It was Ogilvie.

"Say what?" Emily whispered, her eyes on the stage as the curtain went up.

"Our names."

"Mr. and Mrs. Ashford?" She looked at him, and he nodded.

"That was it."

And the play unfolded.

It was the first scene in the most wonderful of adventures, the most miraculous of journeys . . . the rest of their lives.

Visit the Simon & Schuster romance Web site:

www.SimonSaysLove.com

and sign up for our romance e-mail updates!

Keep up on the latest
new romance releases,
author appearances, news, chats,
special offers, and more!
We'll deliver the information
right to your inbox—if it's new,
you'll know about it.

POCKET BOOKS

2800.02

ble. He had not taken her, *she* had taken *him.* Everything was vague, hazy when it came the